POISONED SHADOW

THE SHADOW SERIES

CANDICE BUNDY

LUSIOS PUBLISHING, LLC

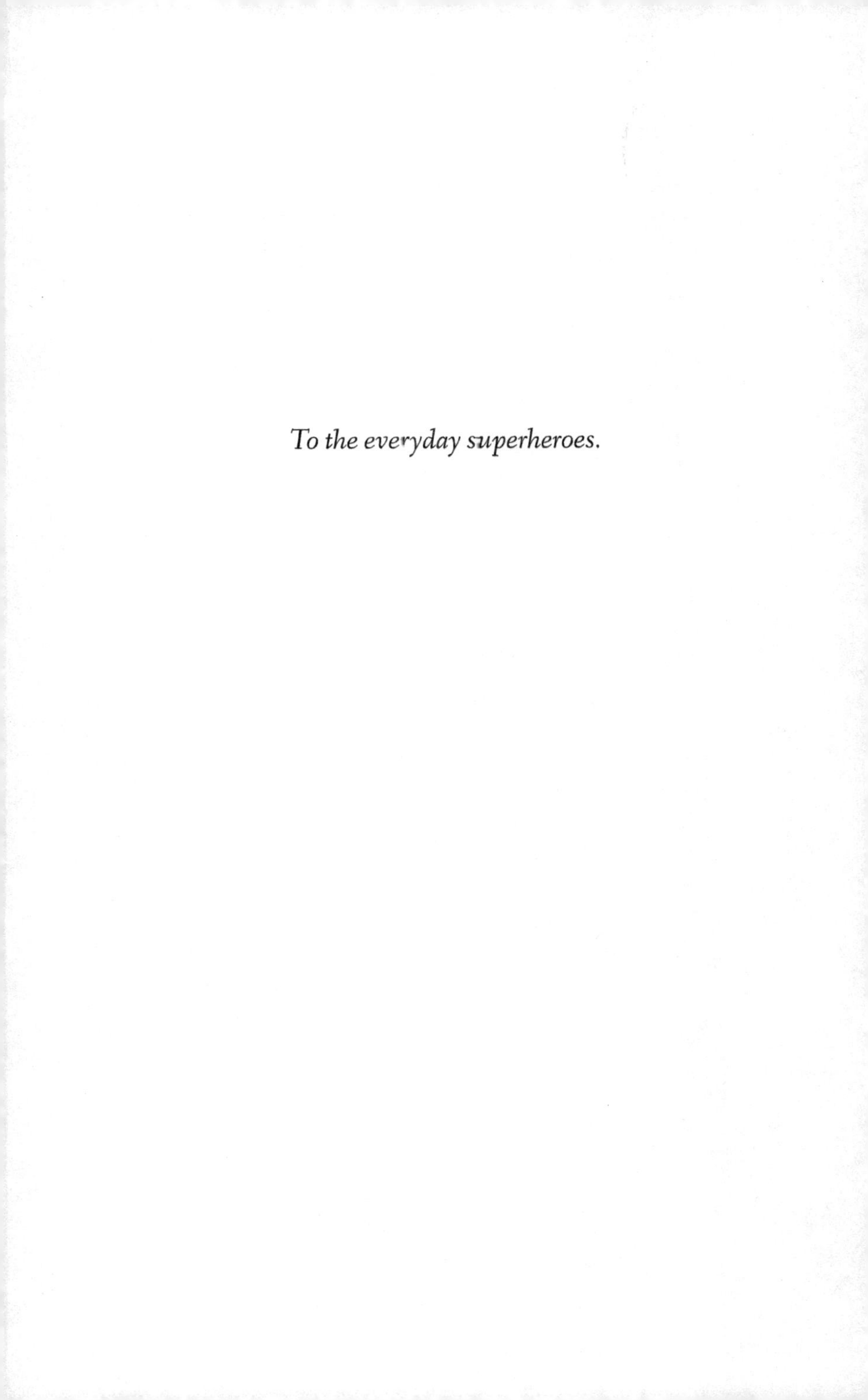

To the everyday superheroes.

CONTENTS

CHAPTER 1

FAE TERRITORIES - HOUSE ROWAN

Becka leaned out the alcove balcony above the great hall, grateful for a few stolen moments away from the crowd. In her youth, she and her twin, Tesse, had retreated to this very alcove to watch the crowds from on high. Observing fae interactions from this vantage point meant they could catch clues about intrigue or flirtations with high-borns who didn't realize they were being observed.

Now Becka used the alcove as a welcome retreat from the magic worn by so many fae, which drilled like porcupine quills into her brain.

Tonight, Becka's heart ached fresh over the loss of her sister. She'd done her best to smile and nod to emissaries from the other houses, trying to make connections via small talk. She'd never appreciated the effort required to chitchat, especially with fae magic everywhere triggering her persisting headaches. After an hour or so, she'd escaped upstairs for this much-needed break.

Fishing her bottle of hot sauce out of a deep pocket in her skirt, Becka flipped open the lid one-handed and took a swig.

She sighed with relief as her headache instantly abated. She shook a stream of the bright-orange liquid into her glass, swirling the fluid into effervescent, sparkling white wine. Becka then tried to flip the lid closed one-handed, but lost her grip on the smooth bottle because of the silk gloves she almost always wore.

While the gloves might protect others from her Nulling magic, they cost her precious grip dexterity.

There was a moment, perhaps two, where she watched the bottle hang in the air, spinning in slow motion before it hit the marble floor below. A credit to its manufacture, the bottle didn't shatter. Instead, the distinctive liquid shot out on impact, peppering those in range with the pungent, fiery sauce. A fae elder from House Hazel screeched in surprise as her pale green boots and layered brown robe took the brunt of the blow.

A pair of muted laughs erupted near the stairwell behind her, reminding Becka that her wolf shifter guards had followed along. From the floor below, all eyes lifted to her position in the alcove. It was a good thing she'd grown fond of the shifters. Becka's usual blunt and direct sense of humor was welcomed by the shifters, unlike her fae relatives, who had little appreciation for it and often took offense.

For a lack of something better to do, Becka waved and smiled down at the crowd like she'd seen beauty queens do on human television. How did it go? Elbow-elbow, wrist-wrist. Smile wide. No, wait – less teeth!

I probably look like I want to throw myself over the ledge, like my hot sauce had done.

If she'd had to name a common emotion on the faces below, Becka would have characterized it as disappointment.

"Way to embrace getting away from the crowd," whispered Saige, one of her wolf-shifter guards. Becka glanced back at them. Saige's green eyes glistened with humor, her pixie haircut accentuating her soft, youthful features in the muted light. "I give her a two."

"Oh, you're being too harsh," Luce replied, also whispering. Her hazel eyes never lost their sharp, determined focus. "She's improving. I'd give her a six." She'd pursed her lips as if deep in thought. Her wild, shaggy mane of chin-length brown hair cast her features in shadow.

"Six out of...?" Becka asked, feeling her smile falter as she continued to wave down to the onlookers below.

"A hundred," Luce replied, and the two shifters giggled.

Below, her mother, Duchess Maura, arched a brow at her while rubbing her temple absently. The ruler of House Rowan, adept at creating illusions as convincing as reality, wore a new dress for the occasion, an off-the-shoulder look which wrapped close around her form in layers of green and gold light, a hue which matched her eyes perfectly. Her hair was swept back into a twist atop her head with a few tiny braids accentuating the curve of her neck. The tips of Maura's layered gown shimmered and shifted in the evening light, reminding Becka of aspen leaves fluttering in the wind.

A water elementalist from House Ash approached the Hazel elder and, fingers twitching with magic, extracted the sauce off her clothes and boots. She deposited it into the sauce puddle on the floor. Not even a stain remained on the elder's clothes, although her expression remained dour.

Becka remembered House Hazel was renowned for training the best dream spinners, crafting messages and experiences for their targets, despite great distances. At least

Becka had no fear of being on the receiving end of a rant in dream form, as her Null ability prevented any such mental trespass.

Her father, Duke Vott of House Rowan but also Elder Vott of House Alder by birth, caught her eye. Even from this distance, his usual gentle gaze held a stony glint. His simple, floor-length robes with embroidered flycatcher birds at the lapels added to his willowy form, accentuating his height. His long hair hung loose except for a pair of thin braids running in front of each ear, framing his regal face. Vott raised his hand and summoned her downstairs with a single swipe of his fingers, a forced smile on his lips.

Becka sighed, wishing she'd had more time to let the pain in her head subside. "Well, I knew it couldn't last." She downed half her drink, and then turned to go down the stairs.

Saige and Luce stood against the wall to let her pass, careful not to brush against the ruffles in Becka's ornate deep-indigo ombre dress. Hers was likely the only outfit in the room which wasn't enchanted in some manner. Except for the shifters who wore tailored, fitted pants with matching shirts in brown tones, which was about as formal as she supposed Vott could talk them into being.

Wolf shifters were anything but typical guards for a fae. Humans? Sure, she'd seen that plenty back in the city. But these wolves were loyal to Vott for reasons she didn't yet understand. Vott had assigned them to Becka after the Shadow-Dweller attack three months ago, neither asking her opinion nor permission, but she'd been grateful for the protection.

Her attire for this event had been delivered an hour in

advance of the festivities with a note from Maura. "*I know this isn't your style, but it's befitting a lady of your station.*" Surely the sheer volume of ruffles paired with the circumference of the skirts might be considered a war crime. But she'd appreciated the indigo hues and was determined to win over at least one dignitary, so she'd relented and donned the dress.

"Could you two teach me to be stealthier? I never hear you coming unless you want me to," Becka asked.

Luce barked out a laugh. "You can't learn the innate gifts of shifters. Besides, we don't need to encourage your sneakiness."

"Not to mention," Saige replied, the two following her down the stairs, "there's no way to sneak about in that dress."

Said the women who moved with the lithe grace of hunters. Becka figured they'd be graceful and silent no matter what they wore.

Becka turned to Luce. "I know why I answer Vott's call, but why do you go when Vott calls you?"

"That's a long story, and it's not mine to tell," Luce replied.

Becka opened her mouth to ask more, but Luce had that determined look in her eye, the one that brooked no argument.

Her feet hit the marble floor of the Great Hall, and while she'd snuck away without notice, her return was the subject of scrutiny. Becka downed the rest of her drink, loving the spicy zing of the hot sauce, and then placed her glass on a nearby tray.

House Rowan hosted the annual regional trade delegation, which drew emissaries from not only all the nearby houses but even ones from farther-flung territories. The group wasn't as large or diverse as those who had shown up for Tesse's wedding and then stayed for her subsequent funeral. Those few months ago, none of the houses had wanted to miss the grand affair of the heir of House Rowan's nuptials. Now, the attendees were bent on more pedestrian matters.

Maura had been busy the past couple of weeks preparing to receive the delegations. House Rowan had made space for all the attendees at the manor, as most planned to stay a few days. After losing Tesse, Maura's concern had turned to strengthening Rowan's relationships with the other houses. She'd confided to Becka that, with the Shadow-Dwellers being a menace, they needed all the allies they could muster for the days ahead.

The Great Hall was full enough that Becka had to thread her way carefully through the crowd, heading for Vott at the far end of the hall. The last thing she wanted was to run into someone, and their magic, sparking another round of headaches for herself.

A tall, imposing man with deep creases around his eyes moved into her path, and Becka rocked back on her heels, eager to avoid running into him.

"Lady Becka," he intoned, bowing his head for a moment. "'Tis an honor to see you again."

Becka pursed her lips. Who was he again? "Oh, Elder Berkeley of... House Birch." She remembered him from those who attended her sister's funeral. "It's nice to see you again too."

He gave her another quick incline of his head, assuring her she'd gotten his name right. "This is a more fortuitous time for an introduction. How have you found your return to

House Rowan?" The glint in his eyes was filled with rapt interest.

Is he being sarcastic? Becka doubted it, but at the speed of fae gossip, no doubt most had heard things hadn't gone smoothly. "The past three months have been a challenge, but I'm sure life at the manor will get easier over time."

"Oh, has it been that long now?" His brows rose, although surely, he could count the time that had passed as well as she could. "I suppose I will receive an invitation to your upcoming nuptials any day now?"

Oh, hells no, not if I can help it!

Becka's breath hitched in the back of her throat, while she searched for the right words. "You're always welcome at House Rowan's festivities."

"Hmm," he replied, but he didn't call her out for dodging the question. "I assume the duchess will be sending you to us for fertility treatments?"

Becka recalled Berkeley's generous offer of fertility treatments to Maura for her house, but the thought of using one herself gave her a shudder.

"Oh no, I'm not getting knocked up!" Becka blurted out a little too loud.

There were a few raised brows around her. It was as if she could see others' pointed ears twitch toward their conversation.

"Knocked up?" he asked. "Whatever do you mean?"

Becka pinched the bridge of her nose with her fingers. She kept forgetting the fae-touched lacked the vernacular she'd become accustomed to in the city. "I meant to say I'm not planning on having children anytime soon."

Berkeley's eyes lit with understanding and his smile

turned poisonous. "Ah, some city-speak, I suspect. How... quaint and colloquial."

Irritated over his condescending tone, Becka searched for a reasonable response. "I lived there for the last third of my life."

"As you say," he replied. "But why would you not wish to contribute to the lineage of your family as soon as possible?"

Becka didn't even know where to begin, but, remembering her promise to Vott and Maura, she held her tongue.

"I'm sure it will work itself out in time," she replied, holding to an enigmatic and thus fae-approved response.

He smiled and inclined his head. "You are welcome at House Birch whenever you are ready." His gaze shifted to the two shifters behind her and then back to Becka, confusion knitting his brow. "Pardon, but why are Vott's shifter guards with *you*?"

Grateful for the change in conversation, Becka smiled. This was an easy explanation. "He assigned them to me after the Shadow-Dweller attack."

Having uttered the words, Becka didn't miss how the rhythm of conversation around her hiccupped when the phrase Shadow-Dweller left her lips.

"How curious," Berkeley replied. "I admit I find the shifters' presence most unsettling. It's so rare to see them within fae territory. Unless they are working with the enforcers, of course." His frown spoke volumes.

You know the shifters can hear you, right?

A short for-a-fae and curvy woman stepped into their conversation, as if invoked. Becka took a half step back, and she sensed the shifters behind her stiffen.

"What a curious excuse! Shadow-Dwellers are but a story

told to children to make them behave. Why would Elder Vott feel the need to protect you from boogeymen?" The lady's arched brow and sneer reeked of contempt

Becka held her breath a moment and then exhaled slowly. "The Shadow-Dwellers are very much real. Woden... I mean Lagan, proclaimed himself one of them."

Elder Berkeley's eyes grew wide with the glint of humor. "You can't be serious," he said, incredulous.

The woman's countenance filled with an icy fury. "I have seen no independent proof of your claim, which you had every reason to invent to justify your transgressions. I grew up with Lord Lagan and he was never anything but kind and generous to me. The word of a city-living fae-touched will never be enough to change my mind."

Who is this woman?

"You're from House Holly?" Becka asked.

The fae drew herself up to her full, if diminutive, height. "Indeed. I am Lady Cordelia and I will not tolerate your lies concerning my kin."

Could Cordelia also be a Shadow-Dweller like Lagan? Or was this just proof at how well they'd integrated within normal fae society?

"You are welcome to read the enforcers' reports as well as anyone. It's all in there," Becka replied, keeping her voice even.

Cordelia held her hand to her throat. "Oh, I *have* read them, and from what I can gather, the two of you fought an unsanctioned duel and poor Lagan lost. Most likely defending himself from your dangerous new gift. I know we consider declared duels lawful and a fair test of powers, but since when has a fae died during one?' She shook her head and fanned herself vigorously. "I'm still confused why you weren't jailed over his death!"

Heat radiated from Becka's ears, and she had to work to keep her balled fists at her sides. "I told you, he admitted to being a Shadow-Dweller!" Her voice came out louder than she'd intended. Definitely too loud for polite company, based on the heads turned her way.

Elder Berkeley held up his hands. "Now, now... Have some decorum, my dear."

Ignoring him, Cordelia leaned closer and whispered, "Eventually, you will be held to account." She backed away and barked out a bitter laugh. "Your house may entertain your wild fantasies, but no one else is required to."

"Believe what you want," Becka whispered back. "Lagan was a psychopath." The memory of her blood running down her leg. His blood on her hands. Even months later, the stark images were still fresh in her mind, pulling her focus inward.

Dazed, Becka ambled off towards where she'd last seen Vott, continuing across the hall and needing a few moments to settle herself. This time others made way for her with no prompting. She strode through a group from House Oak, which she assumed based on their stocky builds, who quieted and parted ways as she passed through. No doubt their stoic intuition informed their actions, discouraging engagement.

Catching sight of Duchess Maura, Becka headed in her direction, taking a moment to compose her thoughts. Her Aunt Astrid, head trainer of the Illusionists Guild, stood next to Maura, deep in discussion with a handful of fae.

As Becka drew near, Maura raised her hand, a silvered orb of energy launching from her fingertips towards the ceiling. It exploded like fireworks, full of harmless, dazzling sparks which drew everyone's attention.

When the room quieted, Maura spoke. "House Rowan is delighted you've made the journey and we welcome you to our annual regional trade negotiations. At this time, all delegates are invited to the council chambers to introduce their terms for discussion. I look forward to hearing your proposals and aiding in the mediation process. Shall we?" She gestured towards the rear staircase.

Lady Wynne of House Ash, who Becka had met briefly yesterday, noticed her and then smiled her way politely. "Will Lady Becka be joining us tonight?" she asked Maura.

Maura's face was as placid as a lake. "No, she will not. Although she is my legal heir, she's not yet guilded."

Wynne's eyebrows shot up. "Oh yes, I had forgotten she'd blossomed into her powers at so advanced an age."

What am I, a spinster? I'm not that old!

"Does it take longer to train when they start later?" Wynne asked Astrid.

"It varies," Astrid replied, resplendent in her floor-length red silk dress. "In Becka's case, the lack of understanding about the unique aspects of her power adds to the challenge. But those who develop later often take longer to fully grasp the complexities of their powers."

Maura turned to Astrid, "Will you join me?"

Astrid nodded, and the two headed to the council chambers. Lady Wynne was not far behind them.

Becka watched them go, feeling kicked in the shins and more than a little embarrassed. When would she feel like she belonged here? Would she ever? Becka shook off her thoughts, again trying to find Vott in the crowd.

Which was when Alain Hawthorne, her fiancé, found her.

"My dearest Lady Becka," he intoned, his voice smooth with confidence. He reached for her gloved hand, depositing a chaste kiss on the back of it with a flourish. A fiery phoenix perched atop Alain's shoulder, stretching its wings as if to maintain its balance as he bent forward. But, as the creature had no intrinsic weight, the display was all for show.

It was a lovely fire elemental, intricate to behold, but the presence of the phoenix so close to her made Becka's head throb. Worse, she'd told Alain it pained her when she encountered other people's magic, and yet he didn't seem to realize that his magical displays also caused her pain. Did he think showing off his skill was going to impress her? All it did was demonstrate that his need to look good eclipsed being considerate to Becka.

A cheerful lady accompanied Alain, full of smiles for Becka. "May I introduce my cousin, the Lady Hanna Hawthorne?" he said.

Hanna reached for Becka's gloved hand and grasped it firmly and fearlessly. "I am so grateful to make your acquaintance, Lady Becka. Alain has told me so much about you, and I can't wait to get to know you better."

Alarm bells went off in Becka's head. No fae was this over-the-top ingratiating and sweet, at least not without an ulterior motive. What did Alain have up his sleeve?

Just then, Becka spotted Vott talking with her brother Calder and his lady friend of the month.

"Lady Hanna, how lovely to meet you. Now, if you two will excuse me, I'm afraid Vott sent for me."

More the spirit of the truth rather than the letter, but any excuse would do at the moment.

"Of course," Hanna replied and gave her a slight bow.

Alain's slight frown was the only sign of his disappointment. "Tomorrow, then, we'll speak more? I must be off to the meeting anyway. I'm the designated envoy for House Hawthorne."

By the way he puffed out his chest, Becka guessed she was supposed to be impressed. Hanna's smile shone up at him, which made Becka even more suspicious of this overly cheerful Hawthorne cousin. Becka wondered at the reason for Hanna's visit. Would she be expected to spend a lot of time with Hanna?

"Lord Alain," Becka replied, neither confirming nor denying any obligations for tomorrow, and then with a nod she headed towards Vott.

She'd moved so quickly towards Vott that when she stopped, her skirts whooshed forward around her, the multi-layered dress rocking against her legs.

"Vott," she said. "Calder." She nodded briefly at both of them.

"Eloquent, as always, sister Becka," Calder replied with a shake of his head. "Have you met my paramour, the Lady Alvilda?"

Becka could see why Calder appeared captivated by this new girl. Alvilda's hair hung loose down to her hips, her platinum tresses so shiny they were almost reflective in the candlelight. Her dress wasn't as fancy as some Becka had seen tonight, but the understated pale blue sheath highlighted the petite yet curvy fae's form. Alvilda's arm tightened around Calder's, and her perfect heart-shaped lips held a forced smile not reflected in her pale gold eyes.

"Not yet. Pleased to meet you." Becka shot out her gloved hand, to which Alvilda gave a somewhat horrified expression before accepting the handshake, a gesture which was tentative and lasted a mere moment.

Calder didn't appear to be sharing complimentary stories about sister Becka to his lover. *Fair enough.*

"I need to excuse myself for the meeting," Calder said. "Vott, will you be joining us?"

"No. As elder of House Alder, there are no proposals from my birth house for me to present. Maura is well-equipped to manage House Rowan's interests. Besides, the initial proposals are often tedious and long-winded, and the trade talks run long enough as it is for my liking." He laughed, and his genuine humor was so infectious they all joined in. Well, Becka didn't laugh, but she returned his smile. "But you should get going, Calder. It's your first one, and I have a feeling you'll enjoy it. Give me an outline of what I need to know over breakfast before the negotiations begin, yes?"

"As you say, Father." Calder leaned in close to Alvilda and gave her a quick kiss on the cheek. "Join me in my room later?" he asked, not bothering to lower his voice.

"I will eagerly await your arrival," Alvilda replied, a slight flush warming her cheeks.

Was this open affection standard, or were Calder's intentions towards Alvilda more serious than Becka had assumed? Surely, their mother Maura had more lofty plans for Calder's future wedded union, but that wouldn't necessarily limit his dalliances. By her overly effusive smile, Becka was sure

Alvilda had every intention of cementing her place at Calder's side.

Calder bowed to Vott and then excused himself.

Vott, smiling pleasantly as if he didn't have a care in the world, turned to Becka. "My dearest, would you please join me on the rooftop garden for a cup of tea?"

"Sure," Becka replied after a pause. Vott tried so hard to help her, she found it hard to turn him down despite the late hour. "Let me just run by my room first and then I'll be right up."

"Don't dawdle." He wagged a finger at her, and then turned to go, leaving Becka standing with Alvilda.

A few uncomfortable seconds hung in the air between them. Although Alvilda presented as a fawning partner to Calder, Becka suspected Alvilda had lofty aims. Why else would she attend this event hanging on Calder's arm for all to witness? Did she think Maura would take her more seriously if she saw the two looking the part of fae royalty?

Perhaps it was rooted in her own dislike of prestige, but Alvilda's focus on upward mobility made Becka instantly dislike her.

"Give my regards to Duke Vott," Alvilda said with a wink.

How boldly familiar! Just because she was involved with Calder didn't mean Becka had to be friends with her.

"I suspect I'm in for a more enjoyable evening," Alvilda continued. She didn't wait for Becka's reply but swept off in a swirl of gold and gray mist trailing her steps.

"With my stuck-up brother? I doubt it," Becka replied, just loud enough for the departing fae to hear.

CHAPTER 2

*B*ecka was overjoyed to discover a new batch of clothes from her townhome back in the city, freshly laundered, pressed, and hung in her closet.

"You got more!" Becka exclaimed. She popped her head out of the closet, and Saige smiled back at her. "Did you wash them too?"

Saige chortled. "No, you have people for that, and I'm not one of them."

"Thank you!" She'd have given Saige a hug, but the wolves were touchy about personal space.

"My ability to smuggle in your stuff has improved commensurate with your bribing skills. To be honest, this week I took pity on your pathetic self. Plus, I had a little more free time, what with your extra training sessions."

If it wasn't for both Luce and Saige being willing to play along, Becka would have had to give up coloring her hair pink and wearing her favorite boho styles weeks ago. Her shifter friends had also acquired a steady supply of her favorite hot sauce. Maura hadn't asked how she'd managed it, and Becka hadn't offered an explanation.

She'd been well-motivated to buddy up with the shifters, not just because they had leeway to travel freely between territories with no one batting an eye, but also because they were far more approachable than the typical fae. For one, the shifters laughed all the time and seemed to try and find the fun in each moment. Second, they didn't follow strict protocols or get upset if you didn't use their correct titles. Third, she didn't have to fear that any of them could be a Shadow-Dweller. Shadow-Dwellers were born fae, later corrupted by an unholy thirst for power.

"I love it! I'll find more of that whiskey you like." She disappeared inside the closet to change. Becka picked out a billowy pair of sage green palazzo pants with a red embroidered dragon wrapping around the legs and a drapey beige crocheted tank to wear. Then she pulled her pink hair back into a messy ponytail. She slipped on a pair of flip-flops and emerged from the closet feeling more like herself again.

"Those floofy dresses don't suit you at all. You look happy to be back in your own skin," Saige said.

She'd learned the wolves were passionate about being true to one's self, or skin as they called it. "Be true to your skin, right?"

Saige nodded, a single brow arched.

Becka had heard shifters say it to each other in passing, sensing each time the weight of their belief behind the sentiment. The saying reached back into antiquity, often cited in some of the earliest shifter lore. She'd never spoken the shifter phrase before, but Saige didn't seem to mind Becka using it.

"Did you agree to smuggle in my things because of the whiskey or because of the whole shifter skin thing?"

Saige grinned, offering her a shrug. "You may never know. But seriously, trying to be that which you're not causes many issues."

Luce, appearing at the door, sniffed the air and cast her gaze about in a wide net. Alighting on Becka, she nodded. "Isn't Elder Vott awaiting the pleasure of your company, *Lady* Becka?"

She rolled her eyes at Luce and was rewarded with a sly grin. The shifters knew Becka didn't need or want titles, so their insistence on using them at times had become something of an inside joke. Becka had tried to get them to disclose some similar level of titles within their ranks, but if the shifters had titles, they had yet to share them with her.

"Just a moment," Becka replied. She slid on the sea silk gloves Vott had gifted her after her Null gift had been discovered, when she'd touched the Unbreakable and broken it. Vott had these teas with her a few days a week, usually after her training had finished for the day. She wasn't sure how he timed it, but he was always precise down to the minute.

This one was an exception to the timing, and perhaps a prelude to an impending lecture.

Becka swept out of her room, falling into a steady cadence alongside the shorter woman. "Off to the rooftop garden."

Luce glanced at Becka. "It'll be pretty in the moonlight."

"She's worried about getting a talking to," Saige, walking behind them, replied.

"I never said that," Becka replied.

"Didn't need to," Luce said. "There's a stiffness in your movements that tells me you're anxious."

Becka sighed, unable to disagree.

As they headed down the corridor towards the main central staircase of House Rowan, they passed portraits of Rowan ancestors along the way. The rich, vibrant colors and historical settings were something she'd stared at in wonder in her youth, both for the intricacy of the art and the richness of the frames, the wallpaper, the carpet, even the lighting sconces.

Becka wondered if, had the elders still been alive, would they have disapproved of the free-spirited woman she'd grown into as much as her current relatives did?

Near the end of the hall they passed by a fae who, at their approach, stepped to the side and inclined his head to her. Becka smiled at him and returned the nod, but the interaction, one of many she had during each day, grated on her nerves.

Becka wasn't anywhere near used to being heir again of House Rowan. Fae kept strict adherence to their social norms, and she had the sense that it gave them comfort. A feeling of stability, even. She'd tried following along, but it didn't feel right. She'd lived too long finding her own path, and following customs she couldn't even remember the purpose of didn't help her sleep better at night. Sighing in frustration, Becka wondered if she would ever grow used to it all. It didn't help that she had no interest in fulfilling the role.

She wasn't blind to the potential that, as heir, she could hold great sway. She'd have even more power as the future duchess, although that time would be decades away from now.

But Becka didn't want to wait. She didn't want to be patient. Her fire for change was in the present, not some distant, untouchable future.

However, when she'd had conversations with Astrid and Maura about her desire to have more control over her life, they'd both shot her down. Becka had been told she was pushing for too much, too fast, and to wait until her gift was under control before asking these questions.

They passed a young man in the hall dressed in the dark tan and green colors of House Oak. He stepped to the side and bowed as they passed.

Becka skirted around him, lost in her own thoughts.

During the past few months as she'd spent day in and day out with her shifter guards, Becka had grown to enjoy their company and had encouraged their candor. Luce had been the one who'd warmed to her most quickly, but even then, it had taken over a month to convince Luce that Becka didn't want to be treated like some fae princess but rather as a respected peer.

The process had involved a certain quantity of whiskey. Happily, House Rowan's stores were ample.

"Did you mean to slight the House Oak youth?" Luce asked under her breath.

Becka glanced back, but the fae had already continued on his way. "Ugh, I've lived for so long around humans. I forget I'm supposed to nod to everyone."

"Just add polite decorum to the list of customs you've forgotten." Luce shook her head.

Becka laughed along. "Well, aren't we extra cheeky today?"

"What are you going to do, report me to Vott?" Luce waggled her brows, and Becka laughed again.

"You know I don't toe the line. Why would I expect you to?"

Luce nodded. "That's one of your redeeming qualities."

They rounded the end of the hall, entered the stairwell, and then proceeded up towards the rooftop gardens four floors up. Becka loved this staircase with its ornate woven metal banisters and white stone risers. Missing her normal exercise regimen, she loved to pound steadily up and down all four flights at least once each morning. Her shifter guards appeared to like the activity, but she got plenty of raised brows from fae who considered it unseemly behavior.

At the top of the stairs, windows lined the outer wall, filling the space with bright beams of moonlight through the quiet evening air. Cautious about the conversation to come, Becka paused at an ornate gilt stained-glass doorway, peering out onto the open-air rooftop deck. Pergolas laden with wisteria provided a picturesque setting, inviting Becka to breathe long and deep of their perfume.

House Rowan really was a ridiculously gorgeous and well-maintained home. *So why do I still think wistfully of my townhome in the city?*

Becka knew why. In the city, she'd had freedom over her days. Over her life path. Here? As much as she wanted to belong, it felt like the responsibilities falling on her shoulders grew daily.

Maura wanted her on the council and Becka was interested in what that entailed, but as she wasn't guilded yet, that step had been delayed. She'd worked to gain control over her gift, practicing daily, but didn't feel like she was in control of how fast that mastery was approaching. Then there were the site visits to the farms and houses on Rowan territory to assess production and needs, but it still felt like foreign territory. And then there was her duty to marry per her house's agreements, which was something she certainly could not bring herself to do, so Becka had dragged her heels.

With her keen night vision, Becka didn't require any additional lighting besides the moonlight to see Vott reclined on a couch under the central pergola. When he saw her arrival, he rose to greet her, a broad smile affixed to his face.

Surprised by the tangle of nerves in her gut, Becka stepped forward and met Vott under the pergola. A couple of candles on the table cast a meager but warm glow around them.

"My dear Becka, thank you for joining me." He took a step closer to her, but there was no hug or embrace.

"Of course, Vott. I've come to suspect you always know when I'm about to arrive. Since you can't track me, how do you know?"

"It is true, your Null ability blunts the Oracular aspects of my Air Elemental powers, so tracking you has proven fruitless. However, I can still hone in on everyone else in the house. Therefore, I have learned to track you by association. Your guards, for instance."

"That's a clever trick," Becka replied, glancing at Luce and Saige, who'd stepped off to the side but were still within earshot. She held Luce's gaze for a moment, knowing she also understood the significance. Becka made a mental note to discuss Vott's newfound skill with Quinn on their next call. If Vott had figured that out, so could the Shadow-Dwellers. Not that she'd encountered any hint of them in the months since the attack at Tesse's funeral, but she hadn't lowered her guard. Woden had said there would be more.

"Thank you. Please take a seat." He gestured to the couches under the main pergola. The table was set with a pair of delicate earthenware mugs with a matching teapot, next to a pair of water glasses. "We can catch up on your progress."

"What tea are we having today?" she asked.

He clasped his hands together, hunching forward in his excitement. "Oh, I broke out the lapsang souchong today. Are you familiar with it?"

Becka cringed inwardly but schooled her expression. "Yes, it's a fine black tea, renowned for its flavor." Which Becka associated with cured salami. Definitely not something she'd ever gained a taste for, or even wanted to.

"Oh good, you know it!" His smile gleamed. He took a step towards the couches and paused. "One moment, my dear. It appears someone forgot to set out the honey."

"That'll *never* do," Becka replied.

Vott wandered over to a cabinet near the door and rummaged through it, no doubt hunting down the missing honey.

Becka took a seat on the couch across from where Vott had been sitting, grateful for the wafting breeze which danced through the pergola's sheer curtains. The tea set was one she didn't recognize. The delicate quality and artisan green crackle glaze spoke to its superior craftsmanship. She'd never seen this set in use before and wondered why it was out today. Was Vott signaling an elevated importance to this conversation? Ever since her return, Becka had needed to relearn the nuances of fae society. Surely, the selection of this set was no coincidence, but further meaning eluded her.

Leaning forward, she picked up the mug closest to her, filled halfway with the lapsang tea. Shuddering in anticipation of the potent and foul brew, Becka noticed Vott's cup was mostly empty.

Will he notice if I don't drink his favorite tea?

Becka didn't see any harm in adding her tea to his cup.

Glancing over to where he stood at the cabinet and seeing that he was still seeking the elusive honey, she leaned across the table and poured the entire contents of her cup into his. She wiped a stray dribble from the side of her mug against her linen pants, then refilled her cup from one of the water glasses.

She looked to Luce, who was watching her and shaking her head. Becka shrugged at her, and then sat back in her seat, hoping Vott wouldn't notice the pale color of the liquid in her mug, despite the bright moonlight.

"Found it!" Vott announced, returning to the pergola with a honeypot in hand.

"Fantastic."

He sat and placed the honey onto the table before picking up his mug again. "I see you've refilled my cup. Thank you." He settled back into the couch, added a bit of honey to his cup, and took a long sip of tea.

Becka joined him, sipping the water from her own mug. Despite having poured out all the tea, there was still a distinctive tannic residue present. And yet she drank, anxiously awaiting hearing what was on his mind.

"Does the flavor bring back memories?" he asked.

"It certainly does," Becka replied, nodding along with him. "What did you want to talk about?"

His expression turned pained. "Must I always have an agenda planned when meeting with my eldest?"

Becka wanted this banter to feel natural. Comforting. But there was a wall between them from her time spent separate from fae territories that neither quite seemed to know how to breach.

"No, but I'm guessing you're not going to let my earlier faux pas pass without comment. I swear I dropped that bottle of hot sauce by accident."

"It is on my mind, but never mind the hot sauce. No harm came from it." He frowned. "Are you aware it has been three months since you returned home for Tesse's funeral?"

"I'm aware." She took another sip. A cool breeze blew through, rustling the wisteria and perfuming the air. She took another sip of the water, feeling suddenly lethargic. Perhaps the long day was finally getting to her?

"How do you think you are getting along?" He paused, brow furrowed. He took another sip of tea. "I mean, how are you adapting to life back amongst the fae?"

No one had asked her so directly since her return, and she found it refreshing. "I don't feel at ease here. At least, not yet. I'm continuing to struggle to control my powers, despite months of training with Astrid. Perhaps if I'd been another illusionist I'd fit in with the guild and the house better, or be easier to train?"

"Astrid ramps up her training as students progress, increasing their challenges as they gain control. Surely you are farther along than you realize?"

Becka shrugged, noticing a surprising stiffness in her

shoulders. "I know it's only been three months, but I don't think others here see the value in a Null. In my powers. I'm not sure I do either." Becka yawned.

Vott mirrored her yawn. "You are more than a nn-Null. You are Ro... Rowan," he stuttered. "The house needs you."

"I know you say that," Becka drawled out, her words slurring. "You say that every time. But I don't think that most of the fae in House Rowan like me. I think they'd prefer if I wasn't here."

Did I really just say that with my outside the head voice? What's come over me?

"Please do not speak ill of your family. You have not even given most of them the opportunity to get to know you."

"It's hard to find time when I spend most of my days practicing my gift."

Vott's eyes fluttered shut, he slumped over, and then the mug fell out of his hand, rolled along the couch, and hit the deck at their feet with a loud crack.

"Luce!" Becka tried to yell, but it came out as a mumble. The shifter was already there, patting Vott's cheeks and checking for a pulse. His pallor was shifting into shades of gray as Becka watched through eyes increasingly difficult to keep open.

Luce called out and then pressed a button on a radio she carried at her waist. Fae and shifter guards alike filled the space in seconds.

Becka found herself looking up into Brent's grave features, his bulk a wide shadow against the stars shining through the roof of the pergola. In the months since her return, she'd gotten used to Brent's constant presence around her father. The head of Vott's contingent of shifter guards, the stocky, unflappable wolf was nearly inseparable from her father. Brent was quick to smile, and always made her feel safe and at ease.

She couldn't remember the wolf shifter ever appearing so angry and scared at the same time. The wrath in his steely blue eyes alarmed her.

"We're moving you to the infirmary, Becka," he assured her. "You'll be all right."

She tried to answer, but the words came out slurred. Becka tried to stand up, but her limbs flailed in response to her efforts.

In moments she was slung over Brent's shoulder, her bleary gaze connecting with Luce behind her.

"Stay with me," Luce said.

Try as Becka might, her world faded to black.

CHAPTER 3

$\mathcal{A}$nxiety peaked Becka's heart rate, increasing the pounding discomfort in her head. She'd forgotten something important. There was danger. She'd been here before. Stuck. Unable to move. *Trapped.*

She heard herself groan but couldn't move her limbs. The memory of being tied down and helpless shot another spike of adrenaline through her veins, and she jerked and flailed her arms and legs to escape. Was that blood she smelled?

Becka's swollen tongue stuck to the roof of her mouth and her head throbbed with the force of her heartbeat. Through the cotton filling her ears, she struggled to make out muffled voices.

A light touch pressed down on her shoulder. "You're safe here, Becka," came a voice she recognized, but couldn't place. The world spun around her.

She tried to open her eyes, finally gaining a bit of control over her body. Eyelids fluttering open, she looked up to see Illan standing over her, concern knitting his brows. Looking around the room, Becka immediately recognized House

Rowan's infirmary and its healer, Illan of House Birch. An apprentice worked alongside Illan, but Becka didn't know her name. She just recognized the healer's customary long white robes accented with light-blue embroidery.

The upper walls and ceiling of the room had been enchanted to appear as if they were out in the forest, surrounded by pine and aspen swaying overhead in the breeze. An illusory finch flitted by, lighthearted birdsong filling the air as it passed. Additionally, wide windows lined the room, and a few were open to let in the fresh air. Surely most patients appreciated the distracting display, but her head ached at least in part to the presence of the magic around her.

She took a deep breath, which was harder than it should have been.

For a moment, she'd been back in the solitude meditation retreat with Woden. That episode had driven dozens of nightmares, keeping her awake and stargazing until the dawn arrived to chase away the darkness. She'd never feared the dark before, not until the Shadow-Dwellers had found her.

A tremor shook through her limbs at the thought. She worked her mouth, and Illan anticipated her need, producing a small bowl of ice chips. He scooped up a fragment and held it to her lips.

"Try this. It'll help with the dry mouth."

He slid the ice chip past her lips, and the refreshing, cool liquid bathed her tongue and freed it from the roof of her mouth. A relieved sigh escaped her and something about the act, be it the water, the cold, or just the interaction, roused her mind into a heightened state of awareness.

After she'd worked the ice around her mouth until it

disappeared, Becka tried talking again. "Another?" she croaked out.

He smiled, but there was sorrow in his eyes. "Here you go."

Becka gratefully accepted the ice chip. Moving her arms around, she realized one had an IV with a bag of something hanging above her on a pole.

"What happened?" Becka asked, her cracking voice a whisper. A foggy memory of sitting under wisteria with Vott flashed through her mind. That awful lapsang tea. Vott's gray pallor as he slumped over. His mug rolling to the ground. "How is my father?"

Illan fed her another ice chip and then sat down on the bed next to her. He ran a hand over his face, pulling at a light dusting of whiskers which must have taken two or three days to grow.

"You and Vott were poisoned, but you do not appear to have gotten as large a dose as he did. When Vott arrived here, he was catatonic. I was able to do a measure of healing on him, but something in the potency or composition of the poison limited my gift and I have had to resort to non-magical methods to further aid him. I have him in the next room on a ventilator, but I cannot predict his recovery."

Images of Woden's enraged face flashed through her mind. He'd said others would come for her. She'd barely had time to learn about her powers. Becka didn't feel ready for this. Now Vott, her father, had borne the brunt of the attack this time.

Remembering her flippant, hurtful comments to him, her heart wrenched, and tears filled her eyes. What if those were the last words he'd heard? What if he died and she never got to apologize?

Seeing her distress, Illan leaned over her, touching her shoulder. "You're safe, Becka."

"Do you mean you don't know how long it will take for him to recover, or whether he will recover?"

Illan shrugged, his expression pained. "He survived the initial exposure, and in the past two days he has stabilized, so I am hopeful."

"I've been knocked out for two days?" Her head spun again.

He nodded.

Who else would get hit in the crossfire between her and the Shadow-Dwellers? Her heart sank and more tears flowed.

"We are still figuring out what they used. You both responded well to the cures for nightshade, but some signs point towards strychnine also being in the mix. I am not a chemist, but we have people looking deeper into the poison to better treat you both. Samples have also been sent to the enforcer labs for analysis."

Becka frowned. "Isn't strychnine used in rat poison?"

"Yes."

"I didn't think fae used rat poison."

"No, no we do not, which is why I found it so odd. I am used to testing for the nightshade; it is not an uncommon plant for horses to run into, as it's native to our grazing meadows. The enforcer techs will finalize the analysis of the other components."

Becka perked up. *Did Quinn return with them?* "Enforcers are here?"

"Yes, they came as soon as we reported the incident. And yes, Enforcer Quinn is among them."

A mixture of anticipation and anxiety roiled through Becka, followed by the lassitude of exhaustion. She'd only been awake for a few minutes and already it was difficult to keep her eyes open.

She desperately wanted to see Quinn again. It had been months since they'd stood face to face. They'd since communicated via message and email about potential clues to the ongoing Shadow-Dweller threat, but no calls. He'd kept his physical and emotional distance.

And why wouldn't he? I'm still engaged to Alain.

Illan set the bowl down on the bedside table. "You need to rest. We can talk more later."

Becka's gaze drifted towards movement at the door, spying Saige waiting expectantly. Illan strode over to the door, motioning to someone out in the hall.

"I don't think she's up for company right now. I'd prefer that she rest," she heard Illan say.

"I'm afraid we don't have the luxury of time," came the reply, which Becka recognized as Astrid's voice.

A moment later, Astrid and Maura followed him back in. Astrid's face was tear-streaked, and her cheeks were pinked. Maura's pallor was gray, and Becka had the impression her well-groomed poise was the only thing keeping her together.

No doubt nearly losing her husband had pushed Maura to the limit. Looking back at them through her own tears, Becka hoped some of those tears were concern for her and not just for her father. She didn't envy the weight her mother carried on her shoulders.

They walked up to her and took up positions around the

foot of the bed. Becka's anxiety spiked, and for now at least all thought of falling asleep fled.

"We've all been holding our breath for your successful recovery," Maura said. "Illan has determined that your health will recover, but Astrid needs to confirm that your powers aren't altered."

Becka's heart ached at their words. *Oh great, they aren't here to check on me, just my powers.*

"I feel all right overall," Becka replied. Maura and Astrid glanced at her but didn't appear satisfied.

Do they even care how I'm doing?

"Based on how she's rebounded compared to Vott, it leads me to think her dose was nominal. We'll know more once the techs finish analyzing the blood work," Illan explained.

"Doesn't feel nominal," Becka said.

"I am sure it does not," Maura said. "Your father was not as fortunate as you."

Becka felt the tears run down her cheeks, and her next words came out in a rush. "I'm so sorry, Maura. I didn't want to drink the tea, so I poured my tea into Vott's cup. If I'd drunk the tea myself, Vott wouldn't have been poisoned."

A flash of anger contorted Maura's face, but she quickly regained her composure, dabbing at the tears on her cheeks with a kerchief. "We don't yet know how the poisoning happened or who was targeted. Besides, if you had received a more potent dose, then you might be dead now or in a coma next to Vott. I am grateful that you appear to be rebounding, but we need verification that your gift is fully intact, which I will leave in Astrid's capable hands. Now, if you will excuse me, I must get back to Vott."

Becka wiped tears away, struck by Maura's cold reaction.

It felt like Maura cared more about Becka's gift than Becka herself, and perhaps she did? Things hadn't ever been warm and fluffy between the two of them, Maura not being that sort of mother.

This situation had cast a bright light on the strain in their relationship. So why did Becka continue to feel disappointed in the distance between them? Why couldn't she be another aloof fae, not caring what others thought?

Maura swept out of the room while Astrid remained, her focus narrowing on Becka. Her relationship with her Aunt Astrid was even more complicated. They'd moved beyond the initial tension and distrust from Becka's return to the manor, but she still felt like Astrid saw her only as a potential resource for the house. It was as if her Null gift was endlessly interesting to Astrid, but Becka as a person, not so much.

"Help her get dressed," Astrid said to the apprentice healer, who moved to Becka's side and helped her sit up. "We will head to the training grounds and see if your gift has suffered."

Becka eagerly accepted the young fae's help, her limbs still not quite feeling fully under her own control.

"Again, I would prefer to keep her here for observation," Illan said, stress visible in the narrowing of his lips.

"Noted, but the heir is coming with me. The sooner we can confirm that her powers are intact, the better for us all."

CHAPTER 4

*B*ecka crept into the training circle on silent feet as if the speed of her motion would change the predictable outcome. Judging by the sinking feeling in the pit of her stomach, she didn't have high hopes about this trial of her powers. With the shakiness in each step and the exhaustion pervading her every thought, she'd be lucky to have a decent showing.

But she knew Astrid wouldn't let her go rest until she'd answered the question: were her powers still fully intact?

What will happen to me if they aren't? Will I get sent back to the townhouse in the city?

Astrid stood off to the side, flanked by a pair of illusionist trainees who had constructed an elaborate rainbowed layering of magic: Nuisi, a stout but tall young lord, and Grein, a willowy and unusually-tall young lady, both clad in the silvered robes of apprentices.

Spheres of greens and blues rotated and spun past reds and yellows, each on its own separate trajectory.

The training grounds were in a tall, expansive square

structure located a short walk from the manor house. Iron webbing lined the interior of the walls, windows, and roof, preventing all magic from either escaping or entering the building. This provided a safe training space where students of all ages and levels could experiment safe from any magic run wild. Large, black rings painted on the plain flooring demarcated separate training spaces, and today there were students and guilded illusionists in each space, filling the room.

Because I want an audience to witness my potential failure? Argh! No pressure!

Becka wasn't certain of the exact number of Rowan residing in the territory, but there were rankings on the wall for the current roster of students, showing recent trial scores for all those who were not yet guilded. The list had 175 names under the heading: Illusionists. Becka's name was on the list, but in a separate column: Nulls.

Again, no pressure, Becka! Not like everyone could see her standing. *Except they can.*

"Remember," Astrid spoke, her voice a mere whisper, "you are aiming to deconstruct each layer individually."

The illusionists' construction training dovetailed with Becka's Null deconstruction drills. The students would spend all day, or the day before, weaving powerful and elaborate, layered illusions.

Becka had destroyed each in less than three seconds. Could she still?

"Got it," Becka replied. "Let's get on with it."

A snicker came from the far side of the room. She glanced over and recognized Alvilda and Yaeli, a near-inseparable pair of guilded illusionists. Despite their formal training being years behind them, she'd often noticed them practicing regularly together. The pair always wore coordinating dresses, and today their colors were in hues of lavender and deep purple.

Astrid shook her head at Becka's impatience. "Remember, gaining control of your gift is your only path forward. Power unmarried to will lies the way to madness."

Destroying magic had come easier than breathing to Becka. Breaking just the things she wanted to, however, continued to challenge her. Now, Astrid's warning caused her to redouble her focus. Becka didn't want to be one of the unfortunate fae-touched who couldn't control their power and were destined for a life removed from fae society. She didn't want to be doomed to live out her days in a hermitage so others would remain safe from her. Nor did she want to live with a weak power, yet still fae and guilded and therefore forced to stay within the territories.

All or nothing would be preferable.

"Today, we need to see if your gifts are in any way diminished. Come along now, continue," Astrid urged.

Becka growled under her breath, stepping near the spinning orb, and then raised her left hand within millimeters of the outermost ring. She had to work extra hard to steady her arm, which already shook visibly with exhaustion and fatigue. Becka's head ached in response to her proximity to the magic. Her reaction to the magic was less than when she first returned to House Rowan, but nonetheless, she'd been hitting the hot sauce hard.

Since she'd been working with Astrid, Becka had come to a place where she could sense a mild physical resistance of magic to her touch, at least when she was looking for magic.

At this moment, Becka energetically sensed the crimson orb as it undulated mere millimeters away from her hand. A spontaneous smile cracked across her face; the sign of progress was small yet tangible.

"I'm still able to sense the magic without unraveling it."

Astrid nodded, a tense smile upon her face. "That's reassuring. Now, without moving, imagine moving closer to the crimson orb."

Becka took a deep breath, and then let it out in a long, slow stream. She imagined moving close enough to touch the magical red layer.

The red orb shivered as if hit by a hammer and then shattered apart, dusting into the surrounding air.

Relief flooded through her. Her magic was as potent as ever and her control hadn't slipped, despite the poisoning and her present state of exhaustion. "Uh huh, that's what I'm talking about," Becka muttered, drawing her hand back and rubbing her hands together.

Becka glanced over at Astrid and the others. At this point, everyone's attention was on her. Others had gathered to watch, their expectant gazes urging her on as they whispered amongst themselves. Becka knew many in her house weren't fond of her and she'd overheard their questions as to the relevancy of her Null gift.

Were they taking bets, wondering if the poisoning had broken her? Or were they simply curious bystanders, unable to look away from the show playing out before them? Either way, Becka didn't appreciate the distraction.

Frowning, Becka brought her attention back to the sphere, focusing on the now revealed green layer. It rotated slowly, appearing to shiver with increasing waves. Curious about what had changed, Becka tilted her head and noticed small particulates of red dust falling against the green sphere.

Moments later, the green sphere shattered. Becka took a step back, the sinking feeling in the pit of her stomach an all-too-familiar sensation this past month. Why couldn't she master this step?

"Well," Astrid said, talking over the noise of the orange and lavender layers shattering apart. "It's not progress, but your ability to manage your power hasn't suffered, nor has the scope of your gift. Maura will be reassured."

Becka watched as the innermost silver layer turned into dust. She should be happy for not having lost skill due to the poisoning, versus wishing for improvement each time. She'd been Astrid's student long enough to read a lack of forward progress as failure.

Astrid's illusionist students' shoulders slumped, their expressions looking like they'd eaten overly sour food. Surely after spending all day creating this spectacle, having it destroyed in mere seconds didn't help their moods.

"The inner layers seemed to take longer to dissolve this time," Becka said.

Astrid raised a brow at her. "Perhaps."

Across the room, Yaeli and Alvilda shook their heads, animatedly whispering to each other. Then Yaeli grabbed Alvilda's hand and pulled her training partner along, heading out the door. Others followed them, the crowd moving on. The show was over for today.

Becka frowned. It wasn't like either Yaeli or Alvilda displayed rare or potent talents. Illusions came in many forms, not all of them large spinning orbs filled with colors.

She'd seen Yaeli's doppelganger skill a few dozen times now, and although it was amusing, it appeared to be the breadth of her illusionary art. In contrast, she'd learned Alvilda's gift wasn't even creating illusions directly, but in spinning tales that mentally transported those around her into another world or changing subtle elements within her surroundings.

"You are definitely gaining a measure of control, if only millimeter by millimeter." Astrid walked over to her, her gaze tracking the motion of dust in the air. "Perhaps tomorrow you can do sheets of layers and bring in a fan, so the Nullified dust doesn't have the opportunity to behave so contagiously."

"What do you mean by contagious?"

Astrid, the consummate trainer, drew herself up and folded her hands in front of her. Becka had come to infer this gesture as recognition of a worthy question. "Your magic permeates the matter it contacts. Even when the magic destroys an object, the particulates from that changed matter continue to exist and they persist in the Nulling momentum for a short period of time."

"But I don't understand why there's even dust? If I'm Nullifying the magic, why isn't it just gone?"

Nuisi cleared his throat before speaking. "Although these are illusions, there is a basic elemental framework weaving the matrices of ley lines together. Thus, dust, air, water vapor, even heat all form a basic net, if you will, upon which the magic lies."

"Wow, that's... amazing. Wait, are you even supposed to be telling me about illusionist mechanics?"

The boy blushed so deeply the flush reached all the way to the tips of his pointed ears. "Uh," he stammered. "I apologize, Lady Astrid, for my lack of decorum."

Astrid rolled her eyes and waved him off. "They are not used to me training anyone outside of the guild. You are a magical outlier and Rowan's heir. I am not worried about you picking up an odd fact or two."

Becka suppressed the smirk that threatened to spread across her face. Such a breach of protocol would have been unheard of before she returned to House Rowan, and Becka counted each shift away from rote custom a win. Bit by bit, the unusual circumstances of her return were shaking up the old order and protocols. They might not be able to forget her once-outcast status, but one by one the fae were accepting her for her differences even if they'd prefer she be like them.

Having her family accept her for herself was the first step. She was slowly gaining Astrid and Vott's respect. Could she win over more of House Rowan? And how long would that take?

The re-heired Becka had two goals.

One, to regain whatever freedom both fae and human cultures would allow her. She needed to get back to her education. Her research. Dr. Traut had promised to hold her a position with his department at the Institute for a time. Although she suspected he wouldn't be able to hold it forever, Becka wasn't yet ready to give up on that option.

And two, she planned to find a way to bridge the gulf between human and fae. She'd yearned for this dream when she was an outcast and that focus had stayed with her. The shifters had found a way to live in relative peace alongside other races. Surely there was a path forward between the fae and humans besides this ongoing cold war?

To accomplish these goals, Becka needed to find a way to make it easier for other fae to follow in her unconventional footsteps. Then she wouldn't be the only one crossing the boundaries and bridging the gap between fae and human cultures.

"Do you think my magic is more contagious than other forms of magic?" Becka asked Astrid, glossing over Astrid's admission while simultaneously pushing for deeper information. She'd learned long ago to not react to false admissions and instead just accept them as the new norm.

Astrid's frown shifted, her brows raised and expression curious as she studied the dusty remnants of the illusionists' magic. "My observation says the intensity of your power does make the effect persist longer than usual, but I must confer with the testers. When's the next time you meet with them?"

"I'm afraid I lost track of time, what with being unconscious," Becka said, feeling unsteady on her feet. "They are bringing a cursed man into one of the meditation houses to test my powers. Hopefully I'll be able to remove his curse."

Astrid's face lit up. "Oh yes, the Elder Langdon. I heard they had to take precautions to transport him here." Astrid took another look at her, as if seeing her fresh again. "You should go and rest. I'll let Maura know your powers appear intact." Astrid's attention turned to Nuisi and Grein, no doubt to give them directions for the next day's training preparations.

Luce appeared at the door, sniffing the air and casting her gaze about in a wide net. Alighting on Becka, she nodded. "Are you done, Lady Becka?"

"Just a moment, Luce," Becka replied. She slid on the sea silk gloves Vott had gifted her. "Same time tomorrow?" she asked Astrid.

"Indeed. We'll try layered plates instead of orbs and see how that goes."

Becka walked out of the building, feeling steadier on her feet than she had a right to. Saige was there too, concern creasing her brow.

"If you need," Luce glanced at Becka, "I can carry you."

"Heck no," she replied. "Or at least, not until we're out of sight. I don't want to give the rumor mill more to gossip about."

Somehow Becka made it back to her quarters under her own power while the anxious pair of shifters watched her every step. Stepping inside her room, her plan was to get into the shower as quickly as possible, which was why she was surprised to find Quinn's familiar form standing before her.

"Lady Becka, I was hoping to have a few minutes of your time?"

Although it had been three months since she'd last seen him, she would have recognized Quinn's rich baritone anywhere, despite the distance and formality in his tone. Heart leaping into her throat, she drank in his presence.

Becka looked him over, his simple but elegantly tailored shirt paired with the cargo pants he so loved, but now in black. He wore that sexy tactical jacket again, which was also in black. His short, stocky frame and cropped burnished-gold hair were the same as she'd remembered. Hands on his hips, his confidence and swagger were unshakable. Becka couldn't stop the smile spreading across her face, and she held in a breath as heat flared across her cheeks.

She wondered at the shift to black from the prior earth tones he'd favored. Had the enforcer's uniform shifted, or was this a personal style choice?

He stood just inside her room, a notebook between his hands and his gaze trained on her. Fatigue strained his features and the look of concern on his face conveyed the depths of the situation at hand.

"Do I look *that* bad?" she asked, her voice croaking. She needed some water.

"I mean, you have looked better." He smiled, but it was strained. Polite.

Distant.

Becka sighed, frustrated at the situation, which she knew as all her own doing. Despite her best efforts, she was still engaged to Alain. She also knew it might not be in her power to stop the impending nuptials; so far, all she'd been able to do was delay the inevitable.

Awkward didn't even begin to describe the energy between them.

"Luce, Saige," Quinn said, "will you trust me alone with Becka for a short while?'

The shifters looked to Becka as one, and she nodded.

"Okay, but don't wear her out with talking," Luce replied. "She needs rest."

"We'll be just outside if you need us," Saige said, pulling the door most of the way closed behind them.

"Want to sit down?" he asked.

Becka nodded and then plodded her way over to the divan.

"Can I get you anything?" he asked.

"A glass of water would be nice," Becka replied, settling herself down on the divan. Quinn ducked into her bathroom and returned, glass in hand. She kicked off her shoes and pulled off her gloves, laying them on the table next to her.

When he leaned over her and placed the glass on the same table, she caught his musky scent and was transported back to the night he'd crashed next to her and she'd been lulled to sleep by his steady, deep breathing.

Becka hadn't seen Quinn since the weekend of Tesse's funeral, when he'd left for Sirona Healing Springs to heal from his injuries during Woden's attack. She shivered, extra aware of the weakness in her knees remembering how he'd been knocked out by the Shadow-Dweller's concussive fireballs and pierced from the shrapnel of exploding trees. His stout House Oak constitution had no doubt contributed to his survival, but from what she'd heard from Chief Elowen, he'd been off work and healing for several weeks.

They'd been fortunate no one had died during the altercation. Would they be so lucky the next time a Shadow-Dweller attacked?

She and Quinn had spent her first week back at House Rowan constantly together. His abrupt absence after that long, tense week ending with Woden's bloody attack had left her off-kilter. Associating Quinn's presence with her return home had complicated Becka's ability to adjust after he'd left.

They'd sent messages back and forth via phone, but being face-to-face with him again sent an electric thrill down her spine to the tips of her toes. It was even better to see him in person than she'd imagined. Despite the weeks apart, the comfort of his presence calmed her. Or perhaps she'd craved seeing him more because of the time apart.

Beyond the initial thrill of his return an unsure tension hung in the air between them. The reminder dulled her excitement over his return. Sure, he was here, but things weren't the same, and might not ever be.

Becka took the glass and sipped. Immediately the soreness in her throat lessened and she felt a tad more focused. "Oh my goodness, I didn't realize I was that thirsty." She looked around the room but didn't see a bottle of what she really wanted.

There was a glint in his amber eyes as he reached into his jacket and pulled out three bottles of her favorite hot sauce. "When I got my orders to come out here, I stopped and picked these up on the way."

Becka sighed in anticipation, holding her hand out for a bottle. She'd missed his smile. "Please, Quinn, you have no idea how much my head hurts."

He opened the bottle and handed it over. "I'd never even dream of depriving you."

His ready smile faltered when she reached out. Becka snagged the bottle with her free hand and leaned back, alternating swigs between the hot sauce and the water. Quinn set the other bottles on her sofa table, grabbed a chair and pulled it near the divan, and took a seat.

"I'm surprised your house cook hasn't whipped up a fae-based alternative to that sauce."

"Oh, they keep trying! It's like every day I get another option, and many work just fine managing my headaches, but I just adore this brand's flavor."

"Out of curiosity, I tried it. There's no flavor, just heat," he said.

"Not to me." She smiled at the banter, but his expression was grim.

Quinn opened his notebook, studiously reviewing his notes for a moment. "As you can imagine, Vott's shifter guards haven't taken this attack well. Both of you have had constant surveillance since."

Becka wasn't surprised. She hadn't been without a posted guard since she'd returned to House Rowan.

"After this, I'll be lucky to use the bathroom without company," she said.

Quinn sobered. "That's a fine idea. I'll recommend it to Brent."

Becka rolled her eyes. "Kidding..."

Quinn's gaze narrowed on her, his schooled expression and terse formality exaggerating the distance between them.

"I'm aware."

There was a knock at the door. Quinn jumped to his feet and turned to the door. Was he concerned who might see them together?

"Who is it?" Becka called out, her voice faltering.

Brent opened the door and walked over. "Good evening, Becka. Enforcer Quinn."

"Brent." She nodded, continuing to alternate sips between water and hot sauce.

"Alain is in the hall, asking if you're up for company." Brent raised a brow, his gaze drifting to Quinn and then back to her.

At Becka's request, her shifter guards had been giving excuses to Alain for weeks. She knew Brent understood she was avoiding Alain and so she attempted to come up with a fresh reason each time.

"I literally just got back," Becka said. "And I'm too exhausted to deal with him."

"And I'm here in an official capacity, I'm afraid." Quinn frowned. "I need time to question Becka about the incident."

"Uh huh." Brent's hands went to his hips as he looked back and forth between them. Finally, he shook his head. "At some point you just need to come to terms with the Alain situation," he said to Becka. "Discomfort is meant to be faced head-on."

"That's a perfect shifter saying, Brent, but I'm not dealing with my *situation* right at this moment. Can you please tell Alain I'll speak with him tomorrow?"

He shrugged, hands up in the air. "May I suggest instead of hiding, that you rise to meet the challenges of your life? Own it. Putting off action is perpetuating this never-ending drama." He turned and strode out of the room, closing the door on his way out.

"Heck yeah, it's mine. I'll put off Alain for as long as it takes, thank you very much," she said under her breath. Becka set her now empty glass on the table. "At least I'm never left wondering what he's thinking."

"Direct is the shifter way." Quinn's lip twitched and he took a deep breath, as if he was debating his word choice. "I hear you're still engaged?"

Becka sighed. "Yeah, unfortunately I haven't found my escape clause yet, but I will."

Quinn's single raised brow paired with tension in his lips. "Even if you were to find a way out of your engagement to Alain, don't you think your mother would find another marriageable prospect befitting her heir?"

A heavy weight settled in her gut. "Yes, Maura definitely will. But I'd have the opportunity to try and talk some sense into her before she signed the next one."

His eye twitched. "You'd school the duchess using your fine understanding of fae customs and then she'd just come around to your way of thinking?"

Becka groaned. "I may be Rowan's heir, but my gift is too

dangerous for most potential partners. Maura must see reason. Once she's released from the current contract, of course."

"Do you have a list of houses who are immune to your gift?"

"Besides your house?" she asked, and he nodded. "Not yet, but the testers have been debating it at length."

"I would think Duchess Maura would have a list of potentials, even if she has not yet made you aware of it."

"Contingency plans?" Becka replied. "Yes, I suppose she would. But it's not only my gift. I'm a bit unconventional. I've had a difficult time winning over those in my own house, not to mention strangers."

The corner of his lip twitched upward. "Some wouldn't consider your unique character a detractor. And even more would be willing to overlook it for the sake of custom and potentially powerful progeny."

"Ugh," she replied, scrunching her nose at the thought. "Can't I just donate some eggs? I'm sure someone would be willing to carry the future heirs of House Rowan."

He frowned. "The fae don't practice surrogacy, Becka. It's believed power transfers from mother to child during the pregnancy."

She shook her head. "I've been gone too long. Humans do it all the time, but I forgot that fae don't. It's too bad; it would broaden our fertility rates. And besides, that argument makes no sense, as children get the father's powers too."

'Yet it is the custom. I can see you've thought this over." Then, his tone curt, "Did you want more water?"

Becka bit her lip, feeling like he'd shut down the conversation. But what did she expect him to do? He'd warned her that he wasn't interested in someone who wasn't available. The chemistry between them had become some sort of cruel joke.

"No thanks, I'd better take it slow with the water... my stomach is still queasy. And thank you for the sauce. My head is already improving."

He gave a terse nod. "You're welcome. Are you up for some questions?"

He'd gone all business on her, and her heart ached. To have Quinn back but distant was almost worse than having him not back at all.

"From you," she smiled, "anytime."

He flipped open his notebook to where he'd left a handy pen as a place keeper. "Tell me what you remember about the day of the poisoning."

Becka took a deep breath and then recounted that day, including her morning training with Astrid, the muffins and sliced melon she'd had for breakfast, the ridiculous floofy ombre dress, the trade banquet and socializing, her bottle-dropping incident, and finally her end-of-day tea and poisoning with Vott. Everything.

Quinn silently listened to her tale. When her words ran dry, he sat contemplatively jotting down notes.

"Just so I know I have this down right: you weren't there when the tea was delivered?"

"No. Vott had all that in order when I arrived."

"And you didn't see the tea brewed? Or the set put out?"

"Nope."

"And you didn't like the tea, so you poured it into Vott's mug?"

Guilt flip-flopped in her stomach. "Unfortunately, yes."

"Did it taste funny?"

"I hadn't tasted it first. I just hate that tea with a passion. His mug was empty, so I gave him mine and got water instead. I only had a little of the tea left in my cup."

"The tea wasn't poisoned."

Becka leaned forward. "But all I drank was tea and water, and I didn't see Vott drink any water, just tea. It *had* to be the tea."

Quinn shook his head. "We tested the teapot and there wasn't any poison."

She frowned. "That makes no sense, Quinn."

He held up his hand to calm her. "We tested the teapot, tea leaves, mugs, tea, and water."

"And?"

"The tea in Vott's mug was poisoned, but not until after you arrived. By the staff reports, he'd been sitting and drinking tea for a quarter hour before you arrived."

"Wait a second... I didn't poison my father!" she exclaimed.

Quinn's gaze met hers for a moment, just long enough for Becka to realize he was reading her. His innate gift gave him an ear for the truth, and because it was innate, it operated twenty-four seven. All he had to do was pay attention. Did he think she was capable of poisoning her own father? His doubt hurt her heart.

This isn't how things are supposed to be between us.

"I didn't think you had, but thank you for the unequivocal statement. It'll satisfy the doubts of some others, and I believe you." He jotted down another note before continuing. "Our techs found that the entire rim of your mug was covered in poison. Our theory is that you were the intended target.

Since you poured your tea into Vott's mug, that's likely how his tea was contaminated."

Becka's head swam in confusion. "You're saying I *did* poison my father?"

He rocked his head from side to side. "Inadvertently. It wasn't your fault."

Tears filled her eyes. "That doesn't make me feel any better."

He leaned closer, reached out, and stroked her shoulder. "I understand."

Becka reveled in the contact, chaste and brief as it was. "Do the enforcers have any leads?"

"We know nothing definite, so we're casting a broader net in the investigation to make sure we don't miss any potential suspects."

"I'm grateful the enforcers are here. Well, that you're here. I just hope Vott can recover from the poison soon."

He nodded, a grim set to his jaw. "I am also hopeful, but the chances are low. He appears to have gotten a larger dose than you. Plus, there's the nature of the poison."

Her heart skipped a beat. "What do you mean? Illan said it was a mixture of nightshade and strychnine. He also said that he'd used a combination of magic and medicine to treat Vott and that he was hopeful for his recovery."

Quinn fixed her with a look, one she remembered from the last time he gave her bad news. He leaned in and spoke in low tones. "There was a third component in the poison."

CHAPTER 6

"*D*on't leave me hanging," she said.

There was no trace of humor in Quinn's features, his prominent bone structure left harsh and grave without his usual animated personality. "We found traces of the Treatment."

Becka's eyes blinked in quick succession. "You can't be serious. *The* Treatment?"

His chin ducked a quick nod. "The one and only."

Every fae-touched knew of the Treatment. Humans developed it during the Great War as a last-ditch effort to eradicate the fae threat. The fae didn't know how it functioned; the method and formula a closely kept human secret. Rumor said it was a form of genetic warfare. Any fae exposed to the substance had their powers limited. Blunted. Bound. But those weren't the worst of the effects.

Becka had read stories of the devastation to the victims. Cruelly, they still felt a trickle of their powers, but never again had access to them in meaningful ways. They also aged at an accelerated pace, which was a death sentence for those already well along in years. The victims withered, losing their strength, night vision, and agility.

Some killed themselves, unwilling to live without elements of self they considered essential. Those that didn't take their own lives withered away, pariahs of their generation. A warning to all fae-kind not to war with humans ever again.

The Treatment had turned the tide of the war in favor of the human contingent. Fear of being stripped of all that made them fae was a weapon they could not defeat. Thus, the Pax Hominid Treaty was born, or at least enforced.

"That's why Maura and Astrid wanted my gift checked!"

"Yes," he replied. "They were the first I told when the test results came in."

She shivered. "I didn't know the Treatment was still around. I thought part of the treaty was an agreement never to use that weapon again, as long as fae maintained the peace."

He shook his head, his grimace nearing a snarl. "There's an exclusion for when fae are convicted of sedition or violent crimes in human courts. Then a part of the sentence includes the Treatment. It's rarely done; the threat alone is enough to deter most transgressions."

"Is there enough left to reverse-engineer a cure?" Becka asked. "You must have access to labs sophisticated enough to attempt it?"

"The labs are there, but remember they are human-run, even the enforcer labs. Reverse-engineering a cure to the Treatment would not be allowed. Besides, once we realized what we had, all our samples were seized. No fae is allowed access to it."

"Except the one who used it to poison my father and me!" Becka felt sick to her stomach. She sat forward on the divan again. "Poor Vott. *I* was the true target, but he got most of the dose..."

Quinn nodded. "There's still hope for him. We don't yet know how much he received. Only time will tell how deeply impacted his abilities and health will be."

Becka felt the floor drop out beneath her, her stomach flip-flopping with anxiety. "If they'd been successful, at least I'd have gotten out of my engagement."

He frowned, brows drawn together. "There are more side effects from the Treatment than simply losing one's powers. You'd be wasting away, powerless and ailing, even more vulnerable to your enemies. Surely that wouldn't have been worth the cost?"

"When you put it that way, it doesn't sound like an acceptable exit strategy. Quinn, I'm grateful the enforcers assigned you to this case. Seeing you in person is so much better than over the phone."

"I wasn't back on active duty yet, but Chief Elowen called me when she noticed it involved you. She knows I'm proprietary with my cases."

Becka let that hang in the air, wanting to know if he felt that way about her, not just about the case. But after his comments earlier about her engagement, she wasn't ready to broach that topic with him yet. She didn't deny to herself that her affection for him had continued to grow.

"I'm going to help you figure out who poisoned me. I will avenge Vott."

Some of his usual warmth returned to his smile. "Of course you will."

"I'm serious!"

"I know you are."

"When I think Vott got hit with the brunt of it and that his poisoning was inadvertently my fault, I feel so angry and sick all at once. Especially since he's been making an extra effort to re-bond with me."

"He has?"

"Yeah, every couple of days he invites me to lunch, tea, private dinner, you name it. Always with the easy small talk and filled with encouragement over each minute gain in skill performance. He just keeps working at connecting, and I haven't made it easy."

"That fits."

Becka scowled at him. "What do you mean?"

"Every time we communicate, you have repeated your doubts about being accepted by House Rowan. You've spoken wistfully of the city and your persisting education and work interests."

Becka sighed, sinking back against the divan. "I suppose I'm holding back. It's difficult to feel at home here after being gone for so long. It's hard to trust I won't be rejected again."

"I don't know how you'll manage it, but I believe you will find your own path. It might not look like what you expect, but I have faith in you to find your way."

Becka reached out and gripped his arm. His touching affirmation spoke to her at a deep level. "Thanks. I am so glad you're here."

"I am too," he replied, eyes full of emotion.

Seconds passed. Then a minute. Then two. She'd missed him to distraction. Becka studied his features, drinking in his presence. Quinn had earned her trust, and her affection had grown along the way. She hadn't been fully aware of the depths of her feelings towards him until he'd left for the Sirona Healing Springs to recuperate. Now, with him back, her emotions were resurfacing with renewed vigor.

She remembered that night, months ago now, where she'd curled up next to him in bed, filled with fear over the Shadow-Dwellers but able to sleep because she felt safe in his arms. She also remembered their passionate kisses the next morning.

"I missed you," she said. "I wasn't sure when, or if, I'd get to see you again."

Quinn raised a hand and brushed her cheek with the backs of his fingers. "I missed you too."

Silence and words unspoken hung in the air between them for a few moments.

"So, how do we find the Shadow-Dweller responsible for the poisoning?" Becka asked.

"Hold on. We can't assume that the poisoning involves them."

"Can't we? Woden said they would never stop until they had me." Becka shifted onto her side.

"Exactly, they want your gift. Killing you or destroying your power would work against their stated goals."

Becka pursed her lips, licking the still-parched skin. "Perhaps they were just trying to incapacitate me and make my powers easier to grab? I mean, if I was in Vott's shape, then I wouldn't be able to fight them off."

"No, that would still at least erode your ability, if not destroy it utterly. Such a course of action wouldn't make sense. However, as it's an attack on you, their stated target, I don't think we can exclude the Shadow-Dwellers from being involved. But they aren't at the top of my list."

"Well, then, who is?"

"Various members of House Rowan, for a start. I'm sure you have relatives who aren't too happy you've returned to the fold."

"Yeah, but enough to kill me? What have you heard about my return to House Rowan? I'm sure an enforcer would be privy to all the rumors floating around."

Quinn's expression turned guarded. "It's well-known that your return to House Rowan has been bumpy."

"And...?"

"There is concern over your ability to reintegrate into fae society. You eschew fae cultural norms and appear determined to forge your own way forward. Disruptions are anathema to our cultural soul. Not to mention, when you became heir you disrupted the previous lineage. It's been widely noted that you haven't adopted your family's manner of dress and there's talk you spend more time with your shifter help than your immediate family. House Hawthorne and their allies have concerns over your delayed marriage to Alain."

The weight of his words pressed down on her body and mind. Her inability to accept her return to fae society had been transparent. "Is that all?"

"No. There are widespread but quieter whispers of some asking if House Rowan might well be better off with another —for instance, Calder—as the heir."

Becka sighed. *Perhaps it would.* "I have to assume Maura has heard all of this. Why hasn't she brought it up?"

"If she had, would it have changed your behavior?" he asked.

Becka frowned. "Yes, but likely not for the better. She knows I'm stubborn to a fault."

"Then there's your answer."

"Right, and now my brother Calder is next in line, instead of heir himself. Plus, he despises me. I swear I can hear his teeth cracking from that forced smile he plasters on his face around me."

Quinn chuckled. "There's your humor. But that makes Calder a prime candidate, from my perspective."

"Which would be idiotic of him, as he's also an obvious suspect."

Quinn shrugged. "Idiocy is not a typical restraining factor to murder."

Becka rolled her eyes at him. Twice. "Who else is on your list?"

"The shifters."

Becka screwed up her face. "What? Why would they have anything against me?"

"You have a new power. Do you know whether it impacts their innate abilities?"

"I've come into contact with them occasionally, on accident, and my Null hasn't appeared to affect them, but I would never test it out on them just to find out if their innate abilities are safe from my Null powers. I wouldn't want to hurt them while experimenting with my own limits."

"And yet, perhaps the shifters fear that your Null power

can harm them? Do any of them appear standoffish or overly cautious of you?"

"No, not at all. They're loyal to Vott to a fault and have never given me cause to worry about their intentions. If they'd meant me harm, they've had ample opportunity before now."

"Someone fears your Null power enough to have you eliminated before you become more of a threat," he said.

"That could be true of any of the fae houses!" Becka threw her hands up in the air.

"Yes, I have also included the other fae houses in my list. Your new ability has the potential to shift power between the houses. Some would read that as a threat to their standing."

Becka nodded. "The infighting and sparring for power amongst fae is legendary. And here I show up with a new ability no one understands. I've noticed that some non-Rowan fae who live here look at me as if weighing me on a scale. They see me as dangerous or valuable, or perhaps both. Plus, we just hosted that trade delegation."

Quinn scribbled down a few more notes. "I'll prioritize those who aren't born Rowans but who live here, as well as get a list of all recent visitors to the house."

She sighed. "Is that the entirety of your list of potential poisoners?"

"No. We can't eliminate humans either. For similar reasons."

She rolled her eyes. "Humans don't magic. How could *they* see me as a threat?"

"For the same reasons the fae or shifters might. They might fear your gift could upset the power balance between the races."

"So basically, you're implying *everyone* might want me dead?"

"Potentially."

"Well, then, I'm lucky to have the best of the enforcers here to solve the mystery."

"*Best* might overstate my status a tad, but we will solve this."

"Then you accept my demand to work together?"

"We have met." He shook his head, apparently resigned to her request. "I know better than to try to change your disposition. I agree to your terms."

"Good. I didn't want to have to call your chief to force your hand."

He barked out a laugh. "She's too fond of you to refuse. One day you must tell me how you managed to cozy up to her."

She could have explained how she'd talked her mother, Duchess Maura, into sending Chief Elowen a shipment of enchanted silken cloaks as a thank you. The cloaks blended into the background, hiding whomever was wearing them as long as they held still. A perfect gift for enforcers.

Becka calculated that with their *donation* Elowen would put House Rowan's requests for aid at the top of her list. When the chief had replied with a thank you note including her direct line, Becka knew they had an understanding.

Quinn's timely return confirmed her instincts had been right, but she didn't want to delve into that now.

"One day I will."

"Oh, I almost forgot. I brought you some not-so-light reading material." He reached into an interior pocket in his jacket and presented an antique leather-bound book to her.

"We discovered this in the case archives. I wanted to get your opinion on it."

Becka reached out for the book, a wave of pressure hitting her skull like a mini-shockwave, and she swooned but retained her grip on the book.

"Sorry, I should have warned you."

She shook her head. "It's not a surprise." Cracking open the tome, Becka let out a long, slow whistle. "You said you found this in old case archives? Those would be for Shadow-Dweller cases?"

"What tipped you off?"

"It's page after page of the same symbols I found on Tesse's neck. Has anyone developed a translation?"

He shook his head. "It's something the enforcers have worked on for decades. We've had linguistics specialists look at them. We've run the different documents through code-breaking algos. We've tried everything we can think of, and so far, nothing has worked. It's almost as if they're art and not words at all. Which is why I brought it to you. I hoped you might have some unique insight."

"I'll see if I can figure anything out. Aren't you worried I might break it with my ability?"

"At this point we've exhausted our options. We have copies of what's on the pages, just in case something happens to the original. We'd prefer you not break it, but even if you do that will tell us something."

"Well, then, let's hope I find something."

Becka paged through the tome, thinking about their conversation. She almost couldn't believe Quinn had returned, but here he was right in front of her. She wanted to talk about her feelings with Quinn, especially since they would now be working together to solve the poisoning. Based on their earlier conversation about her continuing engagement to Alain, Becka shouldn't even be thinking about wanting to kiss Quinn or how good he smelled. Much less about how his muscles rippled underneath the fabric of his linen shirt and jacket.

Oh boy.

She took a deep breath and crossed her arms, rubbing the flesh of her biceps. The shifters and their talk of being comfortable in one's own skin was getting to her. If she could be honest with Maura about not wanting to stay at House Rowan and not feeling accepted, then why couldn't she be direct with Quinn?

Becka knew the reason. She'd experienced rejection all of her life. She'd learned to parry the blows and rebound gracefully. But she'd never explored an intimate relationship with someone else before. Nothing beyond having fun in the moment.

Besides, Quinn had already shut her down.

Quinn chuckled. "Hmm. I'm curious what you're chewing on over there."

Damn detective.

She gave him the side-eye. "What do you mean?" She bit her lip, and then stopped, flustered. Why was it so difficult to say out loud?

"You appear to be working yourself up to something," he said. "You've never been one to hold back your thoughts, so this one has to be a doozy."

She darted a glance his way and blew out slowly. "I suppose it is a doozy."

Becka had survived, and thrived, though so many hardships. Being declared ungifted. Exile. Tesse's death. And she knew she'd find a way to thrive at House Rowan too... somehow. *Right?*

Surely, she could just ask Quinn if he returned her affections? In this new territory, unsure of herself and lost in her thoughts, Becka faltered.

He frowned in her general direction, and then stood up. "I should be going. I'll check in with you tomorrow on any new developments."

"Wait." She stood up, leaving the book on the divan. "You're not going to stay with me this time?"

He raised a brow and walked towards the door, Becka following at his heels. "You have your shifter guards now, and I seriously doubt your mother would approve of an enforcer having unrestricted access to her heir."

There was the sound of conversation at her door, and Quinn paused and stiffened.

"Don't worry about my guards."

He tucked away his notebook in his jacket. "No?"

Becka shrugged her shoulders. "I regularly bribe them with whiskey from the cellars."

He shook his head. "Of course you do. Fair eve, Lady Becka."

Quinn turned to go, and, not wanting to miss her opportunity, Becka sprang into action. She rushed toward him, and he turned to her, confusion knitting his brows. She threw her arms around his neck and captured his lips with her own, the near electric contact instantly radiating throughout her body.

Quinn stood so still Becka feared she'd overstepped. Then, he kissed her back, and for a few stolen moments she was lost in his touch. She pulled back, sucking in a breath between damp lips. Their eyes met again, a silent admission hanging in the air between them, frustration warring with anger in his eyes.

"Your awkward behavior now makes more sense," he said, a sad wisp of a smile on his lips.

"I'm tired of not being able to have what I want," she whispered.

The golden burnished sheen of his eyes flashed, and he regarded her a moment, as if seeing her in an entirely new light.

For a few moments of shared silence between them, the stresses of House Rowan, the poisoning, and even the lurking Shadow-Dwellers all faded away, replaced with the pounding of her heartbeat, the feel of him pressed against her, and a tingling that suffused her entire being.

"As much as I wish things were otherwise," Quinn reached up to disentangle her arms from around his neck, "this is a complication neither one of us can afford."

She shrugged, refusing to let go. "In fairness, my entire life has been complicated for a while now."

"But this... *complication* of ours .. has a lot of reasons it can't happen."

She opened her mouth to respond and then snapped it shut. She let out a groan. "I told you, I'm working on a fix for that."

"I'm sure you are, but you're back in the world of the fae. You can no longer make up your own rules."

She didn't entirely know what she'd started, but it felt true to herself, and she'd done too little of that lately, even if Quinn was upset with her.

Just then, her door flew open and Duchess Maura

stomped into the room, her lips already pursed in disapproval, and an icy glint in her gaze that promised there would be a reckoning.

Quinn roughly pushed Becka away, a flash of anger in his eyes which was squarely directed at her as he turned towards Maura.

CHAPTER 7

Becka's shifter guards peeked into the room briefly, took in the scene, but then wisely withdrew. Becka had the impression Maura's appraising gaze could see straight through her.

"I would ask what's going on here," Maura said, her fiery stare flitting back and forth between Becka and Quinn. "But I can see well enough with my own eyes."

"Duchess," Quinn said, with a perfunctory bow. "I was questioning Becka on the poisoning and was just now leaving."

She turned to Quinn. Maura looked like she hadn't slept in days, and considering the circumstances, she might not have. "I expect you have all the information you need?"

Quinn gave a single nod.

"I will make sure to reach out to Chief Elowen and mention the attention you've devoted to this case."

Becka could almost hear Quinn's clenched jaw pop. "I'd thank you to do so," he replied.

Becka could only imagine what Maura planned to say to

Quinn's boss. *Will he still have a job when Maura is done? Oh no, will she get him removed from the case?*

"Move along, then," Maura snapped, motioning Quinn towards the door. "And close the door after you."

He cast a single glowering glance back Becka's way, seeming to say *this is why things are impossible between us,* then he turned and strode out the door, closing it behind him.

"It seems my flawless timing is on point," Maura said. "Why don't you have a seat? I have a few things on my mind, and I would hate to tire you out."

Considering her worn appearance, Maura was one to talk. Deflated, Becka walked back over to the divan and slumped down onto it.

Maura sat down across from her on the chair Quinn had been using. Instead of lighting directly into the lecture Becka knew was coming, Maura took a few deep breaths.

Becka hoped Maura was composing herself instead of gearing up. The heated flush across Maura's cheeks was something Becka hadn't seen the likes of before. Maura always kept her wits about her, the epitome of fae control.

Becka had a sense that Maura's finely honed exterior was teetering on the edge of a precipice. If there'd been a day to piss off her mother, this was not it.

"I came here to discuss family business with you," Maura said, her voice measured and controlled. "But instead, I must express how profoundly upset and disappointed I am with you."

"Maura..."

"It would be unwise to interrupt me, daughter," Maura said, cutting her off, and Becka held her tongue. "House Rowan has afforded you broad freedoms. I acknowledge returning to the fold after being gone for eight years is traumatic in its own way. Plus, you've been gifted with a power that is problematic at best. It's why I haven't forced your hand to move forward with the marriage.

"Considering what you've been through, growing up away from the fold as you did and returning under such duress, your father and I felt it wise to handle you gently. We thought that, over time, you would embrace our way of life. Our customs. Our sensibilities."

Although Maura wasn't precisely wrong, her summary shortchanged Becka's experience, telling rather than asking how she was doing or feeling. They sat mere feet apart, and yet Becka didn't feel seen or understood. She felt like the receiver of a practiced speech.

"I'm grateful for your patience," Becka replied. "This has been an emotionally and physically exhausting time overshadowed by the trauma of my return."

Maura nodded. "It's only been a few months to process the change and heal, for both you and the house, but your position as our heir and the future that comes with it is something you need to come to terms with. I must ask, are you under the impression that your circumstances will fundamentally change?"

"Well..." Becka replied. *Am I?*

"Let me be absolutely clear with you. As a gifted fae, you are bound by law to reside within fae territories. That means, for all intents and purposes, living here with your family at House Rowan or on assignment on jobs for the house. Do you understand that this is not something within any of our powers to change?"

"Of course I know that," Becka answered. There was

knowing and then there was knowing. Did she understand the legalities of being a guilded fae? Certainly. Had she digested that those same rules now applied to herself?

Indigestion roiled in her stomach. She didn't want to accept the new order. It felt like she might lose all of her hopes and dreams for the future if she gave in to being heir, and all it entailed.

"You may know it, but I doubt you've fully accepted it." Becka started to interrupt, but Maura raised a hand and waved her off. "I see now that our approach has been flawed. We have been too lax with you when instead you need more structure, even if you do not realize it yourself."

"That's the exact opposite of what I need," Becka insisted. "If anything, I need *more* freedom, not less! I'm stifled here! I don't want to marry Alain. I want to work at my internship and I still want to get my doctorate. And I want to be able to spend time with Quinn."

"I do not think you have any idea what you *need*. You are the heir to House Rowan now. Lucky for you, I am well-motivated to provide you the direction you appear to be craving."

Becka's stomach sank. This Maura was not a woman she could reason with. This was a Maura who had almost lost her husband and eldest living child and would not suffer any fools. This Maura was on a mission.

"It is far past time that you learn the duties of your station. Tesse used to attend council meetings and so shall you. It's what she would have wanted."

The mention of her sister's name wrenched at her heart. "It's not fair of you to use her name as leverage over me!"

"I am past attempting to be gentle with you, Becka. If

Tesse could see you now, she would be embarrassed on your behalf."

"Ha!" Becka barked out a humorless laugh. "Goes to show how little you knew her. Tesse loved hearing about my life! She would never have wanted me to change."

Maura's eyes were filled with rage. Whether from Becka's refusal to comply or her statement on Tesse, she had no idea.

"No doubt Tesse indulged you, because you were an unguilded outcast. No doubt your tales of city life were a thrill to hear. No doubt she missed seeing her twin every day and loved to simply hear your voice and see your words. But Tesse understood the expectations upon her and her role in the family. Never once did she falter in fulfilling those duties."

Becka's knowledge of Tesse had been limited to their calls and a single meeting in the city years ago. Although Tesse had shared her life with her and groused about the strictures of fae society, she'd never spoken of bucking tradition. Only now did Becka realize that, for all that Tesse shared her thoughts with Becka, her sister's behavior had been exemplary. The realization hit her right in the solar plexus. Perhaps Maura was right? Would Tesse have been appalled over Becka's continuing unwillingness to conform? How had she never asked herself this before?

"This is how things are going to be now," Maura replied. "You will start attending the daily council meetings. You will keep the schedule I set for you. You will, of course, answer the enforcer's investigation-related questions when required, but only under the supervision of your shifter and fae guards."

"I'm to be chaperoned?"

"Yes. At all times, as it seems you would benefit from the oversight."

"Then why allow me to talk with Quinn at all?"

"Because it is in House Rowan's interests that the poisoning case is solved, of course, and the needs of the house are always preferenced over personal interests. Enforcer Quinn appears well-motivated to accomplish this task. If he won't stay on target, then I'll have him replaced. He has a known reputation for divided loyalties, but he has also risked his life for you and House Rowan, and so I'll give him an opportunity to prove himself."

"What do you mean, divided loyalties?" Becka asked.

"He is an enforcer, Becka, which overrides his upbringing in House Oak. He works with a team of humans, shifters, and other fae to keep the peace between the races, which obviously clouds his loyalty to the fae."

"Being dedicated to peace sounds like clear loyalty to me."

Maura shook her head. "You have lived apart from us for many years, but some things never change." She stood and paced the length of the divan, her wandering, exhausted gaze full of emotion. "No loyalty is higher than devotion to our own kind."

Becka was well aware her mother was a separatist, although this was the first time she'd spoken it aloud to her daughter. Even though she'd suspected it, having it confirmed hit Becka like a punch to the gut. How could she and her mother be so diametrically opposed on this issue? Sure, having lived so long among humans, Becka had endured never-ending microaggressions and marginalizations, but she'd also enjoyed friendships and connection with other races. She saw the hope beyond the hate and yearned to show others that potential and leave the war behind forever.

What would it take for fae society to recover from losing the Great War, she wondered?

In order to win over her mother, perhaps Becka would need to start by opening herself to listening to Maura's point of view. After all, if she couldn't win over her mother, how did she expect to inspire any other fae to step forward into a new future?

"House first and always?" Becka asked, knowing it to be the answer her mother expected. Now, with Maura's mood piqued in anger, was not the time to discuss the future of the races.

A strained smile spread across Maura's face. "Always. We are committed to peace, but the safety of our people must come first. We must maintain our perspective. The humans would have preferred to exterminate us. Enforcer Quinn has, in the past, turned over fae accused of crimes against human society. You need to be wary of placing too much trust in him, lest he disappoint you. Or us."

She'd heard accusations against Quinn before and he had addressed them all to her satisfaction. Hearing Maura's perspective helped Becka put together the pieces. "Wouldn't all fae-touched enforcers be bound by the same directive to hold our people to the law?"

Maura chuffed. "The laws they uphold are human-written and human-centric. Most fae who serve as enforcers only do so to fulfill their years of community service. Shifters have remained neutral and thus aren't targeted by human laws like we have been. Thus, their Enforcers are more fair. Those fae-touched who make a career out of enforcer service, like Quinn, are a different breed altogether." Maura pursed her lips like she'd tasted something sour.

Becka had heard the converse of that same argument from humans. She'd heard that humans who served alongside fae and shifters as enforcers were either moles intent on catching out fae on any cause or traitors to their own race for working with fae as peers. Distrust between the two races flowed both ways.

But she wanted to understand her mother's perspective better, so she asked, "What do you mean?"

"All of that time they spend away from their house? It corrupts their spirit and blinds their loyalties." Maura let out a mirthless laugh. "They are apt to be as lost as a babe in the woods on a cloudy night. Not unlike you at this moment."

Becka heard her concerns but knew Quinn's dedication to hunting down the Shadow-Dwellers had motivated him to stay with the enforcers. Becka shivered.

Do others in my house harbor those same thoughts when they look my way, that I'm a lost soul?

"I trust him not to betray me," Becka said. Although he'd been distant, she'd attributed that to her engagement. What if he was also reacting to the attitude of those in House Rowan toward enforcers? Surely, he didn't think she agreed with her house, did he? "He's put his own life at risk to help me."

Maura's gaze narrowed on her. "I believe you believe that. What about the rest of us? Is he enforcer, or fae, first?"

Unused to being the sole focus of Maura's indomitable will, Becka steeled her nerves. She told herself not to take it personally, that Maura would pressure anyone to get the answers she needed to ensure the safety of her house. Yet this was no mother asking her daughter to answer a straightforward question. This felt like an inquisitor demanding answers, and Becka could all too easily imagine her mother assuming this role regularly.

Becka was determined this was *not* the dynamic she would carry forward with her mother.

Her hesitation lasted only a moment. "Fae. His focus is on hunting down the Shadow-Dwellers, almost to the exclusion of anything else in his life. That's why he's stayed with the Enforcers' Guild. I don't think he has any bone to pick with fae society."

Unlike myself, she left unsaid. If anything, their conversation had gelled in Becka's mind the need in fae and human society to bridge the gap and move beyond their hate.

Maura reached out and touched her shoulder, a genuine smile gracing her lips. "That's good to know. Thank you for your honesty."

Becka smiled, feeling a touch awkward, considering Maura's prior stern warning.

"You and Quinn appear to have grown inappropriately close. Evading being murdered together will do that." Maura paused, as if considering her words. "In fact, I am confident surviving a psychopath forms a bond unlike any other."

Becka side-eyed Maura. "I think our connection is rooted in more than that."

Maura stopped and turned towards Becka, her expression neutral. "I am pointing out that the intensity of your connection to Quinn is likely a byproduct of meeting during your sister's funeral and Woden's subsequent attack. That makes it likely that there is no indication of long-term viability."

A nervous laugh escaped Becka's lips. *Could that be another reason why Quinn was distant? Does he think our connection is trauma-induced?* "Since when did you study psychology?"

Maura's brow arched, but a hint of a smile lifted the corners of her lips. "I never have, but I'm attempting to put this in words I think you will understand. I am the duchess of this house, as one day you will be. I pride myself on my ability to manage this territory and the people within it. I also pride myself on my ability to build good relations with the other houses. If it happens under my roof, I will know about it eventually. I have eyes everywhere."

Becka pursed her lips. She should have considered that bribing her shifter guards with whiskey likely wasn't enough to keep her secrets from Maura. Not that it mattered, the house was full of staff and family and she hadn't exactly kept her opinions to herself.

"We control neither our emotions nor whom we care for," Becka replied. "Regardless of how my feelings came to be, they are still real."

Maura shrugged her off. "Emotions are amazing and wonderful things, but they are a byproduct of our surroundings. To be clear, I'm not implying that your affections for the enforcer aren't real. What I'm saying is that these feelings are a natural result of the time you've spent together, which has in fact been a very short time, intensified by dire circumstances."

Becka felt led down a series of logical arguments by a master speechmaker. "Sure..." Becka searched for a point to argue with her mother, but Maura wasn't wrong. In fact, she had a solid point. But just because their relationship had started with a trauma didn't mean it wasn't real or worth exploring.

"I'd point out that, if you spent a similar amount of time with, say, your intended, you could develop feelings there just as easily."

Becka rubbed her forehead. "I don't feel you understand the extent of the differences between Alain and me."

"Then illuminate me, daughter," Maura replied.

Maura's expression was receptive, and their conversation had been so direct, that Becka decided to take a chance.

"After Tesse's death, Alain was cruel and nasty to me. Angry with me because I looked like her but wasn't. Sometimes when I see him, his expression mirrors those angry, ranting moments of his, and it brings it all back fresh. And when I was recuperating after Woden's attack, he didn't seek me out. Didn't check on me. Sure, he wants an alliance with House Rowan, but I feel like a consolation prize. Every time I speak with him, the tension between us gets worse. We have nothing in common."

Maura held up a hand, and Becka quieted. "You met him after Tesse's death, a trying time for you both. From what I've heard, you have also rebuffed his efforts since. You need a new beginning."

Becka took a deep breath. "What I need is to break the engagement. It's not something I ever agreed to!"

"Do you have any idea how many agreements and contracts House Rowan has, all of which I inherited overseeing? This engagement is not unlike any of those others."

"But you always said you loved Vott from the moment you met..."

Maura smiled, but sadness filled her eyes, and Becka immediately regretted her words.

"I have always loved him, but understand, our families

arranged our marriage too. It's fae custom. We only met a week before the ceremony."

That morsel was not a part of the story that Becka had heard before. Perhaps, in her childhood naivety, she hadn't thought to question if she'd gotten the full story.

"I know arranged marriages began after the Great War to rebuild our numbers and strengthen our powers, but in modern times we have access to technology which could better serve that goal."

Maura nodded. "I appreciate your education, Becka. It will serve our house well. But you speak of human technology. You must realize it's rare for them to share anything with the fae, especially something which might aid us in returning to our past glory. So, we use what means we must."

"I read the engagement contract. It's antiquated and reads like a boilerplate law contract."

Maura shrugged. "I'm not sure what else you were expecting, but it's good you familiarized yourself with it. Now you know there's only one way out for House Rowan: a right to divorce if there is no progeny within five years."

"That still requires me to marry him."

"As you say. Perhaps Quinn might settle for being your paramour?"

Becka knew better. "Quinn isn't the type to settle."

Maura waved her off. "Then it can't be helped. You'll have to find a way to come to terms with the situation."

Becka felt like a rat trapped in a cage. When she boiled down her stress and anxiety about being heir of House Rowan, the single largest component was her engagement to Alain. Sure, she was concerned she wouldn't master her gift or that she might hurt someone with it. And she woke up from nightmares about being captured by a Shadow-Dweller again at least once a week. But her lack of power over the engagement contract was maddening.

"I don't know how to do that right now," Becka finally replied to Maura.

Maura gave a single nod, and, seeming to understand they'd talked the topic to death, moved on without missing a beat. "Did you know Berak and Saana have requested a session with you when you're feeling up to using your abilities again? They've brought in a cursed candidate who's willing to give your Nulling powers a try, even while knowing the risks."

"Yes, I heard. I'd love to help them," Becka replied.

"Wonderful. I'm scheduling it for tomorrow." Maura sighed, her exhaustion again overtaking her features. "Becka, I need your willing participation, not just as a member of our family but also as heir to maintain our power base. Your head-strong traits will serve this house well, once you know how to apply yourself and then actually do so."

Perhaps Maura was right. If Becka was here to stay, being more connected to the council and daily Rowan affairs would help her adapt. Yet the conversation about her engagement grated at Becka.

Becka needed to leverage her relationship with her mother, moving it beyond the struggle it had been so far into a mutually beneficial partnership. Somehow...

"You're right. This is not the life I've created or braced myself to deal with."

"Be patient," Maura replied. "Once your training is complete, more opportunities will open up for you, including work in the cities. Perhaps there will even be time for that internship you are so intent upon, assuming you embrace your duties here more fully and we find work for you within the city."

"That would be wonderful," Becka replied. "Dr. Traut said they'd put the internship on hold and are awaiting word from us on my availability once I'm guilded. The board will have to review and approve allowing a guilded fae on staff, but Traut is excited for the opportunity."

"Oh, your gift will be quite lucrative for the house, I am sure. But I'm still surprised you're holding onto the dream of your internship with Dr. Traut. Won't you be working amongst humans who fear or hate you?"

"You're right, I'd be walking right back into that fire. I suppose, having dealt with their prejudice for so long, I came to accept it and move on." Becka tucked a stray lock of hair back into her ponytail. "Plus, I think of it fondly because it was a time not so long ago when I got to make my own decisions."

Maura arched a brow. "Learn how to play your cards right, and that time may come again. Also, you are scheduled to have dinner with Alain tonight. I expect you to attempt to get to know him better."

Becka sighed, the breath leaving her like a deflated balloon. Spending time with Alain might be necessary, but she didn't have to like it.

"Do I have a choice?"

"We always have *choices*, not necessarily with the life the fates have chosen for us, but with how we comport ourselves along the journey. And I expect you to behave yourself."

Becka wasn't ready to give up on a potential relationship with Quinn by giving in and marrying Alain. But perhaps, if she went along with Maura's requests, she'd at least buy time to find some way out of the engagement.

"As you say," Becka replied.

"Good. I'll expect to hear from him tomorrow about how it went. And I'll see you at the council meeting, daughter," Maura said, and then swept out of the room.

Although parts of the conversation had been difficult, especially dealing with her mother in command mode, Becka supposed it had been productive. If only she could stop thinking about Quinn's lips against hers or the accusatory look in his eyes as he'd left the room.

She'd hoped to spend the evening puzzling over the Shadow-Dweller book Quinn had brought, but instead she steeled herself for dinner with Alain.

CHAPTER 8

*L*uce stood leaning against the bathroom door directly within her line of sight, so every time Becka paced back and forth she could see the shifter staring right at her. She kept telling herself she was trying to pick out the right outfit for dinner with Alain, but in truth, she was searching for an excuse not to go.

"Something on your mind?" Becka asked Luce.

"Now that you mention it, I suppose there is." Luce took two steps into the bathroom. "You know neither Saige nor I would rat you out to Duchess Maura, right?"

Becka didn't totally understand the shifter's chain of command, but she knew they all reported to Brent, who in turn reported directly to Vott. However, with Vott not being conscious, she didn't know how it worked at this moment. It wouldn't have surprised her if the shifters had been reporting directly to Maura on Becka's movements.

Becka shrugged. "I figured, although I'm not entirely sure why not. She is the duchess, after all. But it doesn't matter much how she found out about my interest in Quinn. What's done is done."

"It matters to me that you know we didn't do it," Luce replied. "The duchess must have assumed, based on your behavior during his prior visit, that you had feelings for him. Then she got lucky today, when she caught you two locking lips."

"We haven't seen each other all this time!" Becka replied. She settled on a bright yellow-and-red jumpsuit outfit with a square pattern. It wasn't proper fae attire, but she liked it.

"Oh, I know. The shifter sense of smell is even more acute than your fae nose. If you'd been messing around, we all would have smelled him on you."

"That's encouraging." Becka made a mental note to shower more frequently.

"We shifters report to Vott, not Maura. Our pact is with him."

That sounded like a formal term, and not one Becka was familiar with in shifter vernacular. "Pact?"

"It's not for me to explain," Luce replied. "But if someone reported you, they had to be fae."

The shifters had never given her reason to doubt them, so Becka took Luce at her word. Although she had to admit, Luce's unwillingness to share hurt her feelings just a wee bit.

"Sure. Okay," Becka replied.

Luce started pacing back and forth.

Becka had been around shifters long enough to know that pacing was a sign they were holding something back and needed to either talk or act to get it out. Besides, the longer they talked, the later she would be to dinner with Alain.

In her mind's eye, Becka could see Maura shaking her head.

"I have a feeling something else is bugging you," Becka said.

"I got to thinking during your conversation with Maura. She mentioned how you need to step up."

It shouldn't have surprised Becka that Luce had been listening, as she'd been right outside the door and they'd been loud at times, but it was still a bit disquieting. "You weren't even in the room."

Luce tapped the side of her ear. "Our ears are better than yours. But I had an idea. Nothing like a shifter display, mind you." Luce laughed to herself. "You fae never throw down and fight each other, unless it's magical sparring. Or maybe House Oak... Anyway, with Vott out of commission, I was thinking I'd recommend to Brent that he name you as your father's replacement until he recuperates. What do you think?"

What do I think? Maura would love it. So will Vott, when he wakes up. Plus, maybe I could learn more about this "pact."

"It sounds like an all-around win. What's involved in the role?"

"Understand, Vott had us mostly manage ourselves. He signs off on payments to our clan and approves details, but it's rare he'd change any of Brent's plans."

"It sounds straightforward and uncomplicated. Plus, I like your clan, so anything I can do to help, count me in," Becka replied.

Luce stopped and squared her stance to the divan. "Will do. Plus, I can suggest to Brent that he meet with you daily to 'review' findings, or schedules, or whatever. That way the other fae will see you as taking charge of us."

"Seems sneaky, yet low-impact," Becka said, and Luce grinned. "I like it."

"A show of force is in the beholder's perception, not the actual power behind the moves."

A single knock on her bathroom door was followed by Saige poking her head in.

"Are you accepting the dinner invite with Alain, or are you blowing him off?" Saige asked. "Because you're about to be late."

Becka groaned. "I was blocking it out of my mind."

Saige tilted her head, as if her reply didn't quite make sense. "So you're going?"

Becka picked up her bottle of hot sauce, took a swig, capped it and then slid it into her pocket. She stretched, feeling soreness in her legs and back. At least the dinner wouldn't include a hike, and she could always beg off early and come back to sleep.

"Yeah, I am, for what it's worth." Becka barked out a laugh and headed out the door, both shifters trailing a step or two behind.

"You look unsteady," Saige said. "Let us know if you need help getting back. It's no problem."

Becka nodded, hoping she wouldn't have to take them up on the offer. Gratefully, Alain had picked a tea hall near her room to host the private dinner, and she arrived within minutes despite her relatively slow, shuffling pace.

Saige opened the door and entered first, Becka following. The room was illuminated with dozens of pure beeswax candles and the windows were open, allowing the scent of jasmine and rose to flow in on the evening breeze. A light evening repast had been set out on the central table. Becka spotted sliced fruits, cheeses, and breads.

Alain stood at the windows, turning to greet her as she entered. His hair was braided at the temples, the rest falling in perfectly kept cascading layers to his waist. His pale golden eyes virtually glowed in the candlelight, and his clothes, a sunset-red shirt and straight-legged amber-toned pants, were tailored to perfection around his thin, willowy form. The embroidered family crest over his heart, the fiery flames of Hawthorne, was unmistakable.

He was the epitome of good grooming.

Alain moved to her and took her gloved hand, placing a single kiss upon it as he bowed slightly at the waist. "My dearest Becka, I am humbled you could make it tonight. Thank you for accepting my invitation."

She almost pulled her hand back in response to the revulsion hitting her gut, but then thought better of it. No doubt Maura would hear how she'd behaved later from either Alain or the household staff.

"Sure, but I don't know how long I'll be able to stay. I haven't gotten my energy back yet."

Then Becka realized they weren't alone.

A short fae female arose from the couches and gave a quick bow in her direction. "Lady Becka, I am Alain's cousin, Hanna. We met at the trade delegation, but I wasn't sure if you'd remember after all that's happened. I'm so glad for this opportunity to see you again."

"That evening is something of a blur, but I do remember you, Lady Hanna." Hanna was the one person who'd been enthusiastic to meet her. Becka recalled. She'd been suspicious at the time and now Becka was even more so. Why was Hanna here? "It's nice to see you again."

"Please, take a seat." Alain motioned to the couch nearest her. "There's no need for you to exert yourself any more than necessary."

Becka sat, and Alain took a seat across from her, while Hanna sat on the section of the rounded couch squarely between the two of them. Saige stood to one side of the doorway, her gaze fanning between them and the corridor outside. Luce must have been right outside, because Becka didn't see her. Alain poured Becka some sparkling juice, placing the glass close to her.

Saige stepped in and used a wipe on the rim of Becka's glass, and then dipped it into the liquid briefly.

"What is that?" Becka asked, her heart skipping a beat. It was one thing to know about the potential of another poisoning, but the reality of having her food spot-checked made the danger visceral.

"You took chemistry at school?" she asked, and Becka nodded. "Then think of it as a type of litmus paper, except this is enchanted to detect a variety of poisons." Saige used another wipe on the silverware and plate before Becka. "Simply put, if it turns black on contact, it's bad."

Is this how all meals are going to be until they catch the poisoner?

"That's clever, but do you really think they'd use the same method?" Becka asked. She didn't miss the worried glances between Alain and Hanna.

"Unlikely, but the testing is Brent's directive," Saige replied, watching the paper strips.

Alain, sitting forward in his seat, cleared his throat. "You aren't suggesting that *we* would poison Becka?"

Saige didn't miss a beat. "It's not personal. I've been directed to test all of Becka's food, no matter the source." She turned to Becka. "You're clean, drink up." She drifted back towards the door, blending into the background.

Alain's expression soured and Becka had the impression that Saige's explanation hadn't placated him.

Becka lifted the glass and toasted them, before taking a sip of the refreshing, sweet beverage.

Alain appeared to force a smile, but his expression remained tense. "How are you recuperating from the poisoning?"

"I got lucky. Besides feeling like someone has knocked me off a horse, I'm otherwise intact. I can't say the same for Vott." A shadow of guilt moved over her, settling in her chest.

"We are all deeply concerned for his welfare," Alain replied. "I've offered House Hawthorne's support to your healer, but please let me know if you think of any way we can be of further assistance."

Becka couldn't imagine what fire elementalists could do to help Vott in this situation. "I'll leave the healing to the healers."

"As you say," he replied.

"It's nice you came to visit your cousin, Hanna," Becka said. "I'm sure Alain misses home."

Hanna laughed, a tinkling sound that reminded her of Vott's wind chimes. "Oh, I didn't come to catch up with Alain. I'm here for both of you."

Becka attempted to drink and breathe simultaneously and instead coughed into her napkin. "Pardon me?"

Hanna smiled so sweetly Becka wondered how these two were even cousins. "House Hawthorne holds the gift of fire, which manifests differently in our members. Alain can control flame and has a keen insight into business dealings. I also have flame control, but I've further been gifted with a rare intuition into the passions of the heart."

It took Becka a moment to process Hanna's words, and when she did, Becka almost felt like she was back in the city. Her favorite magazine, *Boho Today*, always had ads for coaches. Style coaches. Depressed pet coaches. Career coaches. Embrace-your-joy coaches. You name it, there was a coach for it.

It felt like the city had come to her in the form of her very own coach. Becka tried but couldn't stop the laughter that bubbled up from her solar plexus. "So... wait. You're a relationship coach?"

Hanna frowned, taken aback at her response. "I am called a passion-seeker."

Alain sat silent, his jaw clenched. Becka, reminded of her conversation with Maura, suppressed her laughter. She needed to find a way out of this engagement. Pissing off House Hawthorne hadn't worked so far, therefore Becka needed to take another approach.

"Sorry," Becka said, taking a deep, slow breath. She curbed her expression, if not her emotions, holding an image of Maura's disapproving frown in her mind's eye. "It's been a trying week and I'm not quite myself yet."

Alain and Hanna glanced at each other, and Hanna shrugged at him. "She truly isn't."

Alain leaned in, setting down his glass. "Hanna has helped many couples I know find their way to joy. You should know I did not send for her. My father had Hanna visit as a gift to us."

"Duke Eldinrod is a most generous man, but truthfully I wanted to help. I can sense blocks in the heart's realm and advise how to navigate the obstacles blocking forward progression," Hanna said, sitting on the edge of her seat and talking quickly.

Considering the fae disdain for human-based psychology, it surprised Becka to hear Hanna's description. But, she supposed, the fae wouldn't appreciate the comparison to the endless variety of human coaches. Thinking back to her studies at the Institute, Becka wondered if in the pre-war days, would Hanna's gift have been developed, or directed, in a more aggressive fashion? She'd read tales of House Hawthorne strategists who'd executed attacks which had terrified the human troops, causing them to break rank and turn on their own, mired in panic.

Now, Hawthorne focused on business strategy. Financial strategy. Obviously, never war. Perhaps, after she got to know Hanna better, Becka might work herself up to asking about the roots of her magic.

Becka helped herself to some slices of apple and cheddar, taking small bites. Gratefully, her stomach didn't complain this time.

"That's useful." But could she use Hanna's power to somehow prove she and Alain were unsuitable for each other, and would it even matter if she did? "What's your profession al opinion of our issues?"

Hanna smiled, appearing pleased at the question. She looked back and forth between them. Hanna gave a quick shrug.

"I rarely start off like this, but as you're insisting, my first impression is that you are resistant on almost every level to Alain's presence."

Becka paused her chewing and swallowed hard. Comparing Hanna's gift with human life coaches had been a mistake. Hanna's insight was sharp as a laser. "That sounds on point. Anything else?" Becka asked, nibbling on another piece of cheddar.

Curiosity lit up Hanna's eyes. "Quite a bit. I can sense you have a good relationship with the shifter guards you arrived with, but your ties in this house are limited. You have some deep connections in your life, but they are far from here or not within this family. So you can bond, but it takes monumental energy to get past your defenses." Hanna mumbled that last bit.

Is she even aware she said it out loud?

Hanna refocused on Becka, smiling like a door-to-door cookie salesperson. "Alain told me you haven't been back at the manor long?"

"If you mean I've been back for three months, surrounded by the family that cast me out, and now I'm stuck here because I have a powerful gift that scares everyone off because it's not well understood or controlled, then yes, I suppose I've been back just a short while."

Hanna's smile faltered. "Right," she drawled, and then a moment later her eyes lit up and the smile was back in full bloom. "Of course you are not receptive to Alain. You are unable."

"Pardon me?" Alain grumbled, his eyes flashing in the candlelight. "What do you mean unable?"

"Becka has experienced a massive trauma, Alain," Hanna

said. "And she has just come to terms with the loss of the life she knew and has not yet accepted her renewed role back within House Rowan. On top of all that, someone just tried to poison her. There's no path forward for the two of you, until Becka heals the rifts between her heart and her family."

"Finally." Becka blew out a long breath. "Someone who gets me." Becka raised a glass to Hanna, and when neither she nor Alain toasted her back, she drained her glass.

"Are you sure?" Alain asked Hanna.

"I'm afraid so," Hanna replied. "The path of her healing is long."

"I am pained to hear it," Alain replied.

"So... Does that mean the engagement is off?" Becka asked, attempting to keep her voice level.

Both Hanna and Alain looked at her, their confounded expressions like someone who'd tasted salt when they'd expected sugar.

"Why would you think that?" Hanna asked. "House Hawthorne understands you've been through a trial. Yes, you need all the support we can give, but it's not as if you're a lost cause. The circumstances aren't even your fault, you poor thing."

"Support?" Becka asked, fearing the answer.

Alain cleared his throat, and having appeared to collect his emotions, his countenance was once again placid as a meditation pool.

"House Hawthorne is dedicated to upholding the contract with House Rowan. After Tesse's passing, my father spoke with the seers at House Reed concerning the change in heirs stated in the original engagement contract. Their foresight deemed our collaboration as the most fortuitous pairing of our generation. Hawthorne is thus committed to carry on."

"Really?" Becka exclaimed, interrupting his train of thought. Why couldn't she catch a break? "Collaboration is an odd wording, isn't it?"

He shrugged. "House Reed is often peculiar in their phrasing. We both have excellent pedigrees and, although I am not as potently gifted as you, I am considered one of the premier fire elementalists of my house."

"Of course you are." She wasn't surprised Alain was so focused on how advantageous the engagement contract was for his house, but she couldn't suppress her woe. When, if ever, would he see her as a person?

"Indeed, I am," he replied, oblivious to her sarcasm.

"The good news is, I'm here for you, Becka," Hanna said, leaning towards her, eyes full of hope.

Becka shot Hanna a side-eye. "Thanks?"

"Don't mention it," Hanna replied.

"Okay..."

"No really, I'm drenched in your emotions right now. It might be easier for me if you could try to temper things?" Hanna's suggestion hung in the air for a few moments, her raised eyebrows and expectant smile frozen in anticipation.

Becka shrugged and shook her head. "You know, *some* people find my blunt honesty endearing."

Hanna's expression fell, her lips pursed in a slight frown. "As you say." She turned to Alain. "I need you to give Becka some space."

Thank the gods!

Would she get a reprieve from Alain? Perhaps Hanna wasn't as bad as Becka had feared.

"I have been giving her a wide berth, Hanna," he replied, his back ramrod straight.

"And now you will give her even more space. For the time being, you will only interact with Becka at times I deem fit. Preferably also when I am present."

Alain clenched and unclenched his jaw. This wasn't the outcome he'd been hoping for. "As you say, cousin."

Becka placed her glass on the table and rose to leave. "Alain, Hanna, as fun as this conversation has been, I'm afraid I need to call it a night."

They both rose.

"It was wonderful to see you again, Becka. I look forward to working with you." Hanna inclined her head in respect.

"Working with you?" Becka replied. "What do you mean?"

"Why, I will help you to identify your blocks to joy and find ways to move past them."

Becka half-expected Hanna to give her a brochure with that phrase embossed on the cover. She was frankly too worn out to argue further.

"Fantastic. I can't wait," Becka replied, hearing the sarcasm in her tone she couldn't quite seem to keep out. "Good evening."

"Fair evening, Becka. Until we speak again," Alain said.

Becka gave them a quick nod and then fled the room, Saige and Luce close on her heels. She feared what Hanna mean by "support." Yet Becka was grateful for the reprieve from more tedious time with Alain and the further delay of their engagement. She hoped working with Hanna wouldn't be as tiresome as she feared.

When they arrived at Becka's quarters and were safely

behind closed doors, Saige and Luce walked through the room, searching for anything out of place.

A piece of paper lay on her bed, which Luce picked up, read, and then held out to her. "It's your itinerary for tomorrow, from the duchess."

"What's it say?" she asked, knowing Luce had already scanned it.

"It lists a council meeting for you to attend in the morning, an afternoon tea party with Hanna and other ladies of the court, and then a pre-dinner meeting with your aunt, Elder Alaetha."

Becka didn't look forward to the meeting with Alaetha, fearing how Vott's sister would view the niece who'd accidentally poisoned her own father.

"It's the new schedule she promised," Becka replied. "I almost wish the poison had worked."

Luce waved it in the air towards her, a wisp of a smile on her lips.

"Can you leave it on the sofa table?" Becka replied. "I'm crashing. Please inform whoever swaps out with you to let me sleep in." Not even bothering to change her clothes, Becka flopped down onto her bed, exhausted.

She heard the guards whispering, but it soon faded into blackness as sleep claimed her.

CHAPTER 9

The night's restless sleep left Becka feeling slow and groggy. Her guards had swapped out overnight, and although Shamus and Lorelai had come in to check on her when her breakfast had arrived, they'd politely stepped out when she'd asked.

Becka tried to sleep in, but there was too much on her mind fighting for attention for her to fall back asleep. The room echoed memories back to her. Before Becka had returned to House Rowan, this had been her sister Tesse's room. But before that, it had been her room. Even before that, it had belonged to an aunt who'd long since married and moved to another territory. Becka wasn't sure of the provenance of the space before that.

When she'd first inherited the room, Becka had updated the bedding, added a few pictures, and had picked out the forest green couch everyone liked to sit on. After it went to Tesse, her sister had added the divan and the roses lining the wall of windows and changed out a couple of the portraits on the walls.

Becca's sole change this time was adding a painting of Tesse in her bedazzling engagement gown. She was a specter of ageless beauty and power and a constant reminder of the event that had brought Becka back to House Rowan: Tesse's murder. Becka had hung the portrait on the wall across from the divan so she could look upon and remember her sister from the furniture Tesse herself had added to the room.

Her sisters, Ingrid and Sigfrid, thought the painting morbid and had encouraged Becka to overhaul the space to invite in fresh memories. Becka had flatly refused. She wanted to remember Tesse. Besides, she liked the amalgamation of styles that her space represented. And more than anything, she wanted her first and last thoughts of the day to remind her that, if she wasn't careful, a Shadow-Dweller might kill her just like they'd killed Tesse.

Now, after her discussion with Maura the day before, Becka wondered how well she'd known Tesse after all? From Maura's description, Tesse had been not just an illusionist prodigy but also a model daughter, following in her footsteps with gusto. But the Tesse she had spoken to during their secret conversations had loved hearing all about Becka's wild experiences in the city, so much so that she'd often wondered if Tesse would have preferred being there with her. It was impossible to know her sister's inner thoughts and it wasn't like she could ask Tesse now. Based on the general adoration Rowan had toward Tesse, Becka had to conclude that her sister was indeed an exemplary fae.

She could imagine Tesse wouldn't be pleased with Becka's slow reintegration into House Rowan or her persistent refusal of Alain. Her sister might have found Becka's insistence on holding onto her city clothes and pink hair amusing, but she would have had a strong opinion. Becka wanted to do right by Tesse's memory, but how could she do that while remaining faithful to her unique identity?

Becka had resisted the notion of stepping into Tesse's shoes despite being thrust into the role. Not only did it smack of imposter syndrome, but Becka hadn't felt like she truly belonged. Perhaps she'd been thinking of it all wrong? Would Tesse have wanted Becka to step into her shoes?

Exhausted and moody, Becka didn't want to seek out her schedule any earlier than required, so she lay down on the divan with the Shadow-Dweller book Quinn had brought her to test. Oriani, her sister's gold-and-brown tabby with a golden sheen to his eyes, joined her, at first demanding scritches under his chin before he took up a position curled around her toes. Paging through the book, Becka took a sip from a bottle of hot sauce to forestall the headaches that kicked in whenever she encountered something magical.

Becka turned her focus back to the book. Wearing the gloves that had become her daily habit, Becka opened the book carefully. She was intent on not damaging the book despite Quinn's apparent lack of concern. And wow, was this book layered in magic! The first time she'd touched it, something had been knocked loose by her Nulling ability and given her a heck of a headache.

Quinn had asked her to find something, anything, of consequence in these pages. Becka was determined to help, especially considering the trouble she'd gotten him into. Besides, like she could turn down a good mystery?

Each page was covered in the glyphs she'd become all too familiar with. There was no known translation for them; the enforcers had exhaustively searched to no avail. Yet Becka couldn't help looking for some sense of a pattern between the pages.

A few rare pages were blank. A handful had only one or two glyphs. Most were covered with the arcane symbols. Becka couldn't determine any rhyme or reason to it. There didn't appear to be chapters or sections. Each page felt random. More like artistic styling than a language.

One thing she'd learned from research was to keep asking questions to find the answer beyond the answer. Focus on what you observed and look for patterns and meaning based on what you'd seen later.

Was she looking for the wrong thing?

Switching gears, Becka focused on the energetic signatures of the pages and how her gift reacted to each. Using this method, she discovered that not all pages felt the same energetically. Could separate enchantments effect different sections of the book? She knew the magics were there because they made her head throb when her gloved fingers slid over the pages. She took great care to not loose her powers upon the book. Instead, she selectively moved around those elements, jotting down in her notebook pages that seemed to be more magically complex, as well as those which appeared to have no additional magic imbued. Curiously, the level of magic infused into the pages appeared in no way related to the number of glyphs on a page.

What if the glyphs aren't even important? What if only the magic matters?

She had yet to figure out what the magic did, but she felt like she was getting closer to... something. The magics used were sometimes familiar and sometimes unfamiliar to her. Some patterns felt like the illusion magic she trained against daily. Others reminded her of the more subtle movements of Vott's air elementalist patterns. Still others were completely foreign to her. The combination reaffirmed her understanding of Shadow-Dwellers; they alone wielded a spectrum of stolen magics.

Becka felt like she was on the cusp of putting the puzzle together and the answer was floating around the back of her mind, just needing the right push for it to float to the surface of her consciousness.

Becka bit her lip, wishing she could talk with Quinn and tell him what she suspected. Perhaps he'd have ideas on things to test out.

She thought about venturing out of her room to find him, but would he even want to talk to her right now?

Just then there was a knock on her door, and Becka set the book aside and jumped up to get it, hoping Quinn was on the other side.

Swinging the door open, Becka came face-to-face with Maura Rowan and Hanna Hawthorne.

"From the disappointed look on your face, I am guessing you were hoping for someone else," Maura replied. "May we come in?" she asked as she stepped in. Maura motioned for Hanna to follow her, which she did a bit reluctantly, appearing less willing to invade Becka's personal space.

Becka closed the door behind them.

"You have such a lovely room, Becka," Hanna said.

"Thank you, Lady Hanna," Becka replied, grateful for Hanna's upbeat presence.

"I see you haven't gotten dressed for the day yet," Maura said, taking Becka by the elbow and walking her in the direction of her changing room. "Hanna, why don't you wait for us here while I help Becka finish getting ready?"

Once they entered Becka's bathroom, Maura gently shoved her toward her changing room.

Still stinging from their conversation yesterday and moody from her thoughts of Tesse, Becka didn't protest. She was determined to move forward with Maura, which right now meant placating her. "Are you planning to accompany me all day?" Becka asked.

"No, but I thought I'd check on you. What have you been up to this morning?" Maura asked.

Becka looked around her closet, searching for the perfect outfit to match her mood.

"I had breakfast and was engaging in some light reading. I'm still feeling worn out and didn't want to tax myself before the long day ahead." Her red tracksuit and neon green sports bra were calling her name.

"That's sensible," Maura replied. "You'll be thrilled to hear Lady Hanna has offered to act in the role of your political and romantic advisor."

"That sounds..." Becka started to reply, pulling the sports bra over her head. She searched for the right words, wanting to be snippy, if only because Maura wasn't giving her an option. But, to her own surprise, Becka liked the idea.

"Generous and gracious of Lady Hanna, don't you agree?"

"Yes, it does," Becka replied. "I could use her perky energy at my side."

A brief smile graced Maura's lips. "How... refreshing. Now, let me appeal to you, Becka, on a topic I know you care about," she spoke in low tones. "I spoke with Chief

Elowen last night. If I push the matter of Enforcer Quinn's breach of behavior, then I can get him reprimanded. Fired, even."

Becka's heart skipped a beat. Quinn lived to be an enforcer and hunt the Shadow-Dwellers. "Wouldn't a formal complaint embarrass House Rowan as well?"

Maura smiled, broadly this time. "I do appreciate how you are thinking of your house first. And yes, it would, but do not think I would not do it. Do not push me."

Becka tugged her hair into a messy bun and emerged from her dressing room looking ready to run a marathon, which was exactly how she thought about the day ahead.

"Fine," she said to Maura, walking around her back into her bedroom. "Lady Hanna, I hear we'll be spending a lot of time together going forward. I must say, I am grateful for your company."

Hanna's brief frown at Becka's attire lasted only a moment, and then she was all smiles again. "Yes, I am so excited to learn what your days look like. Your schedule looks so entertaining. Are you ready to go?"

Becka tucked the Shadow-Dweller book and her journal into her bag, which felt heavy slung over her shoulder. There was some clue she was missing. Something that didn't quite fit together. Maybe the book's simple presence, as a constant reminder, would help her subconscious surface whatever clues it was trying to puzzle out?

She remembered her schedule, steeling her nerves for the upcoming day. She luxuriated in a long, deep yoga breath. "I'm ready."

"Do not forget your meeting with Elder Alaetha later today," Maura said, her still-exhausted features otherwise placid and calm. "She is keenly interested in meeting you. And please, for the love of all things sacred, be polite to her."

"Dearest Mother, there's no other way I know how to be," Becka replied as sweetly as she could muster.

Hanna looked back and forth between the two of them, brows knit in confusion. "Your words and your emotions are wildly disparate."

Becka smiled at Hanna, feeling genuine mirth. "I think we'll get along fabulously, Hanna Hawthorne. Shall we get going?"

"Remember, Becka," Maura said. "Leave the investigation to the enforcers and keep your focus on your duty to House Rowan."

Like she'd needed the reminder? She'd understood Maura's threat to Quinn's career loud and clear. "There's nothing else on my mind, Mother."

"That's not at all true," Hanna replied, progressively looking more confused.

"I know, isn't it exciting?" Becka smiled, her mood brightening. She took Hanna's hand in hers, dragging the bewildered woman along with her. "We're going to have such fun today."

CHAPTER 10

It felt like a veritable host of guards trailed Becka as she walked the halls with Hanna at her side. She hoped her first council meeting wouldn't be as dreadfully boring as she feared, but perhaps with Hanna along for the ride she'd at least have someone on her side, even if that side was also Hawthorne's and Maura's side.

Becka's desire to avoid arriving at the council meeting early meant they'd walked in circles, but Hanna hadn't complained.

"Who are they again?" Hanna whispered, leaning towards Becka.

"Which set of guards do you mean?" Becka asked, her voice at deliberately normal levels.

Hanna frowned. "Start with the ones who aren't fae."

"Sure. They are wolf shifter guards who are pledged to Vott. After the attack on me a few months ago, he assigned some to me. Shamus, despite looking so attractive and inviting, is a brooder, while Lorelai is the friendlier one of the pair."

"I would not have guessed it," Hanna replied. "My gift does not work reliably on shifters, thus why I asked. She looks so grave."

She wasn't wrong. Shamus, sporting a fresh frown, always seemed to be waiting for the other shoe to drop. His pate of wild curls and perpetual five o-clock shadow was worthy of a magazine ad. Becka had tried to get him to laugh, to no avail, so she mostly ignored him.

Lorelai laughed, the sound filling the hall. Becka looked back and the wolf was threatening Shamus with the end of her long braid. Sure, her angular features made her look perpetually stern, but her attitude was always upbeat.

"Nah, Lorelai is a blast." Talking with Hanna, Becka realized she seemed different than other fae. Perhaps it was her focus on bringing joy to others, but she appeared to genuinely care about Becka, which came as a welcome surprise.

"What about the others?" Hanna asked, motioning to the guards.

Becka looked back. The fae guards were clad in their everyday uniforms, the standard tan form-fitting outfit with an Illusionists Guild sash running right shoulder to left hip.

Becka shrugged. "The fae guards? That's Elena and Oba, part of the family house guard." Her interactions had been relatively perfunctory with the house guards, who'd rejected her overtures of friendship. But why wouldn't they? As the heir, they couldn't relate to her without the customary deference lest they risk their jobs.

Hanna's eyes widened. "Oh my! Are you in that much danger?"

"Yes, I'm afraid I am, but you don't have anything to worry about."

Most likely. Just don't drink after me!

Ascending the stairs to the third floor of the manor where the council chambers were located, Becka watched a pair of Astrid's students creating an elaborate waterfall illusion cascading down one side of the stairs and over the banister. The water danced as if a living thing, color-shifting through a rainbow as it hit obstacles, leaving nothing wet despite its appearance of being water.

Becka altered her course to the far side of the stairs, knowing an accidental footfall could break their illusions into dust. It wasn't like she was stepping on eggshells to avoid conflict with her housemates, but neither was she oblivious to how other fae reacted with fear or caution to her approach. She tried not to take it personally, but she couldn't deny the ache in her chest every time someone jumped out of her way or turned and walked away to avoid her. No one wanted to accidentally run into her, lest they suffer the consequences of lost time, effort, and intention.

The students, both male teens, eyed them with caution as they walked up the steps. She had seen them in the training hall but hadn't yet learned their names.

"Don't worry," Becka said to them. "I won't break it."

The shorter of the two rolled his eyes at her. "I told you this was a bad location," he said to his friend. "She loves walking these stairs."

The other boy nodded back. "Let's go."

They turned and ran off down the stairs, leaving their illusion for her to appreciate. Becka made a point of staying out of its way. She was happy when she passed it without ill effect.

"So there is a fair amount of friction between others in your house over fear of your power?" Hanna said.

"It's inevitable due to the nature of my gift," she answered. "I may be valuable to the house, but people fear what they don't know. They don't know me, and they don't know how my gift works."

Hanna placed a reassuring hand on Becka's arm. "That must be terrible for you."

"It does suck. I wish I could step into a future date where that's all behind me, but all I can do for now is wade through the murky middle."

Hanna patted her arm and they walked in silence the rest of the way up the stairs.

The council chambers were conveniently located across from the top of the stairs. To her knowledge the closed doors weren't kept locked, yet only council members and visiting dignitaries were allowed within. The ornately carved pine doors recounted the long history of House Rowan. She'd spent hours in her youth staring at the scenes and learning the stories. Becka recalled wondering what secrets were held within the chamber, knowing in her youth that one day, as heir, she'd be privy to the inner workings. But that day never came, as she was never guilded. When she was cast out, the loss of her potential inclusion within these hallowed halls had been the least of her concerns.

But now, standing with her gloved hand on the handle, Becka paused. Lorelai and Shamus backed off and stood across the hall, at the ready for when she returned. As shifters, they could not follow her into the chambers. Guards were not allowed inside. Elena and Oba, her fae guards, stood at attention against the wall down the hall, to silently await her re-emergence.

She turned the handle and walked into the room. Becka was met with a series of nods from the short list of fae inside. It was clear everyone had gotten the memo that she'd be attending, likely even before Maura had delivered the message to Becka.

She ushered Hanna in beside her and closed the door behind them. It took Becka a moment to absorb the room. Duchess Maura stood near an ornately carved chair at the head of an oblong table, which ran lengthwise nearly the full length of the room. The table was ringed by plush and carved chairs from the same material as the table, a lightly stained rosewood with a stunning sap grain, varying in ripples from beige to dark rose. Portraits lined the stone-walled room, images of former influential members from the house over the generations. The wall across from the doors was filled with bookshelves and tomes covered in a fine layer of dust, and predictably the scent of musty library filled her nose. On the wall with the doors hung a map, fifteen by ten feet in size, of the world of fae territories, each boundary marked with a distinctive and separate color.

A vellum tome lay open before Maura on the table, where she was taking notes. In the middle of the table was another map in a raised box. This one she recognized as the Rocky Mountain fae territory, where House Rowan's lands resided. It was a topographical map, with mountain peaks and placid lakes part of the landscape. A black border delineated the space at the outside of the territory, and dotted, colorful lines within the territory marked the borders of four different house lands. One paved road ran adjacent to the east of the area, north to south, and was the only route connecting them to the human cities beyond.

Everything here felt antiquated and old-fashioned. Becka wondered if they'd considered adding a whiteboard for posting the daily agenda.

Could I get one delivered?

Becka also recognized Calder and Astrid but couldn't remember the names of the other three council members. Seeing Calder there made the pastries she'd eaten that morning sit heavily in her stomach, but she forced herself to smile at him.

"Now that everyone is here, let's begin," Maura said. She reached over and patted the chair to her left, and Becka didn't hesitate. "Becka, this is now your seat and I'd like Hanna Hawthorne to sit next to you. Hanna is here at my request to serve as Becka's political advisor. Calder, can you please move down?"

His cheeks flamed and his gaze narrowed at Becka, but Calder did as he was told.

Astrid took the seat to Maura's right. The other three sat in the seats across from them.

"Everyone, I'm sure you know Becka," Maura said. "Becka, I know you're familiar with Calder and Lady Astrid. In case you're not aware, to his left is Lord Cedric, Elder Eirian, and then Lady Wynne. All are illusionists, the best in the guild. Duke Vott's chair is held open until his safe return."

"Forgive my question if this isn't appropriate, but I'd like to understand. As Vott isn't an illusionist, his place in the council is by rank?" Becka asked.

Lord Cedric leaned forward, elbows on the table, and

spoke. "You should always ask for clarification when needed. We reserve a place in the council for the duchess's partner and for the heir apparent."

"Thank you for your inclusion," she replied, feeling a slight flush hit her cheeks. So it wasn't just Maura's insisting she attend the council to give Becka some busywork; the heir's presence was customary. Which Becka would've likely known, had she asked before now.

"It is our custom," he said. "But, Duchess, we must discuss your son's continuing inclusion. As he is no longer your eldest guilded child, his seat is forfeit."

"This is an unusual circumstance, so we will vote upon his continuing status," Maura replied. "Are there any other perspectives we should consider?"

The council members shifted in their seats, each looking to Calder, as if weighing him in their minds. In return, Calder glowered at Becka, obviously blaming her for his precarious position.

Seeking a path to move forward, not just with Maura, but with all of her family—grouchy brother and all—Becka considered her next step. She felt no fondness towards Calder, but he wasn't going anywhere, either. If she could improve their dynamic, perhaps she'd dislike being around him less.

"If I may? My return is an exceptional occurrence, with my further delay in being declared guilded a part of that equation. In the past few months, Calder has been privy to the council business. Have there been any issues?"

"No, not at all," Aunt Astrid replied.

"Are there other common reasons for removing council members?" she asked.

"We only remove members when they can no longer perform their duties," replied Lady Wynne.

"In that case, I move Calder remains, unless you consider him unfit for duty?"

Calder's brows shot up, and he regarded her afresh, surprise and confusion warring on his features.

"I second the motion," Maura said, a pleased look on her face. "All agreed?" Everyone raised their hands. "Calder remains on the council. Next item of business?"

Hanna shot Becka a toothy smile, reaffirming to her that lobbying to keep Calder on the council was definitely the right move.

"As you're new here, Becka, I'd like to clarify the role of this council," Maura said. "We oversee all who live within House Rowan territories, as well as all members of the Illusionists Guild, whether they live here, in another house's territory, or are on assignment within the cities."

She thought of her engagement, and how House Hawthorne wasn't within the local Rocky Mountain fae territory but instead hailed from the Newfoundland fae territory. "Who's in charge if there's an altercation between houses or guilds?" Becka asked, because it was worth knowing who might mediate any potential disputes between them.

"Both parties pick a mutually agreed upon third entity to mediate," Maura replied.

"That sounds straightforward," Becka muttered.

"It almost never is," replied Lord Cedric with a wry smile. He turned to Maura. "Has Becka been brought up to speed on the current state of our territory?"

Maura shook her head and waved him on. "Keep it succinct."

He rose and picked up a wooden pointer. "The Rocky Mountain fae territory encompasses approximately forty-five thousand acres and nearly six thousand fae. As I'm sure you recall, four houses share this territory. Rowan," he tapped on the space to the upper left, 'Birch," he tapped on the upper right zone, "and then Apple and Pine," he said, tapping on the two smaller, lower sections. "What you may not know is that House Apple suffered a great loss a few years ago and is now a protectorate under House Rowan."

The boundaries of the four houses reminded Becka of the ventricles of the heart. "What happened?"

"A group of humans managed to infiltrate Apple's border undetected and attacked their central manor. The fae living there were shot, artifacts were stolen, and the manor and outlying buildings burned to the ground. Their loss was a great tragedy for all fae, and the remaining members of the house have not yet recovered. Since the tragedy, House Rowan has overseen the day-to-day elements of trade for the area and the remaining patronage. The territory has rallied and rebuilt their structures, but no one can replace the lost lives or history that was destroyed."

"That's horrid. They're pacifists." Becka's heart ached for the people of House Apple. She'd played down by the river with children from their house when she was young, remembering them as an easygoing and kind house. Angst and rage gripped her ribcage, making drawing her next breath painful. The humans couldn't have picked a less aggressive house to attack. "Were the humans found and punished?"

Sorrow filled Cedric's features. "Oh, certainly. They were caught by enforcers soon after the attack and jailed for a year. Some of the stolen artifacts were recovered, but even those were damaged."

"That's nowhere near adequate," Becka replied. "But having lived in the city, I've seen how normalized aggression towards the fae is. It's as if some humans think the Great War never ended."

As much as she'd liked her freedom in the city, Becka couldn't deny that most days she'd felt measurably safer here in fae territory. Like she had a chance against the threat of the Shadow-Dwellers. At least, that's how she'd felt before the poisoning.

"As you say," Cedric replied. "All houses within the fae territories have taken this as a warning. It's why we keep such a large contingent of our own trained guards and no longer rely on the enforcers, who are stationed within the cities. We must police our property and protect it from threats rather than waiting for help to arrive from afar. As House Rowan is the largest of the four houses within our territory, we oversee and coordinate activities for the protection of all."

So it wasn't just Becka's imagination. There were indeed more guards than she'd remembered in her youth.

"What do you do with trespassers?" Becka asked.

Cedric shook his head. "We use reasonable force to catch them and then lock them in a holding cell. The enforcers are quick to pick them up, which doesn't usually take long. But we do not expect the culprits to get punished for their crimes. All we can do is remove them and hope they do not come back."

"Let's refocus on the tasks before us today." Astrid thunked a heavy tome down upon the table and opened it, the spine cracking with age. "We have another youth whose illusionist skills have been unremarkable. Her name is Iona, daughter of Tove."

"I know the girl," Maura replied. "Are you certain her gift won't progress further?"

Hearing Iona referred to so dispassionately hit a little too close to home for Becka. Was it just Maura's way of managing bad news, or did she not care for the girl if she wasn't gifted?

"She's been steady for the past year, and if something changes we can always reassess, but she's nearing the age of civic duty."

Everyone nodded, and Becka assumed this was a familiar conversation. She knew gifts came in the full range from none, to not much, to 'oh my goodness put a lid on it'. Having once been declared ungifted, Becka would have given anything to have had just a whisper of power versus being an outcast. However, she doubted young Iona felt grateful for her diminished gift.

"What civic act can she perform, considering her depth of talent?" asked Elder Eirian.

Once their guild training had completed, all fae were required to perform three years of community service in the cities as an act of subservience and acceptance of human rule. Becka knew some students had passed and become guilded with just barely a passing grade, and yet they were still expected to serve in whatever capacity they were able. What wasn't discussed was the additional human prejudice they'd be subjected to in the cities for being low performers. Becka had seen for herself how humans considered fae useless if they didn't have gifts to be used for their greater, or personal, good.

"Well, the arts and beautification district won't want her. They've requested only the most skilled of artisans," Astrid replied.

"A better question is, what serves House Rowan best?" said Calder.

Becka's emotional feathers ruffled again, not just at the perfunctory nature of the conversation but at Calder's profit-focused question. Were they always this callous?

"May I suggest we send Iona to serve with the transport and infrastructure sector?" said Cedric with a sly smile on his face.

"What would that gain us?" asked Becka. "And what would it gain Iona?"

Cedric held up a single finger. "Iona would learn the current patching and repair techniques used on roads, bridges, and other projects. The Civic Board has a call out to House Oak for earth elementalists who can move and repair large objects, but I would guess they need help to visually improve where repairs have occurred. From a distance, slight imperfections within an illusion wouldn't be as noticeable. Iona is skilled enough to perform that level of illusion, and she's clever enough to take detailed notes on how they are repairing their infrastructure and what types of weaknesses are surfacing within the city's systems. What think you, Astrid? Would she be up to it?"

Becka's internal radar pinged. Lord Cedric was suggesting espionage!

Astrid wobbled her head from side to side. "Iona has sufficient skill to blend colors and hide repairs, which would save the humans time and materials, and the magic will last for the life of the structure. Plus, she has a quick wit to learn more than they might guess. It's a fair suggestion."

"I'd like you to discuss this with both Tove and Iona," said Maura. "I want to make sure they are receptive. You're right, Eirian, this could be a good opportunity. Even though Iona's skills aren't great, this gives her an opportunity to contribute to the house as she is able." She turned to Becka. "What are your thoughts, daughter?"

Becka tapped a gloved finger against her nose, debating with herself. How direct should she be with her concerns? Maura raised a brow, and Becka pushed forward. Subtlety had never been her strong suit.

"Let me make sure I'm understanding the potential. It makes sense for Iona to serve her allotted time with the Civic Board in a relatively low-impact capacity. If she learns anything pertinent to systemic infrastructure weaknesses, what would House Rowan do with that information?"

The other members of the council exchanged glances, but it was Calder who answered her.

"First, we share our learning with the other houses. Second, we consider how such information could be used defensively, if ever there was cause."

"Do you mean we track weaknesses in human city infrastructure for potential later exploitation?" Becka asked. Hanna nudged her foot, but Becka needed to understand what was being proposed. Any information gathered with a "defensive" mindset could cross the legal threshold into an act of war.

"Yes, that is what we mean. But we'd only use that knowledge defensively, of course," Calder replied.

"Of course... But doesn't that border on the legal edge of

sedition against humans?" Becka asked, needing to make sure she understood.

Calder shrugged. "Which is why we do it as a purely defensive gesture."

"Okay," Becka replied, and then took a moment to process what she'd heard. Plotting against humans, or raising arms against them, directly violated the treaty. Having lived within the cities for the past several years, Becka didn't want to think about fighting against her fellow students and library lovers. But she could imagine needing to defend their territory, especially given the attack against House Apple. It never hurt to be prepared. Did it?

"I suppose it never hurts to build one's defenses," she replied, knowing full well that wasn't the case. She'd read the history books. She knew arms races inevitably led to wars. *Preparing against* looked a lot like *preparing for*, and then it was just too tempting to have a tool and use it when things got heated.

Anxiety and disappointment clenched her gut. This conversation did not feel like a path forward between the fae and human races. Becka had a lot of work ahead of her.

Lord Cedric openly frowned at her. Becka felt like she'd crossed the line with her question about sedition.

"We must do what we can, where reasonable," Astrid said.

Becka nodded, stupefied. She sat at this table, sharing in the decisions. She'd only been back three months, but she'd paid attention. Did they think she bought their story of using information only for defense of the house? She wasn't ready to rock this boat, so she withheld her questions. For now.

Lord Cedric cleared his throat. "Have we heard from House Ash on our engagement proposal for Lady Sigfrid?"

Maura nodded. "Yes, a firm denial. They have eligible males of her age but remain offended we offered our heir to House Hawthorne instead. They suggested we look towards House Oak."

"I doubt we will see peace between the House of Thorns and the House of Time within our lifetime," replied Lady Wynne. "But they are correct in that House Oak has some suitable prospects, although not as highly ranked. I can speak with my cousin-in-law who lives there, to see how receptive they might be?"

"They aren't my favorite at the moment," Maura replied with a swift glance to Becka. Was she miffed at all of House Oak because of Quinn's presence? "But reach out to your cousin. And let's do our best to not ruffle any more feathers along the way?"

"As you say," replied Lady Wynne, her chin bobbing.

"Becka," Maura turned to her, "remind me to walk you through the present state of the fae-touched political land-scape sometime soon. The last thing we need is an incident because you're not up to date with current affairs."

"Sounds scintillating." Becka figured she might need an entire bottle of hot sauce just to make it through that lecture. But she could take notes. Lots of notes.

"More so than you might imagine," Maura replied.

The conversation moved on without her, while she was occupied within silent contemplation. She couldn't blame her house for acting to defend themselves, but did they ever cross the line? Becka was certain humans would consider the act they'd discussed crossing the line.

Humans had eliminated houses for failing to bend the knee to human oversight. In the cities, she'd heard tales first-hand of how the humans had clawed back their lands and bent the fae to their will. If House Rowan wasn't careful, they'd be sanctioned. But perhaps Becka could think of palatable excuses to use should the humans ask questions.

Becka's stomach churned and flipped. Life in the city as an ungifted had been so much less complicated.

The council discussed a few more generic matters, such as a seed swap for winter crops with the nearby House Vine. House Vine had varieties of squash that House Rowan's head gardener had deemed might do well in the local climate. Despite having slept all night, Becka was having a difficult time paying attention to each of the votes. She did her best, but there was a level of fatigue she couldn't quite shake off.

After about an hour had passed, Maura placed her hands on the table and rose. "That's enough for today. Until midweek?"

Becka rose with the others, but instead of staying around to chat, she exited the room and came face to face with an expectant Brent.

CHAPTER 11

"Lady Becka, would now be a good time to review this week's roster?" Brent asked.

Astrid and Calder had also emerged from the council chambers and stood behind her, listening to the exchange. Calder's paramour, Alvilda, came sauntering down the hall, her attention trained on him. In turn, he greeted her arrival with a wide smile. Astrid frowned at the two of them and then went the other way.

What's that about? Does Astrid not like Calder's choice in girlfriends?

"Brent, this is Hanna Hawthorne. She's acting as an advisor for me. Hanna, this is Brent Douglas. He's the lead wolf shifter here."

"Pleased to meet you." Hanna gave a quick bow.

"Same," he replied. "Would you mind giving Becka and me a few moments to speak about her security?"

Hanna frowned. No doubt Maura had instructed her to remain by Becka's side.

"I'll find you right after," Becka said.

"Oh, all right, then," Hanna said, returning her smile.

"Walk with me?" Becka asked Brent.

He gestured for her to take the lead, and, craving fresh air, Becka led them upstairs and out to the rooftop garden. Her bevy of guards followed them. At the top of the staircase, Becka walked through the doors to the rooftop garden, feeling drawn back into this space... the couches where she and Vott were poisoned days before.

"Are we going to review the shifter duty roster or is this all for show?"

Brent shook his head. "This isn't for show. Luce recommended to me that you take over Vott's oversight of wolf shifter operations here at House Rowan, and I think it's a smart idea."

"You do?" Becka took a seat on one of the couches, motioning for Brent to sit across from her, mirroring Vott's placement.

He nodded and took a seat. Shamus and Lorelai walked the area, giving them the space to speak privately. Elena and Oba did the same, walking the perimeter of the roof.

"Luce has good instincts. We shifters do more than you are likely aware of. Also, we don't yet know if Vott will recover. I prefer to plan for the worst-case scenario, so I can be surprised, and frankly relieved, if things go better than expected."

"Have you heard anything new about Vott's condition?" she asked, and he gave a simple shake of his head in reply. Poor man, she knew he and Vott had a close bond. No doubt this was doubly hard on him, knowing the poisoner had gotten by his team to Vott. She'd do whatever she could to make things easier on him. "So, what do you need me to do besides approving expenses?"

Brent gave her a halfhearted smile. "Traditionally we settle out at the end of each month, so that's not on my mind today. As you know, Vott ramped up our security detail when you were declared gifted and it was clear there was a threat to your life."

She nodded. During the last few months she'd appreciated having their presence twenty-four seven. Becka felt safer with them than the house guards.

"Do you want to change anything?" she asked.

"Not the frequency or number of guards, no. Look, you faced down Woden, a Shadow-Dweller, who wanted to steal your powers."

Becka shivered, remembering Woden drinking blood from her wrist. "I remember."

"I was talking with Quinn earlier. I don't think this poisoning fits with the Shadow motive."

At the mention of Quinn's name her heart skipped a beat. "You talked to Quinn?"

"He's been all over this place. I swear he will start ripping it apart brick by brick to hunt down proof for his theories."

She smiled. "Sounds like him. And you're right, this doesn't seem to fit the Shadow-Dweller motive. I discussed the potentials with Quinn, and he asked me to think about more, but I'm at a loss."

"I want you to keep notes. Or make a mental list and communicate to my staff whenever you add someone to it. I have my own list, of course, but you might think of someone neither Quinn nor I have previously considered."

Quinn had hinted around this topic, but hearing it from

Brent, her father's longtime guard and trusted confidante, hit home.

"Of course. You and your shifters will be the first to know."

Brent steepled his fingers, his entire focus on her. "I know this is stuff you've covered with Quinn, but off the top of your head, who might want you dead?"

"Anyone who might feel threatened? I mean, could they be afraid of my powers? So maybe Aunt Astrid?"

"I've thought about her, but it seems like she adores taming powerful gifts. It's her vocation."

"Yeah, but my power is wild. She's warned me about the potential for madness if I don't harness my powers adequately. So many warnings. Perhaps she fears for the house?"

"Okay." He shrugged. "Next?"

"What about Calder? He's not happy I'm back as heir; he's enjoyed his temporary stint as the eldest guilded progeny. Once I am declared trained and guilded, he goes back to being number two. I'm taking his position as next in line, and that's got to burn a bit."

"I agree he has a strong motive. Who else?"

"What about Alain?" *If he was behind the poisoning, surely that would be a way out of the engagement contract?*

"Your fiancé? That's not someone I would have pegged. Why do you think he would want you dead?"

"It would get him out of the engagement! And, I'm nowhere near the 'pedigree' Tesse was. I'm a disappointing second-place prize. I'm sure he'd prefer a new arrangement, if he could. Perhaps Ingrid, or Sigfrid? Or another house's heir?"

"I'm not sure anyone sees you as second place, Becka. Besides, why would he wait three months?"

"To see if we could get along? To set up the poisoning? I don't know."

"I'll make a note of it. Anyone else you can think of?"

Becka shrugged. "I don't know. All of those options sound potentially plausible to me."

Brent leaned back and scrubbed a hand over his face. "Okay, I'll get started tracing Astrid and Alain's movements in the days before the poisoning. I was already looking into Calder. I'll report back to you and Quinn once I know more. And if you think of anyone else, if you even just have a wild thought cross your mind, report it to any shifter and they'll pass it back to me."

Reviewing her potential poisoners had brought with it memories of the event. Distressed, Becka took a deep yoga breath and held it for a few seconds before blowing out slowly.

"Will do. Thanks for looking into it."

Brent stood up. "The enforcers aren't the only ones who can hunt down their prey. Besides, Vott was poisoned on my watch. I have an oath to keep, and I'm taking this as a personal attack."

Becka was glad he was on *her* side. "There's something I've been wanting to ask, but the timing just never felt right."

Brent shrugged. "Ask away. I have no qualms telling you if you've crossed a line."

Becka didn't doubt him for a second. "How is it you came to work for Vott, and what's this oath you talk about between the two of you? I mean, from what I understand, your agreement is rare amongst fae and shifters."

"Oh, I guess you wouldn't know." His hands came to rest on his hips and his features softened as he smiled at her. "In my adolescence, Vott stopped by our clan during one of his journeys."

Did I hear him correctly? "Vott used to go on journeys? I'd thought he'd lived here since his twenties."

"Yes, it's common for House Alder. Soon after they come into their seer powers, they are sent on a two-year vemhel, where they wander around, have visions that may help others, and learn how to read the signs. It's part of the process of learning how their powers manifest."

"Wait, I remember hearing about his vemhel, but he never shelled out details. The vemhel is how House Alder performs civic service, because of the nature of their gift. But I always thought of it as a formal series of visitations."

"It is exactly their civic service, but it's not at all formal. I guess if they stay home, their seer gifts aren't developed in the same manner, so out they go. Think of it like a magical road trip without a destination."

"Okay, that's not at all how I think of my father. But it's lovely. Charming, even. I suppose his visit was to your lands?"

"Yes, and my dad, Barric, wasn't having any of it. As clan chief, he didn't welcome fae within our walls. He always felt you all were a batch of troublemakers and were apt to bring the wrath of humans knocking on his front door."

Becka shrugged. He wasn't wrong on that count. "So what did Vott do?"

"Vott accepted Barric's refusal. But instead of leaving, he bedded down with a herd of elk on our property for a week."

Again, did I hear him right?

"He denned with elk?" Becka couldn't imagine Vott doing any such thing.

"In the winter, no less. Even for shifters, it convinced us he'd lost his seer-loving marbles."

She couldn't wait to hear what happened next, wondering what other secrets Vott had up his sleeves. "Don't leave me hanging. What happened?"

"A week into his stay, he got the elk worked up in the middle of the night. You know how loud rutting elk can be? It wasn't even rutting season, but somehow he managed it. He woke the entire clan."

Imagining Vott hooting and hollering with elk under pale moonlight made him sound a bit looney, and Becka burst into laughter at the thought. "Why would he do that?"

"The night nurse had died in the middle of the night, knocking a chair over into the fireplace in her death throes. Luckily, since the rutting elk awakened us, we quickly noticed the smell of the fire. My father was burned badly, but he was the only casualty, besides the nurse. All the babies were saved."

Awestruck, she couldn't speak for a moment. Vott was always understated, but she'd never dreamed he'd gone to bat for a shifter clan in his youth. No wonder they were so dedicated to him.

"I had no idea he did that for you."

"We still don't talk about Vott's exploits with the elk, but Clan Wolf owes multiple life-debts to your dad."

"And so now you run security for him to pay him back, so you can fulfill the life-debt?"

"Precisely, and he insists on paying us. Until recently, it

was boring work. Once you showed up, things got interesting."

She knew he meant once Tesse's death had happened, but Becka didn't mind the omission. "Thanks for the explanation, Brent. That's a side of Vott I'd never guessed existed but am blessed to know."

"Sure thing."

Becka looked at the light streaming in through the windows. She had an hour before Hanna's tea party, and she knew how she wanted to use it.

As he turned to go, she threw one last question Brent's way. "Do you know where I can find Quinn?"

Brent looked back over his shoulder, his penetrating gaze not missing a thing. "Stay here. He knows where you are."

Becka gave a single nod, unable to form a response over the intensity of her insides clenching.

Of course he knows.

Becka pulled out the Shadow-Dweller book, leaned back, and cracked it open, laying it across her lap and preparing to fill her wait with a bit of research.

CHAPTER 12

Gloves still on, Becka paged through the Shadow-Dweller book, and the nagging sensation that she was missing something struck her again. She was missing something obvious. Something that was most likely the key to this tome.

Despite the low-level headache lingering at the back of her skull, she couldn't stop paging through, taking in the aged parchment covered with arcane symbols. The same symbols which had covered Tesse's throat and shoulders. The longer she looked at them, the more they almost made sense.

She'd seen these symbols in the historical manuscript of the Great War in the campus library archives, but with no frame of reference at the time she'd assumed they were an illustration or decoration. Now she knew there was more to it.

Shamus and Lorelai moved towards the entryway to the rooftop garden, and a moment later Hanna emerged from the house. At first Shamus blocked her, but then Becka motioned her over and he let Hanna pass.

Hanna sauntered over, a seemingly genuine smile on her face. "How did your talk with Brent go?"

"Quite pleasant, although he's all business."

"As one would expect of a hired guard! Oh, what in the world is that?" she asked, pointing at the book in Becka's lap.

"It's part of the Shadow-Dweller investigation."

"How wonderful!" Hanna laughed, amusement dancing in her eyes. "I heard the enforcers are investigating monsters from children's stories now."

Becka had to bite her tongue. She liked Hanna, and knew she wasn't trying to be spiteful, but her words stung.

She took another deep breath, getting her emotions under control. "This book is very real." Becka turned the open book towards Hanna so she could have a quick glance, and then placed it back on her lap. "It's a piece of a puzzle I've been trying to figure out. My gift might help lead to insights about this ancient tome that's not well understood."

"Oh, I love puzzles! With all of those geometric designs, it looks like someone's sketch pad. What's the mystery?"

"Well, I'd love to be able to translate this, but I don't think the glyphs are words after all. So I'm focusing on the magic instead."

"Do you think you're on the verge of a breakthrough?" Hanna took a seat across from her, which just happened to be where Vott had sat when they were poisoned. She arranged her diaphanous skirts around her like a work of art, her gaze focused on the book in Becka's hands.

"I wish. I mean, maybe I am? It's that sensation where you have a word on the tip of your tongue, but it just won't surface."

She nodded. "I know what you mean. Like there's something floating out there just outside the range of your perception?"

"Uh huh." Becka left the book open on her lap, insulated from her Null magic by mere layers of fabric and her now ever-present intention.

"How are you feeling?" Hanna asked. "You still look a bit tired."

Hanna's genuine concern was a welcome gesture, and Becka felt herself smiling.

"I'm almost back to normal. Fatigue is still dragging my energy down, but I mostly have my stamina back."

"That's good to hear. Have you checked in with Healer Illan today?" Hanna asked.

"I am going to, but he didn't seem to have any concerns about my progress. Wait, did Maura tell you to ask that?"

Hanna scrunched her nose. "No, silly. That was just my general concern for your wellbeing. Are you sure working with that book is safe? It sounds like it might be just a smidge dangerous."

At that moment, movement between and underneath Becka's fingers caught her eye. Simultaneously, a low throbbing kicked in at the back of her skull.

"You like a bit of danger, do you?" Hanna asked her, nodding almost imperceptibly to herself.

Becka frowned, more interested in the book than Hanna's line of questioning. Moving her gloved hands to the edges of the pages, the movement clarified. The arcane symbols on the pages faded ever so slightly as squiggly lines undulated underneath the blockish forms, like worms crawling around the page. She flipped a page and then back again.

Is the book reacting because of Hanna's presence, the change in location, or some other factor?

Similar squiggly worms appeared on the other pages. Their movement slanted toward Hanna.

The forms reminded Becka of words.

"I suppose it might be a smidge dangerous," Becka admitted. She picked up the book and showed Hanna the open page full of squiggles and now transparent glyphs. "But I'm more curious than afraid. What do you see?"

Hanna laughed. "It looks the same to me, Becka. It's just a book. An old, faded book."

Becka returned the book to her lap.

There must be some illusion that hides it from Hanna, but I'm immune to it? Just like before, with Quinn not being able to see the marks on Tesse. It must have some illusion or obfuscation spell that doesn't work on me.

Becka felt the smile spread across her face. Finally, a breakthrough! She sat back in her seat and looked with renewed interest at Hanna, suspicion peaked. What was the book trying to tell her and why was it reacting this way towards Hanna?

She paused a moment; what if Hanna was a Shadow-Dweller? How would Becka know? And if so, would Hanna be able to see the squiggles too? But if that were true, Hanna would never reveal it, obviously!

Becka decided to err on the side of caution and not mention the squiggles to Hanna, just in case. Instead, Becka continued to study the page. All at once, the squiggles froze and she could make out a word, repeated along the lines, again and again.

TEA.

Did it mean the tea she'd had with Vott? The upcoming tea party this afternoon? It wasn't lost on Becka that they were sitting on the couches where she and Vott had been poisoned.

"Hanna, what do you remember about the tea?"

Shock and confusion pinched Hanna's delicate features. "What an odd question to ask. I suppose you're asking about the lapsang souchong tea I brought to Vott?"

Wait, what?

"*You* brought Vott the tea?" Becka asked, pulling back from Hanna as she tried to calm her suddenly speeding pulse.

The squiggles on the book had lost the word TEA and returned to their sunburst alignment.

"I did. Alain had shared with me Vott's love of rare teas, so I brought some of his favorite flavor from home as a gift."

Excited, Becka felt a puzzle piece move into place in her mind, one she didn't yet know the importance of but was certain it mattered.

"You did it to curry favor with Vott?" Becka asked.

Hanna frowned. "It's customary to give gifts to allies. I didn't feel a need to curry favor or get him to like me, since my mere presence here is a gift from House Hawthorne."

Becka bit her tongue to keep herself from laughing. Surely, Hanna was referring to the gift of her services and not just her august presence. *Right?*

And she knew from Quinn that the tea itself wasn't poisoned, so...

"Hanna," Becka asked. "what happened when you gave Vott the tea? Where were you? And was anyone else there?"

The squiggles shook as if hit by lightning.

Is that good or bad?

"Well, let's see. I presented Vott the tea in his study. Calder was in attendance but didn't seem interested in my arrival nor the gift. His focus was entirely engaged with his paramour, Alvilda. In fact, he wasn't receptive to me at all. But there was nothing particularly noteworthy about the conversation. Oh, there was a female shifter guard at the door; I don't know her name. She wasn't introduced."

She'd have to ask Brent who was on duty that day. Perhaps they'd seen something?

Why did the gift of the tea matter? She now knew Hanna had brought it, but since it wasn't the source of the poison, who cared?

As she wondered these things to herself, the squiggles mysteriously faded from the pages and the glyphs lost their transparency, solid once again. The book must be done with her for now, the fleeting moment of discovery rendered complete.

"Oh my gosh," Hanna said. "We need to be going. The tea party is starting shortly."

Although she didn't relish the idea of the gathering, Becka didn't want to see what Maura's next move would be if she kept refusing her. Becka stored the Shadow-Dweller book in her bag and rose to go.

Becka couldn't wait to talk to Quinn about the squiggles.

CHAPTER 13

"Lady Hanna!" exclaimed Sigfrid. "May I sit next to you?"

"Please do, Lady Sigfrid." Hanna popped a black-skinned grape into her mouth as a young serving girl filled her glass. The fiery relationship coach appeared well at ease, all smiles and poise.

Sigfrid plopped down next to Hanna on the light-green linen blankets which were spread out on a natural ringed formation of flat-topped sandstone. It relieved her when her quieter sister, Ingrid, sat to her right without preamble.

Focused on conserving her energy, Becka had been the first to take a seat. Everyone arranged themselves around her. Hanna to her left, Ingrid to her right, and Yaeli and Alvilda across from her. Perhaps she could get through this social occasion by smiling, nodding, sipping, and snacking.

Becka tried to enjoy the chatter of the other women but couldn't help being distracted by watching Lorelai test the food on her plate and her glass for poison. But the day was pleasant, the rocks radiated warmth against her legs, and a soft breeze caressed her skin. A group of finches endeavored to sneakily steal crumbs, and as the fae wouldn't shoo them away, were guaranteed to share in the feast laid out on the central table.

When Lorelai gave her a curt nod, Becka picked up a glass of strawberry-basil shrub and sipped at the tart, refreshing beverage. The others appeared oblivious to Lorelai and Shamus. Another two fae guards walked the perimeter of the meadow, close but not underfoot. Becka sighed, wishing Quinn had accompanied them.

For all appearances, this gathering seemed like a casual ladies' afternoon tea. Hanna wasn't hovering over Becka, for which she was grateful. Shamus was doing his part to glower at everyone, although she couldn't tell if anyone paid him any mind. From her discussion with Brent, Becka knew Vott's relationship to the shifters was a unique one. Did other fae have shifters living among them? From their nonchalance, she'd have thought the practice commonplace.

Ingrid stood and raised her glass in Becka's direction, breaking Becka out of her reverie. "In honor of our heir, I propose an einvigi!"

"Yes!" Alvilda replied, a sure smile on her lips and competitive glint in her eye. "It's just the thing you need to uplift your spirits."

Becka's stomach did a flip. An einvigi was an age-old fae contest of wit and skill, but because of her years away from House Rowan and her unguilded status, Becka had never taken part in one. She wanted to feel thrilled at being included, so why was her gut churning with anxiety?

"What are the einvigi's conditions?" Sigfrid asked. "Wait, who won last time?"

As if she didn't already know. Based on the way everyone turned to look at Yaeli, a more obvious rhetorical question could not have been asked. Yet from Becka's point of view, it was a revelation. In fact, she realized she didn't know their gifts well or in depth. Today could prove to be more informative than she'd expected.

Yaeli blushed and fanned her face as if to hide it. "Why, I believe I had that honor." Her confident smile betrayed her demure reply.

"Then the choice of terms falls to you," Sigfrid replied, raising a glass to Yaeli.

"Hmm." Yaeli cocked her head to the side, pursing her lips in concentration. "Oh, I have it! I propose each of us changes an element of our surroundings. The change must blend in and appear to be what nature intended. However, once noticed, it should be unmistakably flawed. Bonus points for humor. The one whose illusion is the most subtle wins the round."

Ingrid groaned. "You play to your strengths!"

Yaeli shrugged. "As if you wouldn't?"

Everyone laughed except Becka. *Am I in over my head?*

"Lady Hanna, would you judge?" asked Sigfrid. "You're the only non-Rowan present."

"Oh, what fun!" Hanna replied. "I'll play arbiter."

"But wait." Alvilda frowned. "We aren't being fair to our heir, Lady Becka. She's guilded but no illusionist. We'd be leaving her out with this challenge. It wouldn't be right to exclude her."

An air of disappointment settled over the group, and in unison they glanced over to Becka and then took quick sips of their drinks or bites of food to distract from the palpable discomfort.

Had Becka imagined the condescending edge to Alvilda's voice, or was it her own lack of self-confidence in her gift that ruffled her proverbial feathers? Surely, the heir to House Rowan should be able to compete in mere parlor games?

Couldn't she?

Becka cleared her throat. "I think Yaeli's challenge is fair. I only ask the honor of going last."

She was answered with silence, surprised glances, and arched brows. When she met Alvilda's gaze, her pursed-lipped frown transformed into a demure smile and a nod of encouragement.

Could she be any more fake?

"Is that acceptable to everyone?" Becka asked, daring the others to challenge her. Which she knew they wouldn't.

"Certainly," Hanna replied. She leaned over and whispered, "I'm excited to see what you have planned."

So am I. Becka forced a smile, glad to have at least Hanna's encouragement.

Hanna raised her glass to the group. "Let the einvigi begin! As the prior champion, Lady Yaeli has the honor of going first."

Yaeli set her glass down and stood, her gauzy pink dress almost floating around her as she moved. She cupped her hands together in front of her, brow furrowed in concentration. Between her hands, a spinning ball of energy grew from a speck to the size of her head in seconds, sparks of light illuminating the golden sheen of Yaeli's eyes. A few moments passed, and then Yaeli tossed the orb up into the air, where it exploded into countless sparks flying in all directions.

The shifters, the birds, and Becka didn't shy away from the miniscule points of light as they floated down, slowly dying out like embers from an unstoked fire. Becka felt the impact of the energy like tiny pinpricks against her skin. A light band of pressure encircled her head, her telltale alert of coming into contact with magic. Becka had become used to a persistent, low-grade headache at House Rowan. If only she could find a way around it.

Yaeli's display was met with polite clapping.

All of the secrets of the illusory arts hadn't been disclosed to her, as she was a Null and not an illusionist, yet Becka understood a few precepts. In order for the magic to work, an illusionist needed to either be in contact with the item in question or cast an energetic net through which the illusion could travel. Therefore, anything in range of the ball or the caster's immediate vicinity could be the target.

Yaeli scooped up her glass and sat back down. "Anyone?"

Becka looked around but saw nothing amiss. At least, not yet.

"Give us a minute," Ingrid said, her gaze scrutinizing every detail. "We'll find it."

"Or you won't." Hanna scrunched her nose. "Either way, the contest continues. Alvilda is up next."

Alvilda straightened her skirts, took a deep breath, and then closed her eyes. She wore her hair in big, thick braids swirled around her head, and they bobbed slightly along with her breathing. After another moment she exhaled and looked up, a pleased smile upon her face.

Becka looked all around Alvilda but detected nothing amiss.

Everyone looked around, but no one spoke up. The

tension had Becka at the edge of her seat. She hadn't imagined she'd enjoy this as much as she was.

"Next," was all she said, serenely sipping her bubbly beverage.

"Sigfrid, it's to you." Hanna gestured her way.

"Anyone catch them out yet?" Sigfrid asked, standing up.

Becka cocked her head to the side. "Are you delaying?"

Sigfrid jokingly frowned at her and the others laughed. "Never!"

Like Yaeli's method, Sigfrid held up her hands and created a spinning ball. Instead of lightning, this one appeared to be some disco-inspired glitter ball wobbling wildly out of control. Moments later Sigfrid threw her hands outwards and the energy ball exploded in all directions.

Alvilda and Hanna both attempted to shield their faces from the energetic shards, but there was no need, as they disappeared on contact. By the time they looked back up, Sigfrid was sitting again, eyes on Ingrid.

Becka joined the others in a round of clapping, knowing the magical net was cast by the ever-increasing pressure inside her head. She debated pulling the hot sauce out of her bag, but waited, keeping her focus on the game at hand.

"Ingrid," Hanna said. "It's to you."

Ingrid stood and held up a single hand. A moment later a single, enormous jasmine blossom appeared, glistening with morning dew. The flower shuddered, and then exploded, particles flying in all directions.

Again, Becka's head felt the impact of the tiny particulates. Again, she saw nothing amiss. Again, she clapped and smiled along. Becka sighed. *Is it just my inexperience, or am I just not very good at this game?*

"Becka," Hanna said, breaking her reverie. "The last turn falls to you."

"So it does." She stood and stretched, aware of how different she was from the other fae-touched women. Her pink hair and ear piercings. Her red track suit, neon green sports bra, and running shoes. Her occasional human or city phrases. It was kind of them to include her when everything about her stuck out like a fox trying to blend in with the chickens.

She gazed back at her seat. Who was she kidding? Perhaps she should give up before she embarrassed herself.

That's when she noticed the design shift in the fabric she'd been sitting upon. When she moved, the fabric shifted, almost imperceptibly. Once she noticed it, she couldn't un-notice it.

She moved to the outside of the ring, walking behind the others. "The blankets we're sitting upon. The fine linen now has a pattern that matches the creases and whorls in the sandstone underneath."

"Oh, good catch, Becka!" Hanna said.

Was she a relationship coach, or a cheerleader?

"I can see it now too," Sigfrid said. "Whose was it?"

Alvilda raised a hand, shaking her head in disdain. "I hate it when I get caught out first. But where's your entry to the einvigi, Becka?"

Becka's stomach flipped. She had an idea, but no clue if it would work. But what harm could come from trying? It wasn't like her reputation would take a hit.

"I'm going to try something." She squatted down next to the fabric and removed her right glove. Becka held her hand out over the blanket, focusing with all her might.

"You can't win by destroying our creations," Alvilda snapped. "Those aren't the stakes."

By the edge in her tone, Alvilda appeared to be taking this contest more seriously than the others. It was good she didn't care for the woman or Becka might have felt hurt over her tone. *Maybe.*

"I'm well aware," Becka replied.

Over the past few months, Astrid had trained her rigorously to control the extension of her Nulling gift to minute detail. It wasn't as perfect as she'd like, and the process always caused her head to ache, but what better opportunity to test her finesse?

Hovering her hand over the fabric, she could sense the warp and weave of the magic running through it. She didn't understand what all the components did, only how they entwined with the fabric on a structural level.

"I'm so excited!" Hanna blurted out.

"Shh!" Ingrid shushed.

"Sorry," whispered Hanna, head slumped down.

Becka ignored them all, her interest enraptured by the elemental magic woven through the fabric. That's when she noticed something odd. Another layer of magic.

Ever so carefully, Becka released just a trickle of her energy onto that thread of magic. A moment later, the light-green color of the fabric shook and shuddered. A ripple spread across her blanket, the color fading in places, revealing an uneven and imperfect dye job.

The pattern of the sandstone remained, all the more out of place on the mottled beige and green blanket.

In the following moments of silence, Yaeli laughed out

loud. "I mean, you know it's done, but we all prefer to pretend in the perfection."

"Your control is remarkable, removing the maker's spell but leaving Alvilda's," Ingrid said. "You've come so far in such a short time."

The genuine compliments touched her. Becka had had such a difficult time feeling connected. Perhaps Hanna and Maura were right. She needed to be open to connecting with her family.

"A clever feat, to be sure," Alvilda replied. "But does it qualify for the einvigi? I mean, we all noticed your change right off."

There was some general hemming and hawing amongst the crowd, but Becka broke the silence. "I agree. I'll give it another go."

She walked around the group, alert for signs of the others' magic.

"Eww," cried Hanna, who spat a grape out into her napkin. "I thought the last one was a little off," she said to the serving girl, "but these are too bitter to eat." She leaned forward and dropped the few she had in her hand onto her plate.

Yaeli raised an eyebrow, but then quickly grabbed a bite of cheese and bit in. Her nose wrinkled with disgust. "All right, who tainted the food?"

Sigfrid shrugged. "I did." She sipped from her glass. "Ugh! But I got the timing wrong. I'd meant for the bitterness to fade in slower." Sigfrid held up her hand, appearing to grab the air, and then shook it and waved it away.

Hanna picked up her discarded grape cluster. "At least

the food is good. That leaves two remaining: Yaeli and Ingrid."

Becka cleared her throat.

"And Becka!" Hanna giggled.

Was Hanna always this bubbly? Becka shook her head. Which was when she noticed Shamus shooing away a bee above his head.

Shamus stood at the edge of the grove leaning against an aspen tree. Despite standing in the shade, his silhouette dappled by the sunlight, Becka could still make out tiny bright white petals atop his head. As she neared, Becka recognized the distinct forms of miniature jasmine flowers blooming off of the peaks of his curly hair. Shamus greeted her approach with a growing scowl.

"Ingrid," Becka asked, glancing back over her shoulder. "I take it this is your doing?"

Ingrid nodded. "I thought, with him in the shade, that no one would notice."

"It's a good catch, Becka!" Sigfrid said.

"Need I remind you," Shamus interrupted, "shifters have no interest in your magic. Whatever you've done here," he gestured at the top of his head, "is non-consensual."

Ingrid blushed deeply. "Apologies, Shamus, I forgot myself." She held up a hand and blew across it in his direction. A moment later the petals fell from his head and dissipated into dust.

"You okay?" Becka asked Shamus. He shouldn't have to endure being treated as an ornament in a party game. At least Ingrid's apology had sounded heartfelt.

"She can't hurt me," he replied.

It didn't exactly answer Becka's question, but his expression had returned to neutral.

Becka gave him a quick nod and then walked back over to her seat.

"That leaves us Yaeli's illusion and whatever else Becka comes up with," Hanna said, popping another grape in her mouth.

"If you can't find it, that's all right. I'll happily claim my win." Yaeli's smug grin was met with frowns from the other contestants.

Tired of enduring the low-level magic-induced headache, Becka took a moment to pull a bottle of her hot sauce out of her bag. This raised some eyebrows but didn't shock anyone, as her predilection for hot sauce as pain reliever was well-known at this point.

At that moment, a bird landed on the blanket next to her, seeming to be interested in the bright coloring of the bottle in Becka's hand. And in that moment, Becka saw Yaeli's illusion and cried out in alarm.

Yaeli had reversed the nap on the bird's feathers, causing the bird to somehow appear put together backwards, and yet in the proper shape. The effect disturbed Becka at a deep level, although she couldn't quite put a finger on why. The finch just looked wrong.

She heard others ask what was amiss, but Becka's attention was entirely on the bird. Missing not a beat, she set down the bottle in front of the bird, who then moved in for a closer look. Becka reached out a single finger, her focus tuned, and just barely touched the bird. In that millisecond she attempted a partial removal of Yaeli's magic, just to see what would happen.

Instead of reversing the feather nap 180 degrees to the correct direction, Becka had managed to turn it halfway back to normal so each barb along the shaft stood out at a right angle, causing the bird to appear perpetually startled.

Becka shrank back, appalled at her impact on the bird. Yaeli's laughter pealed out, startling the bird from its seat. It flew up and then came back down, picking at a seeded cracker it no doubt took as bird food. The others leaned in for a closer look.

Alvilda's look of dismay was accusatory. "What have you done?"

"We should rename it the puffball!" Yaeli exclaimed, having caught her breath.

"It looks like you electrocuted it!" Ingrid said.

Hanna, laughing, choked a little on her grape but seemed fine.

Sigfrid had joined in with Yaeli's laughter. "Electrocuted... or like a stable man did its hair!"

There was another round of laughter, which Becka joined in on this time.

Hanna cleared her throat. "It's remarkable, Becka. Disturbing, but remarkable."

Becka pulled on her glove, and then took a swig from the bottle of hot sauce.

"Hmm, who shall I name the winner? Yaeli or Becka?" Hanna asked.

Yaeli stood and gave a short bow in Becka's direction. "I yield to our heir. Although we all noticed her magical change right away, it was unexpected, and I haven't laughed like that in ages." She held up her hand, pointed at the bird, and then wiggled her fingers, restoring the bird to its original state of being. "Any objections?"

To Becka's surprise, there were none. She'd somehow won her first einvigi.

Mother would be so proud. Come to think of it, Becka was proud of herself too. She'd never imagined she could compete with illusionists.

As Becka bade them farewell, Hanna rose to go with her.

"May I accompany you to your next appointment?" she asked.

"Definitely!" Becka replied, smiling with the confidence of her recent win.

"This was a lovely picnic. If you were to ask, I would advise you need more of these types of events to help increase your feelings of connectedness with your family."

Considering her upbeat mood, the fact that she'd laughed plenty, and had spent time engaging in conversation with women her age over the past hour, Hanna had a point Becka couldn't discount.

I think I agree with her. And I like it.

Turns out Hanna wasn't a bad relationship coach after all.

CHAPTER 14

Hanna, Shamus, and Lorelai accompanied Becka across the grounds to the sun patio outside of the infirmary. Becka entered, motioning for the others to wait for her.

Although the windows of the infirmary were expansive and opened daily to bring in fresh air and sunshine, the patio allowed patients quick access to lounge in the sun for its healing properties.

Today, the only occupant of the patio was Elder Alaetha, her father's sister. She lay back on a chaise, feet up, gaze trained into the distance. She'd pulled her silvered hair back into a bun made from a single, large braid. The elder's frame was slight, and Becka remembered Alaetha was Vott's older sibling by a good two dozen years.

Her willingness to travel at her age was a testament to Vott's poor condition, but Vott had always spoken of Alaetha and their correspondence fondly.

"I was not sure you'd be able to meet with me," Elder

Alaetha said, not looking her way, yet motioning for her to take a seat.

"Elder Alaetha," Becka said, sitting down on a couch across from Alaetha's. "I am honored to make your acquaintance. Vott always spoke of you with warmth."

"Lady Becka," Alaetha replied. Her piercing gaze turned towards Becka, taking her measure. "I am afraid I can't say the same."

Becka held her tongue, unsure of what to say, and so let Alaetha make the next move.

"I've been here just two days, niece. Can you guess what I've learned?"

Her shoulders tensed and Becka folded her gloved hands in her lap, bracing for Alaetha's response. What *could* Alaetha have learned in two days? Did she know about her relationship with Quinn, such as it was? Had Maura recounted to her all of the ways Becka hadn't yet stepped up? Did she also think the Shadow-Dweller attack was an inflated children's story?

Becka didn't want to know.

"I would love to learn," she lied.

"It is a deep shame that my brother was poisoned as part of an attack on you. It looks like he will survive, but most likely at great personal cost. My first inclination was to grieve for you both equally. Through my many years I have witnessed the fae-touched jockey and vie for power for all manner of reasons. Sometimes it's because of heated emotions. Sometimes because of political or territorial matters. I had assumed this hubbub was just another altercation."

Becka nodded her head, inclined to allow Alaetha to vent uninterrupted.

"But this is no standard power play, just as you are no standard fae. Late to mature and returned from a life in the city, your powerful and dangerous gift has propelled you to singular status within the stream of never-ending back-channel gossip. I suppose you must think you're special?"

The sharp edge of Alaetha's tongue had knocked her joy from winning the einvigi right out of her. Had there really been enough material about Becka to produce a constant flow of gossip? And did she think of herself as special? Becka didn't think so, but she also thought of herself as being different. Separate.

But that doesn't equate to special. Does it?

Alaetha sat, brow arched, awaiting her reply.

Becka answered from her gut, hoping it would appease her Aunt. "I don't feel that I'm special, Elder."

Alaetha burst into a joyless, rebuking laughter. "That is where you are wrong. You are special, if only because others deem you so."

That didn't ring true to Becka. "But I'm not..."

Alaetha raised a hand to cut her off. "You are special enough that others might prefer you dead over risking a future with you in it. And now that I have seen you for myself, I am beginning to understand why."

Her words fell like a weight across Becka's shoulders. She had the impression Alaetha had been preparing this speech, and that she was conveniently responding to her prompts. She didn't want to ask, but couldn't not ask, either. "What do you mean?"

"One expects the heir of a powerful house to behave with

a certain minimal level of decorum. You, however, defy expectations, and not in a good way. Your gift is novel and powerful, but don't think for a moment that your gift is the only thing fae hold in esteem.

"You refuse to present yourself in the manner of your house. You shrug off our customs and avoid gatherings. You have a wonderful, high-born fiancé who you treat like dirt. You appear to prefer the company of shifters and enforcers over your own family.

"There is a general concern over the mental stability of any fae-touched who would behave in this manner, ungrateful to her house and holding a power few yet understand. I have heard other houses whisper the question: is Lady Becka the best House Rowan can do?"

Becka's limbs felt heavy, almost as if the rumors and gossip from Alaetha's lips had dealt her a physical blow. Somehow, the criticism coming from Alaetha after seeing Vott unconscious hit her fresh and at a whole different level, like she'd already been ripped open and wounded, then her aunt stepped in and poured on the salt.

Alaetha was known for being a no-nonsense straight shooter. It was one thing to hear the same feedback from Maura week after week. But from an aunt she hadn't seen in forever? It was an unexpected level of emotional impact. This time she felt it viscerally and Becka had to force herself to breathe deeply.

As biting as Alaetha's comments were, they weren't cruel. If this was truly her reputation, she'd rather know. "I've attended council meetings. And I just came here from winning an einvigi at a tea party."

"An einvigi, how lovely!" Alaetha replied, a harsh bite in

her voice. "And all it took was you and your father's poisoning to make you finally step up?"

No one could dish out guilt like an elder from the House of Whispers.

Becka was too embarrassed to respond with the truth, which was that Maura had *demanded* she step up. "I have sworn to make an effort."

Alaetha shook her head. "I'm sure Vott will find that comforting. I too look forward to seeing the fruits of your esteemed labors. You would do well to heed my warning. If they visit more pain upon House Rowan, it will be because of you."

Alaetha's words hit literal home for Becka. As much as she hated to hear it, Becka knew she'd needed to hear Alaetha's perspective.

"Speaking of duty," Becka jumped up, eager for any excuse to exit this conversation, "I forgot; I have a curse to cure. Perhaps we can discuss this further at a later date?"

Alaetha shooed her off like a fly. "Do not let me stop you from being of use to your house."

"Elder Alaetha," Becka replied, dipping her chin low before she spun and sped off.

Flummoxed and heavy-hearted from Alaetha's rebuke, Becka breathed a heavy sigh. "I didn't even get to find out how Vott is doing."

"Do you want to go ask?" Lorelai replied.

"No, I would have heard from Illan if there had been a change. Besides, I don't want to be late for Berak and Saana."

CHAPTER 15

They had added a few chairs to Berak's testing chambers, which was convenient because Becka had Hanna and her entourage of guards. At least the fae guards remained outside the door.

"Fair day, Lady Becka," Berak said, taking in the group. "I didn't know you were bringing an audience."

Hanna, Shamus, and Lorelai stood behind her.

"I didn't know either, Berak." *This is getting ridiculous!* "Good to see you too, Saana."

The wizened old lady's face wrinkled with a broad smile. Next to her sat an elder in a chair. His creased expression and downturned mouth made him look like he had a constant case of heartburn. He must be the one with the curse? His robes ran to the floor, and his frizzy hair was long and unkempt.

"It's no worry, dear," said Saana. "Although I would recommend they remain in the viewing chamber, just in case something... unexpected happens."

Becka looked to her guards, who were an immediate no

for whatever reason. Hanna fanned herself and shot her a smile.

"We'll leave you to it," Lorelai said. "Luce and Saige are handing off with us." She and Shamus were going off shift, and the other two walked in the door.

"Thanks, Lorelai."

Lorelai inclined her head, and then she and Shamus showed themselves out. Berak shut the door behind them.

"You're staying too?" she asked Hanna.

"I don't see any point in leaving when they're staying." Hanna motioned to the shifters. "I'll be safe with them. Besides, I'm here to support you. To work my magic, I need to learn all about you, your daily challenges, and what drives you. Only then can I heal the rift between you and your betrothed."

Becka smiled back at Hanna, grateful for her support. "Thank you. Hopefully you'll get to see something special."

Hanna took a seat with great flourish, arranging her skirts in the shape of a perfect sunburst pattern on the floor in front of her. Becka shook her head, not even understanding how such a thing was possible, but perhaps it was trained into all fire elementalists at an early age.

Becka placed her bag next to the central pedestal. "So, what's the plan?"

Saana gestured to the fae in the chair. "Becka, meet Elder Langdon of House Willow."

"It's good to meet you, Elder," she said. His unkempt appearance made more sense now, as she'd heard House Willow preferred to live a more rustic life closer to the land.

"Well, let's wait and see on that count," he replied. "But I've made it here, so let's get on with it."

Becka found his direct manner refreshing and wondered if it was on par for his house or just his personal taste. "Don't sound so optimistic."

"No worries, youngster," he snapped back. "I've had people trying to cure me for decades. You're not the first, and you won't be the last."

Becka grabbed a chair and pulled it across from Langdon and sat in it, her knees mere inches from his.

"What's the nature of his curse?" she asked Berak and Saana.

"Why are you asking them?" the elder spat out. "You would think if they understood it, then they would have been able to cure it by now, right?"

Neither Berak nor Saana said anything, and Berak took a step backwards. Becka bit back a laugh. After all she'd faced, this bitter old man wasn't about to scare her. "My apologies, Elder. This is all new to me. Please tell me about your curse."

He guffawed. "See, how hard is it to give a little respect? Yes, young lady, I will explain my curse. See, it started back when I was a lad."

Becka was appalled. "Who would curse a child?"

"My older sibling, Radford, who I followed everywhere. He couldn't get free of me. So much so, he used his newfound abilities to prevent me from following him around."

"You're from House Willow, so your powers are related to moon magic?"

"Yes, which gets artsy and melodramatic, if you know what I mean."

"I've read about moon magic, but I have no direct experience," Becka replied. Where was he going with this line of thought? "So how did his powers manifest?"

"See, Saana, I like this girl. No one ever asks about Radford much, despite him causing all of this muck."

"Hmm, indeed," Saana muttered.

It was all the encouragement Elder Langdon needed. "Radford was a poet. His powers came on during his teenage years, and like many, were wild and unmanaged during that time. He'd see the moon and stars and opine with such froth that his very feelings would take on physical manifestations."

"That's amazing. Can he still do that?"

Langdon shook his head. "Gratefully, rarely, and nothing like what he could during his years of teenage angst. Honestly, harming me with his gift inhibited his trust of it. He's not been the same since."

She heard a frog croak. Becka looked around, but as no one else reacted, she brushed it off.

"He hated having you on his heels, and in the throes of teenage angst, cursed you?" she asked, fearing it was true.

"Yes, he spouted off some poetry telling me to get rooted in the mud and leave him alone."

Sure, she'd had friction with her siblings, but cursing each other? What consequences had Radford received for crossing that line, beyond fearing his own gift? Whatever they were, it paled in comparison to Langdon's lifelong curse.

"Which damaged your feet?" she asked.

"Well, it wasn't just Radford's magic. My mama was constantly singing these nursery rhymes. There were a lot of us kids, she had migraines, and she would sing this one rhyme whenever we got unruly or raised a ruckus. It wasn't mean-spirited, more like all she could do to hold things together for yet another hour."

"Let me guess, her song was about feet too?" she asked, enjoying the detective work of understanding his situation.

There was another resounding croak. Becka looked around again but didn't find a creature to pair with the noise. Where was it coming from?

"Sort of. When she'd recite it we'd still be running around, but it would dampen the noise, as if our pounding feet didn't even hit the earth."

"Clever of her, if it kept her sanity and migraines at bay. So what do you think went wrong?"

"I know what went wrong. Radford hollered out his magic at the same time as our mother did hers. Somehow, they melded together, causing this." He reached down and lifted his robes to his knees.

For a moment, Becka couldn't quite make sense out of what she saw. Instead of feet, he had wide, bulky protrusions that reminded her of mangrove tree roots. Covered with moss, dirt, and patches of a bark-like substance, the deformity reached up near his knees.

Behind her, Hanna gasped, but everyone else was quiet. Becka shot her a quick look of censure, and Hanna hid her face behind her fan.

"It appears your legs end in... roots? Like you're a tree? Can you still walk?"

"At first I could, but the growths have expanded over the years, so I haven't been able to for some time. I can feel the wee tendrils reaching for something all the time. It feels the best when I soak them in a stream."

Becka couldn't take her eyes off Langdon's legs. Stream soaks would explain that snail hanging onto his... maybe it was a toe? Did he even still have feet under all of that? In fae society, those from House Willow were commonly derided as hillbillies who lived in swamps and mangroves, living lives that were simple but close to nature. Although Langdon looked every bit the part, Becka knew his problem was more than a comedic punchline. As an outcast, she'd been pigeonholed plenty, and knew all too well that people were rarely the sum of their component parts.

"The challenge," broke in Berak, "is in the combination of misaligned magic. Usually when fae work together, there's a good deal of effort put into aligning the intention of the spells. Efforts to undo the magic have been hampered by our inability to untangle the threads."

"So this is less of a curse, and more of misconfigured magic?" Becka asked.

"Is there a difference in practice?" Saana asked.

"I'm just looking for your insight. You're the experts in testing magic and curses," Becka replied.

"They're experts at failed attempts," Langdon said, laughing alone at his own jibe.

Berak and Saana took his jibe in stride, both more or less ignoring him.

A third croak resounded through the chamber. Where was it coming from?

Langdon opened a pocket near his chest. "Pipe down, will ya? I'm doing my best here." He turned to Becka. "These jokers tell me you might be able to do something?"

Did he have a frog in his pocket? Again, no one else took any mind of Langdon, so Becka let it go.

Saana and Berak's callousness toward Langdon's plight worried her. Becka didn't want him going into this without fair warning, which she wasn't sure the testers had been fully forthright about. She needed to put all of the potential outcomes on the table and make sure he understood the risks involved.

"I can definitely do something." Becka replied. "But I don't know what will happen to you once I've destroyed the magic."

"Destroy... so what, will I lose my legs?" he asked, appearing more curious than shaken at the prospect.

Saana cleared her throat. "Although that is a possibility, we really don't know. You've had this disfigurement nearly your entire life. There is a high likelihood that resolving your curse won't change the way your legs function. However, if she removes this magic, other things can be done to restore function."

Langdon groaned. "You don't have any clue. Never have on how to fix me up. What do you say, Becka?"

She hesitated for only a moment. "I can break the magic, but I have no clue what that will do to you. I might even damage your gift. You may well be worse off after I'm done."

A brief look of surprise flashed across his face, followed by a glint of amusement in his pale golden eyes. "I like your candor. Go on. Get on with it. The suspense is killing me."

Becka wished she felt as hopeful as Langdon. No, hopeful wasn't right. His amusement in the face of the facts wasn't him being hopeful. He was *resigned*. He knew the risks and was willing to accept whatever might happen for a chance at leaving this curse behind. She slid off her gloves, tucking them into her pants pocket. "Don't move."

Over the past few months, Becka had become used to holding her powers within her skin. This was a fundamental aspect of her training with Astrid and something she'd become competent doing as her default state without a lot of extra effort. Pushing beyond her skin now took mental effort and focus. She'd gotten a decent amount of control over the past few months.

She still wore the sea silk gloves during the day and didn't know how great her control was when she slept, but at least Becka no longer worried about controlling her Null power every waking moment. When she'd been unconscious after the poisoning, her shifter guards had moved her to the infirmary with no ill effects, and Illan had treated her using gloves of his own.

During the months since they had assigned the shifters to her, she'd come into contact with them many times with no ill effect. They were fearless, convinced her fae gift had no ability to harm them. Becka didn't understand what bolstered their confidence. If their positions had been reversed, Becka would not have risked contact.

The shifters'—and Quinn's—apparent immunity was the subject of ongoing debate within the Illusionists Guild. Astrid continued to push for more control during their training sessions, always aiming for the next level. Her aunt had privately expressed her concern to Becka that newly emerged gifts had, historically, been difficult to predict in their development, and so she wanted Becka to err on the side of caution.

The potential that her gift might evolve sent momentary chills down her spine. What if it grew stronger over time? So strong she lost the ability to control it and it later drove her mad?

Becka shook her head to center her thoughts and moved her chair back a few inches. She then let her gift fill her bare palms. She hesitated. She'd never done magic deliberately on a person before. What if she screwed up, and she left Langdon worse off? What if it worked, and he was also worse off?

"He knows there are risks, Becka," Saana said in low tones. "Sometimes the pain is worth the risk."

Langdon met Becka's gaze and nodded at her to get on with it.

Becka paused. "I have your consent?"

"Yeah, yeah, get on with it, lass," his weathered gaze was grim.

Becka let out a long sigh and focused on the task at hand. She reached down and brought her hands millimeters from the bottoms of Langdon's stumps. With intention, she pushed her gift ever closer to the skin.

She experienced the sensation of pushing against an unseen barrier. The migraine slamming into her skull was the first sign she'd gone far enough, and she immediately stopped. If she needed to do more, there was plenty of time for that. Too much, and she did not know what the consequences might be to him. Even as Becka pulled back and stood, pushing her chair out from under her, Langdon howled. He grabbed at his legs, as if trying to rub away the pain.

His flesh twisted and roiled, the rootlike tendrils of human skin flailing and withdrawing as if burned by an unseen fire. The skin of his legs, which had been covered in knots and a tree-bark-like scale, shuddered and then slowly paled.

Was it working? Despite the aching in her head, a spark of hope leapt in her chest.

Yet Langdon screeched, "Ow! Ow! Stop it!" in terse staccato beats.

Should I have exposed him to more? For longer? Becka wrung her hands.

Another few moments of Langdon bellowing and Becka holding her breath... and then there was a discernible trend towards the better with his feet. Then Langdon got quiet, and Becka knew things would be better when she could make out his toes. Chunks of dirt had peeled off his legs, falling in sodden clumps to the floor. A frog emerged from one clump, a declarative ribbit filling the chamber. And were those more snails? Ugh.

Langdon jumped up, launching himself into the air. He scrunched his toes and danced back and forth on his feet for a few seconds, before grabbing Becka by the arms and scooping her into a boisterous twirl around his chair.

I can't believe that worked! He's no longer in pain. I helped him!

A moment later, Langdon's feet went out from under him. Had he slipped on a clod of mud he'd shed mere moments before? Or the snails? She hoped it wasn't the frog.

Regardless, he lost his grip on Becka, yet the momentum of his dance propelled her backwards and dumped her into Hanna Hawthorne's lap, messing up the pattern of her perfectly placed skirt in an instant.

CHAPTER 16

Despite the fae-born having the reputation for excelling in dexterity, strength, and grace, Hanna and Becka tumbled sideways to the floor. Becka blamed the trajectory of her impact for the rolling tumble, but no doubt the unexpected nature of being tossed onto Hanna's lap was more to blame. Becka reached out to break her fall, grabbing Hanna by the arm as they came to a stop.

Becka pushed Hanna away, her other hand touching Hanna's shoulder. Her head. Already pounding from working her Null abilities on Langdon, it throbbed anew with such intensity she let out a groan. Before she could right herself, hands grasped her around the waist and lifted her off of Hanna. Luce set Becka down on her feet, her arm at Becka's hips to steady her.

"Are you all right?" Luce asked.

Becka held her head in her hands. "I think so," she forced out.

Wait...

Her hands were bare. Gloves off. She glanced at Hanna, her heart plummeting into her stomach.

I touched Hanna. With bare hands. With my gift in full swing.

Hanna had no defense.

Langdon, who'd also picked himself up off the floor and appeared sobered, approached her. "I'm so sorry about that, Lady Becka. I was so excited I forgot myself."

"I'm so sorry..." Becka echoed, not to Langdon, but to Hanna.

"What did you do?" Hanna, who'd sat up and was straightening her braids, but her gaze lacked focus.

Berak approached her and helped her up onto a chair. She sat gingerly, continuing to look around the room as if she'd lost her sight.

"Can someone please fetch Astrid?" Becka asked, hearing the tinge of panic in her voice. *Poor Hanna, she doesn't deserve this.* "And Alain?"

"I'll go get Astrid," Berak replied, leaving at a near run from the testing chamber.

"I think I know where Alain is," Saige said, and then took off at a loping run.

Hanna looked right at Becka, her expression a mixture of fear and anger. "What. Did. You. Do?"

Wait, no. She'd missed the betrayal in Hanna's gaze, and it cut Becka to the bone because she deserved it.

Luce moved Becka a step back and behind her. "Put your gloves back on," she whispered, although everyone heard her in the hushed room. Becka took the suggestion.

Saana approached Hanna. "My dear Hanna, how are you?"

Hanna looked at Saana. "The patterns are gone. The fiery connections between people that bind and repel them. It's as if they disappeared. Or evaporated. But that's not possible, is it?"

Tears ran down Becka's cheeks. She'd saved Langdon from his life of pain, but she had a feeling Hanna's pain had only begun.

Saana pulled up a chair next to Hanna's and gently took her hands in her own. "My dear, I'm afraid you have been touched by Becka's Null powers."

Hanna opened her mouth to speak, shut it again, and then opened it again. "What do you mean?"

"I mean to say, her gift breaks magic," Saana replied.

Hanna frowned. "I suppose I didn't comprehend Becka's powers fully before. Such an odd ability."

"Truly," Saana replied. "And yet so vital for those fae who, like Langdon, are saddled with magic gone awry."

"I suppose so. How long does the effect last?" Hanna looked around at all of them, her eyes full of desperate hope.

A silence hung in the room. Becka could almost hear Hanna's heart rate increase and her blood pressure spike.

"As far as we know, the effects of Becka's magic Nullification are permanent," Saana replied.

Becka heard Elder Alaetha's warning echoing in her mind. All harm Becka caused could invite retribution from other fae. Fate couldn't have given her a crueler example by hurting sweet Hanna. Bile rose in Becka's throat. She pulled away from Luce and ran to the bathroom at the far end of the room, emptying her stomach contents into the toilet.

"You can't be serious," Hanna replied, her tone flat. Lifeless.

Just then Alain arrived, followed by Astrid, Saige, and Berak. Becka washed her face, put her gloves back on, and then returned to the main room. The weight of everyone's gaze followed her, guilt churned in her now empty stomach. Were they all afraid they'd be next?

"Langdon," Berak asked, "are your gifts impacted?"

Alain sat close to Hanna, holding her shoulders as she sobbed against him. His nostrils flared and his eyes shone with the fire of his gift. Saige must have filled him in on the way to the testing chamber.

Langdon's red-brimmed eyes sparkled with unshed tears. "I don't think so. I can sense the moon in the sky and her pull on the water. But I won't try to alter the flow right now. It wouldn't be proper." The frog who'd been freed by Becka's magic hopped to Langdon's feet, and he scooped it up and popped it into the same pocket on his chest he'd been talking into earlier. "Shh, you. Now's not the time," he whispered.

Face hot and sweaty, Becka worked to control her breathing, but her throat was as raw as her emotions. At least she'd been able to remove Langdon's broken magic. Hopefully his gift would remain intact. This level of Null control was what Astrid had been training her for since her return.

Astrid and Berak exchanged glances.

"Then it sounds like your cure for Elder Langdon's curse is a success, which is very good news," Berak replied. "It's deeply unfortunate Becka injured you, Lady Hanna."

Hanna sobbed anew against Alain. Becka's heart ached for her.

"It's not at all fair!" cried Langdon. "They prepared me to live my life without my magic if it meant being healed. It's my fault Lady Hanna got hurt, and yet here I am, restored to my proper self. I take full responsibility."

"House Willow will make restorations to House Hawthorne. As will House Rowan," Alain said, the fire in his voice brooking no argument.

Becka wished she'd already had that promised talk with Maura about the current state of the union between fae-touched houses, just so she could fully grasp how wrong things just went.

Pretty darned wrong, Becka. Sure, coming into contact with Hanna had been an accident, but Becka was responsible for her magical loss. Becka had broken Hanna, and her heart ached, knowing she had no way to reverse the harm she'd done to her friend.

"House Rowan will do all we can to make amends," replied Astrid. She turned to Langdon. "I will have Duchess Maura speak with House Willow to ensure they do."

"Our house stands by its compacts," Langdon said, his voice certain despite the fearful look in his eyes.

Hanna pulled away from Alain, wiping her eyes with a kerchief from her pocket, and stood.

"How can you keep her here?" Hanna asked Astrid. "She's a danger to any fae she touches!"

Hearing the venomous words from Hanna broke Becka's heart. She wanted to run, to flee the room and Hanna's accusations, but staying to bear the brunt of her ire was the least Becka could do. She owed Hanna that much in this moment.

Is Hanna right? Am I too dangerous to live amongst other fae? If so, what will become of me?

"You have every right to be upset, Hanna," Astrid replied. "And I cannot imagine the profound depth of your loss. But it's unfair to label Becka so. Houses have been blessed with profoundly powerful individuals in the past and have learned to accommodate them."

"Your house won't consider itself so lucky after she blights one of your own!" Hanna's raised voice filled the room. "She could maim any of you."

"Perhaps you should rest?" Berak said. "I could give you something to ease your nerves."

Hanna glared at everyone. Elder Langdon shrank back, attempting to hide behind a chair.

"I want nothing more from you," Hanna replied. She looked to Alain, who glanced back at Becka for a lingering moment before accompanying Hanna from the chambers.

"That could have gone better," Astrid said, rubbing a hand against her temple. "Langdon, I take it you're well?"

"Yes, Lady Astrid."

"Then if you wouldn't mind excusing us?"

"Oh! Yes." He approached Becka and reached out for her gloved hand. She flinched, but then took his hand in hers. He bowed at the waist, his long, unkempt hair reaching the floor. "Lady Becka, I am forever in your debt."

"You're welcome, Elder Langdon," she replied, searching for and unable to muster a more eloquent reply. She'd had too many shocks in too short a period, and falling back on rote protocols learned as a child was all she could muster.

He left, leaving Astrid, Becka, Berak, Saana, and Luce and Saige in the room.

"I'll speak with the duchess," Astrid said. "Saana and Berak, I want you to monitor both Lady Hanna and Elder Langdon daily until they leave. Let me know if there's any change in their respective conditions."

"As you say," Saana replied. Berak nodded his agreement.

"This isn't any fault of yours," Astrid said to Becka. "It was an accident."

Becka tried to see Astrid's point of view, but Hanna's censure and rejection, which Becka had earned every inch of, had shaken her to the core. She didn't intend to hurt anyone, but it just kept happening. First Votr and now Hanna. Who might she hurt next? Meanwhile, Astrid's callous focus remained on what Becka's power might mean to the house, first and foremost.

"It was my gift. It pretty much feels like my fault."

"Try not to blame yourself. It was your power, but someone else literally forced your hand to use it."

Becka groaned. "I wish I understood why it damages some gifts and not others."

"I understand your frustration," Astrid replied. "But you must be patient. In time, we will have the answers you seek."

"I know we've spoken of this many times. Is there some way we can do more testing? I need to know why my powers don't impact House Oak's innate powers or the shifters," Becka said.

"Shifters don't count," Luce said, her tone brooking no argument.

"What do you mean?" Becka asked. "Shifting is your own sort of... gift?"

"Shifting isn't magical. It's an aspect of our nature. An artifact of our covenant with the earth. Fae magic can't touch it."

She blinked at Luce, who had just delivered the longest speech Becka had ever heard from her lips. She'd heard about the shifter covenant and knew it had to do with their creation stories, but had never heard a shifter explain in more depth. Despite her curiosity, Becka knew better than to press for more information. No doubt Luce had revealed all she'd intended to.

"So, that's not a thing, then?" Becka replied. Both Luce and Saige gave curt nods. She sighed in relief. At least she couldn't hurt her shifter friends. "Well, all right."

"Berak and I will puzzle over the vagaries of immunity to your gift, Becka," said Saana. "But in the meantime, please avoid further contact with both Quinn and the shifters. There may be some threshold we don't yet understand."

The idea that some level of increased contact might harm Quinn turned Becka's stomach. If she damaged his powers, Becka would never forgive herself.

"I wouldn't dream of it," she replied.

Astrid moved closer to Becka. "Will you come with me to see the duchess? I know she'll want to hear about your success today."

"Yes, it would be wise to have a quick word. Although I'm more interested in speaking to her about the accident with Hanna than I am about my success with Elder Langdon." Her head still throbbed from using her Null power. She needed hot sauce. A whole bottle might not do the trick. Becka grabbed her bag and then fell into step beside Astrid. "After that I'll head back to my quarters, order dinner, and then take a bubble bath."

"Don't be so hard on yourself. I've been head trainer for House Rowan for more decades than you've been alive. I could tell you stories of failures, perhaps not as awe-inspiring as today, but you'd be... suitably appalled. Life is not perfect, and neither is magic."

Becka didn't doubt Astrid's experience, and, thinking back through her training, this might have been the kindest thing she'd ever said to her. Which was either a piece of reassurance or a censure of the position Becka found herself in. Perhaps both?

"That sounds like a discussion to be had over a bottle of wine," Becka replied.

"Or whiskey?" Astrid laughed. "I heard you're fond of it."

Becka glanced back and saw Saige and Luce trailing behind them, knowing where all the whiskey had actually gone. Luce shrugged her shoulders. She shook her head in return.

CHAPTER 17

"I would ask you to explain it all again, but I can't bear to hear it and I doubt you're up to it," Maura said. She sounded as tired as Becka felt. At least she didn't appear angry.

After being ushered into Maura's chambers, Astrid and Becka had run through Hanna's accident with her in excruciating detail. Becka had done most of the talking, aware of the tears running down her cheeks and the emotional waver in her voice.

"As I'm sure Astrid has told you, accidents happen, even to those with profoundly powerful gifts. I agree with Astrid; you need not blame yourself. Take responsibility, definitely, but do not torture yourself."

Becka nodded but held her tongue.

"Unfortunately, harming one of House Hawthorne's places us in a very delicate position." Maura paced, lost in thought and no doubt strategizing their next move.

"I would never hurt Hanna." Becka spurt out. "She's been so kind to me."

Maura looked at her thoughtfully. "I would not imagine you capable, daughter. You may be my most stubborn child, but you are much too altruistic to harm another without great cause. And yet, Hawthorne may stringently disagree with my perspective. We must handle this with all due caution."

Becka nodded again. "What would you have me do?" The irony that it had taken this tragedy to bring her into step with her mother brought a heated flush to her cheeks.

"Whatever you do, do not engage with the Hawthornes directly. I will set up a meeting with them and drive the conversation of reparations. We will, of course, offer generous compensation, but I need a few hours to think on it and I need to speak with Elder Langdon on expectations of what House Willow will be able to offer. Until then, keep your head down. Let me handle the next move with them."

Becka nodded in quick agreement. She had no need to seek out the Hawthornes' accusing glares.

"There are promises we made in the contract," Astrid suggested. "Offers of requested trade goods from our territory. I could arrange to have an advance shipment prepared?"

"See to it. It is a wise move before we begin negotiations," Maura replied.

"Not to distract from the seriousness of the situation, but Becka's performance today with Elder Langdon means we can move forward with identifying a vocation for her."

"Vocation?" Becka asked, shocked that Astrid would be thinking of house profit at a time like this. "Shouldn't we be concerned about my ability to control my powers, lest I cause another horrifying, life-ruining failure?"

"Do not be dramatic, Becka," Maura replied. "It was an accident, after all, and life will go on for both you and Hanna.

Life will also go on for Elder Langdon, because of your work today. Think of the others you can aid. Besides, now you will be even more careful, likely to a fault."

Becka was speechless. Perhaps her mother was right, perhaps she should just focus on the next person she could help. But her heart still ached for the pair she'd brought to Hanna on this ill-fated day.

"We have not come up with a title yet, but how does something like Magic Remover sound?" Astrid asked them both.

Becka stared in shock. How could she flip her emotions around like that? "That title makes me sound like a cleaning tool."

"I'm open to other suggestions," Astrid replied.

"So, what, you will send me out to remove all the flubbed spells, conjurings, and curses? Sounds... like a lot of travel." On second thought, it was an opportunity to learn and see the world. Which could be amazing. Her interest was piqued.

Thinking back on Hanna's tears and anger, guilt weighed heavy in Becka's gut. How could she be thinking of such things after what had happened today?

"It sounds," Astrid leaned in close, "like a lucrative opportunity for our house. You think keeping rich humans looking like they're in their twenties is... exciting?" She barked out a laugh. "I can't tell you how many times I've virtually lifted and tucked the same saggy jowls. But never mind. Besides, I won't be sending you out."

Becka frowned. "You won't?"

"No, of course not. Duchess Maura will." She winked at her.

Becka shook her head at Astrid's callousness. When she

was duchess, she'd do better. Assuming she one day held her mother's position.

"What if I can come up with an alternative?" Becka asked.

"Something besides removing curses?" Astrid shrugged. "As long as it's something more lucrative, I would love to hear your ideas."

Becka shook her head. Astrid's idea didn't sound bad, especially the travel element. But Becka still wanted to choose her future for herself, as much as she could.

"Enough, you two," Maura said. "Off you go, Becka. Astrid and I have damage control to do."

CHAPTER 18

Becka had almost reached her room when Calder strode into view with Alvilda wrapped in a diaphanous forest-green silk dress, possessively clinging to his sleeve. Becka forced a smile, maintaining it even when Calder stopped in the middle of the hallway, blocking her passage with the politics of custom.

"Fair eve, Calder. Lady Alvilda."

"Fair eve, Becka," he replied.

Alvilda inclined her head. "Lady Becka."

Calder shrugged off Alvilda's arm and took a half step closer to Becka, and in response Luce moved in closer, mirroring Calder's distance to Becka. Calder didn't appear to notice Luce's reaction.

"I heard there was an altercation with House Hawthorne?"

Becka's heart sank into her stomach. "I see news of the accident has traveled unusually fast."

"So it's true?" His frown was mirrored on Alvilda's features.

"Unfortunately, yes. Hanna was injured, but Elder Langdon of House Willow has claimed fault for the accident." However, Becka would always feel responsible. How could she not?

"That is quite unfortunate. Mother has endeavored for years to gain an alliance with House Hawthorne, who, as you likely know, can be powerfully temperamental."

Becka considered pointing out that fire elementalists couldn't be expected to be anything but temperamental, but it didn't seem appropriate at the time.

"Both Rowan and Willow will make reparations," she replied, but it sounded hollow, even to her ears.

"Pride cannot be bought," Alvilda said, concern etching her features.

Alvilda's words caused Becka to pause. "I trust Maura can smooth things over, or at least buy forgiveness."

Calder frowned at Alvilda, who shrugged in response. "Are you on your way to dinner?" he asked Becka.

"No, I'm wiped out," Becka replied. "Besides, I spoke with Maura and she advised I keep my head down."

He shook his head. "That is too bad. It would be an opportunity to publicly apologize to House Hawthorne. I have come to know Alain during these past few months; if you delay, it will only worsen the situation. I think this is a time to not follow her advice."

Alvilda gave her an encouraging smile. "I'm sure our heir would love to help smooth things over."

"I will be happy to apologize, but will not undermine Maura's plans. I'm sure you want me to follow her lead?"

"I do not think this is wise, Becka," Calder replied. "Alain will see any delay as a slight."

Sure, they were due a profoundly penitent apology from her, but the last thing Becka wanted was to act without Maura's approval.

Will Alain call off the engagement over this fiasco?

The moment the thought crossed her mind, a wave of guilt washed over her. She wasn't proud of herself for this line of thinking. It felt a twinge mercenary. Hopefully Astrid's callousness wasn't rubbing off on her.

"I hear what you're saying, but I can't make a move without Maura's go-ahead. She was explicit."

Alvilda looked like she'd bitten into a lemon. She huffed and turned her gaze away from Becka.

"You have picked a curious time to toe the line, sister," Calder replied.

They'd hit an impasse, and Becka was done with this conversation. "If you'll excuse me, Calder? I'll see you at the council tomorrow."

"As you say." He stepped aside, Alvilda following his lead, allowing them to pass.

An hour later, Becka was up to her ears in bubbles when she heard a knock on her bedroom door. After a few minutes, the scent of lemons and roast sweet potatoes wafted into the bathroom. It was enough of an incentive to motivate Becka to exit the tub, quickly towel off, and wrap a silken robe around her mostly dry self.

She swept into the bedroom, her mood buoyed somewhat by the bubble bath and the promise of confections. Brownies were a balm to the soul. Luce, Saige, and Quinn stood around a large platter of food.

Seeing Quinn again, anxiety prickled at her skin. They hadn't seen each other since Maura had walked in on them.

The plight with House Hawthorne faded into the background as her experience with the book rushed back to her. "I have to tell you something about the book!"

Quinn gave her a quick nod.

"It appears they didn't bring enough servings," Luce said. "I'll call down and ask for another."

"Although the sweet potato hash looks amazing, it looks like they got *my* order right," Becka replied. She reached between the shifters and picked up the platter of desserts nestled in the middle of the dinner plates on the tray.

Saige laughed, her hand rubbing the back of her neck. "I thought the desserts were for sharing?"

"This is my dinner. Order your own desserts if you'd like some."

"You're having three desserts for dinner?" Quinn asked.

"It's been a long day, Enforcer," Becka replied. "Between Langdon, Hanna, and then Calder and his not-so-sweet lover, I'm ready to call it a day. Plus, I skipped an entrée. The calories net out."

She carried her platter over to her bed with all of them watching her movements.

"You're dripping on the floor," Saige said.

"You're eating in bed?" Luce asked.

"You'll get the bed wet," Quinn said.

Becka frowned in their general direction. "Why is everyone being so judgy?"

"Mmmph. I told you, Saige, the fae are bourgeoise savages," Luce said.

"Uh huh," Saige mumbled, downing a mouthful of hash. "Complete heathens."

Quinn walked over to the couch across from Becka's bed

and took a seat. "Would you ladies mind giving Becka and me some time to talk in private?"

Luce put her plate down and walked over to Becka. "No can do, Enforcer."

"Pardon me? You can't imagine I'm a threat to Becka."

Luce's deriding snort filled the room. "You're no threat to her health, Quinn. But the duchess has ordered us not to allow you a private audience with her heir."

"They're chaperoning us, as if they're paragons of virtue," Becka replied.

"If the term fits," Luce replied, hands in the air.

"Don't I oversee your assignments with Brent now?" Becka replied.

Luce leaned over the bed, testing strips in hand to check Becka's food for poison. "Are you paying our bills? 'Cause I'm sure that's the duchess."

Becka frowned. "Ouch."

Luce carefully pressed her testing strips against the lavender lemon bars, then the brownies, and lastly she came to the croissant bread pudding with raspberries and chocolate drizzles. She frowned and then used the spoon to scoop up a chunk of the ingredients, glaze dripping from the spoon. Luce smashed the test into the gooey goodness, a look of disgust on her face.

"This looks... decadent," Luce muttered, extracting the strip by the end with her sharp fingernails to avoid covering her fingers with glaze.

"Do you need to smash some raspberries too?" Becka asked.

Luce shook her head. "They laced your teacup with poison via a liquid poured into the mug. But that doesn't mean it was one of the kitchen staff. Besides, we've been watching them and have seen nothing untoward. The working theory is that it's someone who has access to the kitchen, but that's anyone in the house. This one is all clear."

"Thanks," Becka replied, digging into the bread pudding.

"You discovered something about the book?" Quinn asked.

"Uh huh," she mumbled around a mouthful of warm glazed croissanty goodness.

Becka grabbed her bag from the floor, tossing it onto the bed. She opened the bag and then motioned for Quinn to pull out the book, as she didn't have her gloves on. He fished around for the ancient tome, found it, and then placed the book on the bed at her feet, opening it to a random middle page.

"What are you thinking?" he asked.

Becka recounted her experience earlier with the tome, how the glyphs had gone transparent, how there were curious squiggles that had spelled out the word TEA over and over, and then how the book had gone back to normal after Becka had asked Hanna her questions.

"I was hoping we could try getting the book to give up another clue. I feel like it somehow knew about Hanna's connection to the tea, and I'd like to see if we could learn more," Becka said.

"Keep in mind this book is a Shadow-Dweller artifact. I'm thankful it alerted us to Hanna's connection to the tea Vott used, but how can we know why it revealed what it did?" Quinn asked. "We can't trust it, but perhaps the book can still be useful. We need to understand the pattern of what it does. Only then can we guess at the why."

"Agreed." She took a bite of the fragrant lemon bar. "Oh, oh my gods. The lavender in these bars is truly inspired. It elevates them into another dimension entirely."

Quinn raised a brow in her direction. "You're devouring those with such abandon."

Becka raised a brow right back at him. "Does my lack of decorum offend thee?"

His rich baritone laugh rolled over her. She could almost forget the ache in her solar plexus. Almost.

"Never."

Saige tsked in their general direction, a not-so-gentle reminder of Maura's directive.

"Maura's not going to kick the enforcer out during an active investigation."

Saige and Luce both shrugged.

"It's unlikely you'd be disowned," Quinn replied. "But, based on the conversation she had with Chief Elowen, she may still try and get me removed."

Becka held up her hands, one of which held a brownie while the other had a lemon bar. "In my defense, I apologize."

He sighed, shaking his head. "I accept, and I implore you to put down your weapons so we can focus on the book."

"I'll shift my focus, but I'll never give up my lemon bars," she replied, putting down the brownie and focusing her attention on the tome. Becka pulled on the blankets, moving the book a little closer to her leg. "I see nothing other than the glyphs right now. You?"

"Just the glyphs. Let's see, last time you were talking to Hanna and it started to act funny. What if you talk about Saige or Luce right now and ask them something?"

"You mean what if I started talking about Saige and

asking her if she's involved with the poisoning?" Becka watched the book, but nothing happened.

Saige walked over to them, finished with her sweet potato hash, frowning at them both. "I'm not sure I enjoy being the subject of your testing with that thing."

"It's not like you have anything to hide, do you?" Becka asked.

On cue, the squiggly lines returned to the pages, surfacing under the glyphs once more, which again turned transparent. The lines slid around, their sinuous forms reminiscent of worms or snakes skulking about. But, unlike the episode with Hanna and the tea, they didn't point towards Saige. Instead, they wandered around the page, seemingly without aim.

"The lines are back," Becka told Quinn, "but they don't seem super interested in Saige. Let me try something else. Saige, is there anything Maura asked you to do besides chaperone Quinn and me?" she asked.

The squiggles reacted, moving around as if agitated or excited. They formed patterns across the open pages, but not in a sunburst like before. This time the pattern reminded Becka of waves in water, as if the truth was trying to surface through the squiggles.

"And don't explain it to me," Becka said. "Just give me a yes or no answer."

Saige's gaze narrowed at her. "I don't like where this is going, but yes."

"Did Maura ask you to watch Quinn and me for other reasons?"

"Yes," Saige replied.

"Why would Maura want Saige to report on us?" Becka asked him.

"Perhaps to be the first to hear updates on the investigation?" Quinn asked.

The squiggles churned and heaved, roiling over each other. Words formed in the morass, coming and going almost too quickly to track. Becka caught a "first," and then an "ear." The last word she could make out was "more."

"I can make out the words first, ear, and more." Becka looked to Saige. "Quinn is correct, but is there more to it?"

She gave a curt nod. "Yes."

The lines swirled and swirled backwards upon themselves, and then settled into a sunburst pattern, but they didn't angle towards Saige, as Becka had expected. Instead, they pointed to Quinn with a single word, repeated in every line.

Informant.

Becka gasped, and looked up at Quinn, who had no idea what the book had revealed. Was Maura worried Quinn wasn't just here for the poisoning but to dig into House Rowan affairs?

"What is it?" he asked.

She recalled the council conversation about sending Iona out to gather defensive information for the house. Becka had questioned it as borderline sedition at the time. If Quinn found out, would he report them?

She hesitated for only a moment. "Maura thinks you might be an informant, I would assume to the Enforcers' Guild about private House Rowan affairs?"

Becka looked to Saige to confirm, and she gave Becka another quick nod.

"Clever toy you have there. I wouldn't trust it." Saige wandered off towards the door where Luce was standing.

Quinn sat back on the sofa while Becka grabbed another brownie. She took a small bite, but her stomach had soured, and the brownie suddenly tasted too rich. She took her plate and placed it on her bedside table. After wiping her hands thoroughly with a napkin, Becka ran her fingers through her damp hair, working out the tangles.

"Aren't you going to ask me if Maura's concerns are valid?" Quinn asked.

"No, I'm not. I know you're here working the investigation and I'm not concerned about your intentions otherwise. I trust you."

Quinn held her gaze for a few moments. She knew he had a reputation for holding his loyalty as an enforcer above the interests of the fae, but he'd proven himself to her. Maura could think what she wanted.

"Wait a moment," Becka said. "How is your investigation going?"

He wobbled his head from side to side. "It's been challenging working under the duchess' guidelines."

"So she thinks you're an informant, and has put limitations on you?" He nodded. "Which means what specifically?"

"I am accompanied by two fae guards who report my activities back to Maura. I'm limited in not only who I can question but am also only allowed to question with a council member present. Unfortunately, they are often not available. I've been relying on Brent and his team for assistance, but I'm not making a ton of headway."

"Let's speak with her together tomorrow," Becka replied.

"I know she wants the poisoner found. There's got to be a middle ground."

"That might help," he replied. "Thank you. While I assume you're mulling over all the reasons you don't agree with Maura about me, keep in mind this revelation came from a source whose motivations we do not understand."

Squiggles continued to wander around the book's pages. "What could it gain by revealing honest answers to questions? I mean, what's the point?"

"First, it only works for you, a fae with a powerful gift and also the first of your gift's lineage."

"You're saying this was created with me in mind? But, it's really old. Look at the aging of the pages!"

"Okay, possibly just for someone like you. Second, the most skilled liars deceive using selected components of the truth, omitting facts to sway you to their perspective. In other words, just because the book is sharing truth with you doesn't mean it's the full story or that you know its motivations for sharing," Quinn replied.

"You're saying it thinks and has motivations?" Becka asked.

He shrugged. "You can't know."

She gazed at the tome, wondering if it was a boon or a venomous snake. How could she know? And what damage could the book do by answering questions truthfully?

"If you don't mind, I need to step outside and give Chief Elowen a call." He stood up, pulling his phone from a jacket pocket. "I'd like her to know what we've discovered about the book and see if she can get a couple of agents to research the mechanism."

"By all means," she replied.

He walked out the door to her balcony, a gust of crisp night air sweeping into the room with his passing. She heard Quinn's voice on the phone, the low tones carrying indistinctly through the open door.

Lost in her reverie at the book, Becka didn't notice the faint knock on her bedroom door nor the young fae clearing their dishes until the girl swept near her bed and cleared her plate from her nightstand. She murmured out a quick thanks, but the youth was well on her way out and didn't acknowledge her.

Becka's attention was rapt with the moving patterns upon the pages of the open Shadow-Dweller book.

She took a drink of water, but the sour taste in her mouth wouldn't go away. Her mind kept lingering on the day's events, specifically when she'd been deposited into Hanna's lap. How bad would the fallout with House Hawthorne become? When Quinn was here, she'd been distracted, but with him gone the doubts, fears, and pain had returned.

Her heart ached. Her stomach ached. Her mind ached.

She leaned back against her pillows and groaned, reaching for her glass of water. Next to it sat a small bowl of butter mints in the center of the nightstand. Perhaps one could ease her stomach, or at the least, dispel the foul taste of bile in her mouth for a time?

Becka popped a single mint into her mouth, the clean, bright flavor of spearmint washing down her throat.

A heartbeat, perhaps two, passed. A distinctive and all-too-familiar counterpoint to the mint kicked into her senses.

Instinctively, Becka threw herself across the bed and spat the mint onto the floor. It came out as a gummy slurry. She grabbed for her water glass, pouring water into her mouth as fast as she could spit it out.

She wasn't fast enough.

The glass fell from her hand, hitting the carpet and somehow bouncing instead of shattering. Her center of gravity shifted a moment later, and she tumbled out of bed, hearing her head hit the floor with a loud thump.

Voices bellowed. Feet pounded. Something, someone, rolled Becka onto her side and lifted her up. Her head rolled against a familiar shoulder. A familiar scent filled her nose, one she'd recognize anywhere. Surely Maura wouldn't approve of this intimate moment?

"Quinn," she whispered.

"Run ahead to Illan," Quinn said to someone.

"Hold on, sugar," he said, his voice cracking.

Now she felt him running, her body rocking against his, step by step.

And then she felt nothing at all.

CHAPTER 19

Hours later, Becka lay on a cot at the infirmary, shivering as sweat poured off her body. Something cool pressed down on her forehead, and the cool night air moved over her, a welcome chill against her heated skin.

She looked around the room, which was dim, lit only by a few candles. Quinn sat beside her, his hand on the cool compress over her head.

"Where is everyone?" Becka croaked, her voice rough from hours of retching.

"Brent is meeting with his staff, doing a top-down room-by-room search of the entire manor. He left you under my protection."

"Can I have some water?" she whispered.

He picked up a cup from the bedside table. "Just a sip. Illan warned you to take it slow." Quinn helped her sit up, and then she took a small sip of water. Then another.

"I don't even remember last night," she said. "I remember you running me here and then throwing up for what felt like hours. Didn't Illan give me a shot or something?"

Quinn nodded, dabbing at her forehead again with the damp cloth. "After the last time, the enforcers stocked your infirmary with a couple of poison treatments. Specialty items we have access to."

"Lucky for me you did."

His furrowed brow was marked with shadows in the dim light. "Luck had nothing to do with it. I figured that until we caught the poisoner, another incident was inevitable."

Becka thought about that for a few minutes, grateful for his forethought and yet terrified for her future. If they couldn't catch the poisoner, how long before it would happen again? What if she wasn't as lucky the next time? Would she end up in a coma like Vott? Or dead, like her sister?

She couldn't just wait and hope for the best. Becka needed to join in the investigation. But not right now. Now she needed to rest.

Quinn ran a hand down her arm, his grip comforting. "I have some ideas for other things to try. Ways to keep you safer."

She sighed, grateful for his reassuring touch. "Whatever you think best."

"What, something Becka of House Rowan won't argue with me about?" He smiled, but it didn't reach his eyes, which appeared anxious and sleep deprived. "That's a miracle, but I'll take it."

Fear gripped her, her chest tight, making it difficult to breathe. "Don't you worry, I'll get my spunk back soon enough," she said, forcing a smile, knowing the alternative was too dark. Becka was glad for the distraction of his presence. "Wait a second. I remember something. Did you call me sugar?"

"Certainly not." He shook his head. "The impropriety! Whatever would Duchess Maura say?"

"Uh huh," she replied. "I mean, if you had, I don't think I'd mind it."

"I'll make a note of it," he replied, gripping her hands in his own.

A cool night breeze blew in through the open windows, causing the candles to flicker. The fresh air was a needed distraction from the aching in her body. In the distance, a lone owl hooted softly, distinctive against the quiet of the night.

Becka groaned. "I can't believe I ate that mint. It was so thoughtless of me. It was as if they appeared out of thin air."

"Except they didn't. They were put there specifically for you."

"Have you figured out if the girl brought them?" she asked, unable to wrap her mind around the possibility of a child poisoning her. What was this world she was living in?

"Yes, her name is Sorrel. She's a niece of Astrid's by marriage. I questioned her a few hours ago. All she seems to know is that they placed the mints on her platter to be left with you when she cleaned up the dishes in your room. There were dozens of those bowls of mints in the kitchen. None of the others had poison in them. Brent did exhaustive checks, including the mints that had been sent out to other rooms already."

"I can't imagine the girl is to blame. I don't even know her." She reached for the cup of water, which Quinn refilled and then handed back to her. The chilled liquid cooled the burning in her throat. She sipped slowly to make the sensation linger.

"We agree. Someone must have tainted just the ones in your bowl, knowing Sorrel was going directly to your room. Sorrel remembers passing a few people in the hall, but none of their behaviors stood out to her. Brent is questioning everyone the girl remembers."

Becka handed back the empty cup. "I am so over this crap, Quinn."

He set the cup on the bedside table, his expression stormy. "You aren't the only one."

She stretched, acutely aware of the sore and strained muscles lining her torso and stomach. "Let me know what you hear." Becka's lids fluttered as she struggled to keep them open. "Every time this poisoner acts, they risk exposure. Their luck will run out," she reasoned. But was she trying to reassure Quinn, herself, or both?

He brushed a stray lock of hair from her face. "Get some sleep. If we learn anything, I'll wake you."

"You're staying?" she whispered.

"Nothing could make me leave your side," he replied, his voice uncharacteristically thick with emotion.

Becka reached for his hand and sighed when he took her hand in his own, gently massaging her palm. In the dim candlelight, his eyes appeared to glisten. Or was that just her imagination?

No. The intensity of his gaze and raw emotion creasing his face hit her in the solar plexus. She'd almost died. Again. So much for the safety of being home again.

Becka's eyelids fluttered as she fought to stay awake. "I don't know why you're safe for me to touch," she mumbled. "But I'm grateful."

Quinn gripped her hand. "Always be thankful for small graces."

Becka meant to agree, but sleep pulled her down into its depths once more.

*M*orning had returned and along with it, a trio of disapproving frowns. Brent, Quinn, and the healer stood around her bedside watching her like hawks.

"Why is everyone just standing around?" Becka croaked out, her throat dry.

Illan held out a cup of water, which she took and sipped. "Thanks. Where are my clothes?"

Their frowns deepened.

"I'd like you to stay for observation another day," Illan replied.

Becka pushed herself up on her own as the three men frowned even more. Their looks of incredulity to each other and shared shrugs didn't dissuade her.

"Clothes. Now," Becka said.

Because of Becka's insistence that she get up, dress, and go back to her life, they handed her clothes to wear. When she dressed and then made it clear she planned to leave the infirmary, that's when the scowls started.

"I would truly prefer you stay the day," Illan said. "I know you're feeling improved, but why not rest today? Why risk pushing yourself?"

"Sure, I'm tired, but otherwise I'm okay. You said there's nothing more you can do for me here. You injected me with all of those treatments, and they worked. Now, since I'm stable, I'm leaving. I need to see Maura and I will *not* give my attacker the satisfaction of seeing me appear weak."

Illan smiled. "You're more like your mother than I realized."

Becka offered a side-eyed glare to the healer. Sure, she knew Maura was iron-willed, sometimes to a fault. It was certainly a trait Becka didn't mind having in common with her mother. "Wait a second. Are you comparing me to Maura to try and keep me from leaving? Do you think that'll work on me?"

His suddenly blank face and rounded eyes confirmed her suspicions.

"Nice try, healer. Trust me, when I start to feel tired, I'll kick my feet up and take a nap." Becka walked toward the door, blocked by Brent. "You think you can keep me penned in?"

"Yes," Brent said, "if we choose to do so."

"Do you somehow think me staying in a small room makes me any safer?"

"Yeah, I do," Brent replied. "If you're only exposed to vetted contacts, then I am confident we can minimize or eliminate the threats."

"That's where you're wrong." Becka sat on the edge of the bed. "The person who's after me has made it clear, with Vott's poisoning, that they're fine if those close to me are hurt too. The same goes for this attempt. Anyone else in the room could have eaten those butter mints instead of me. If you lock me in a room, it endangers whoever is in there with me."

"I'm not sure I agree, but what would you have us do?" Quinn asked.

"I need to appear strong while the investigation continues. And for that to happen, we need to go and see Maura. Now." She pointed at Quinn and Brent.

"You want to talk to Maura right now?" Brent asked.

"Yes, right now." She stood up, fatigue multiplying the required effort, but she wasn't about to back down. "And the two of you are coming with me. Let's go."

Brent sighed and shook his head. "Lead on, Lady Becka."

CHAPTER 20

Calder stood between her and the door to the council chambers, looking taken aback by her very presence. He blinked as if he'd seen a ghost.

Becka squared her shoulders and walked right up to him, bracing for a showdown. Knowing Quinn and Brent were behind her helped her confidence, which was shaken after yesterday's repeat poisoning.

Well, she was mostly ready. If she had to remain standing much longer, Becka might have to lean on the wall to pull it off.

"Sister Becka!" he exclaimed. "I assumed you would still be recuperating in the infirmary." He shook his head, looking her up and down. "You appear a tad pale. How are you faring?"

"I'm pushing through," she replied, unable to keep the sharp edge out of her voice. Calder remained a prime suspect in her poisonings, although only because of the potential motive of jealousy over her return to status as the heir. "And still alive, despite certain efforts to the contrary."

"I'm grateful to hear you're recovering, again." He offered her his arm, his expression a mixture of anger and concern. "May I assist you to your chair?"

It took Becka a moment to process his statement, long enough that he raised a brow, and damn if he wasn't about to repeat the question for her.

"Uh, sure. Thanks?" She threaded her arm through his, leaning into him. "I'm surprised to hear you upset. I haven't exactly been on your list of favorite people."

He paused for a moment. "Whoever harms you also attacks House Rowan."

Becka barked out a short, hoarse laugh. "I didn't think you liked me. At all."

A slight smile curved his lips, and he blew out a breath before answering. "Pardon, but I can't say as I do. Your years living outside of these walls have changed you, not necessarily for the better. But you are family. What kind of monster would I be to not accept you, or at the very least, have your back, despite your flaws?"

He appeared genuinely concerned for her safety. Perhaps she'd been too quick to name Calder as a suspect? Either his show of concern was a very good act designed to put her off the scent, or he was innocent.

Becka sighed. Nope, she still didn't trust him.

"Your candor is, as always, refreshing, Calder."

They walked into the room, arm in arm. Everyone else was already there and there was a collective double-take of initial confusion, followed by smiles. Elder Eirian gave her an approving nod, most likely for powering through and showing up. Lady Wynne smiled; did she even like her, or was she just happy to see Calder and her getting along better? Lord

Cedric's astute gaze narrowed on Becka, and she raised a single brow.

Maura's reaction was inscrutable to Becka, as she appeared to have no reaction, while Astrid raised her chin and gave a single nod of encouragement.

When Quinn and Brent followed her into the room, the collective gazes turned sour and conversations were brought to a halt.

"Unannounced visitors is not our standard protocol, Becka," Duchess Maura said, greeting the newcomers to her council chambers with an imperious frown. "This chamber is for council members and their invited guests only."

Becka grabbed a nearby seat, not waiting for anyone else to join her. Although she was determined to make a show of strength, wise energy conservation was key to today's plan.

"Lucky for them, I invited Enforcer Quinn of House Oak and Brent Douglas of the Sawatch Enclave to join me. I understand it may be unusual to have them present, but I feel like we need to address roadblocks in the investigation."

Maura's pique appeared to fade as she graced Becka with a rare nod of approval. "As you say. I agree we need the investigation to produce results, especially after repeated attempts on your life. It's unfortunate it has drawn out this long." Maura took her usual seat and then motioned for the rest of the council to sit, which they did one by one. Brent and Quinn, not having been offered seats, remained standing.

Once the council members settled in, Becka cleared her throat. "Enforcer Quinn, what's holding up your investigation?"

Quinn cocked his head at her. "To put it bluntly, I have

not been allowed to question members of or visitors to the household."

"That seems like a simple request," Becka replied. "Council, Mother, may the enforcer directly question members of the household?"

"No," Maura replied. "Thus why I constrained his actions. Quinn's unique ability to discern falsehoods could be used for purposes not related to the hunt for the poisoner. I do not trust the enforcer to remain on topic and fear he will use this moment of weakness to broaden his scope." She uncharacteristically thrummed her fingers on the table. "I also do not wish House Rowan to be the subject of an investigation that draws progressively more fish into its net."

"I'm in agreement with Maura," Astrid replied, wrinkling her nose in Brent's direction. "You know fae dislike the intrusiveness of your races... scans."

"It's not scanning," Brent bit back. "Your emotions naturally permeate the surrounding air. We can't avoid picking up hints of what you're feeling, just as you can't avoid emitting those scents. And we can't read thoughts or catch lies."

Becka did a slow double-blink, Brent's words shaking something loose in her mind. "Reading emotions is the nature of being a wolf. It's as natural as breathing to them, or magic to the rest of you."

Brent inclined his head to her. "Just so."

Astrid waved a hand in the air, as if she could wave away their rebuttal. "It's invasive. Vott may not mind it, but I don't have to like it."

Becka shook her head, holding up a hand to stall the discussion. She had to find a middle ground between these two. "Quinn. Brent. Can you offer a compromise? Perhaps something with… oversight?"

Quinn took a deep breath. "I would like Duchess Maura's permission to bring in two additional assets."

"Go on," Maura replied.

"I know this is a big request to House Rowan, but with two more enforcers on site we can interview every person in the household. The interviews can be done with a council member present to ensure no irrelevant questions are asked. I wouldn't even need to be a part of the interviews."

Maura's jaw clenched so hard Becka swore she heard a tooth crack. "Why not just utilize our fae guards?"

"We can't use your household guards, as there is the outside risk they're compromised by Shadow-Dwellers."

"But I thought the Shadow-Dwellers were not implicated in the poisoning?" Maura replied.

"That is correct, but we know the Shadow-Dwellers are a long-term threat to Becka. The potential for them to infiltrate your household and guards remains," Quinn explained.

Maura frowned and crossed her arms, unmoved by his argument.

Quinn shifted his weight between his feet and ran a hand across the back of his neck. "I give you my personal guarantee that my enforcers will focus solely on the hunt for the poisoner."

Becka had heard enough talk within the council chamber to understand Maura likely feared Quinn or his associates would report House Rowan's anti-human sentiments to the government. But right now, Becka needed Maura to trust Quinn.

"Enforcer Quinn has my implicit trust. If he vouches for his team, that's enough for me," Becka said.

Maura's gaze narrowed. "You've proved your loyalty to Becka, and perhaps by extension also House Rowan, so I've given you a certain leeway. How am I supposed to believe you have adequate pull with Chief Elowen or your fellow enforcers to make such a guarantee?"

"I have demonstrated I have the pull with Chief Elowen already," he replied.

He paused for a moment, and a few of the council members shifted in their seats. Maura's eyes widened in surprise at his implicit admission that he'd already either hidden information of their seditious tendencies or that the chief had at his request. Maura gave a quick nod of understanding, and then he continued.

"I would personally choose the enforcers. Only those I trust implicitly."

Lord Cedric leaned forward in his chair. "You are alluding to excluding grievances from your reports. Additionally, you claim to know other enforcers who will do the same at your request. All enforcers take oaths to uphold human laws. If you have broken those oaths, how are we to trust you will keep your word to us?"

Quinn shrugged. "You can interpret my statements as you please. I prefer to focus my efforts on finding your poisoner."

Brent side-eyed Quinn and gave him an appreciative nod.

"I need more than your word," Maura replied, and Calder, Cedric, Wynne, Eirian, and Astrid all nodded.

Quinn shook his head, and Brent held up a hand.

"Duchess Maura, do you continue to accept the word of my wolf pack?"

Her eyes widened. "Of course, Brent. Vott trusts you, and therefore so do I."

"Then I would propose that these two hand-selected enforcers of Quinn's be paired with shifter escorts. Then we can ensure they don't deviate from their scope of seeking the poisoner, even outside of the formal interview process."

Maura held up a hand, stopping Brent. "Is there anything more about your proposal that the council needs to know before discussing our options?"

Brent and Quinn shared a look, their sour expressions reflecting the likely poor outcome of their request.

"No, Duchess," Quinn replied.

"Then I would thank you to vacate my council chambers. You will be informed of our decision."

Quinn opened his mouth as if to argue, but appeared to think better of it.

When the door closed behind them, Becka couldn't tell if they'd said enough to sway Maura or the council. If they wouldn't hear reason, what more could she do? Becka couldn't back down, fear of another poisoning driving her forward.

CHAPTER 21

Calder, true to form, was the first to speak. "Mother, you can't be considering his request! Quinn has turned fae over to the human courts, including Elder Bjork of House Alder, cousin to Duke Vott. And he wants to bring more enforcers into our home?"

Maura held up a hand to silence him, and he quieted, but his face remained flushed.

"In case any of you have forgotten, my will presides within these walls."

"Thank you, Duchess, for your level-headed oversight," Lord Cedric replied.

She waved him off. "What are your thoughts?"

Lady Wynne held her hand to her chest. "Do you think we can trust them?"

Maura shrugged. "Quinn has displayed an adept hand with fact-finding and appears quite committed to protecting Becka. Brent has earned Vott's trust, and ours, over the years."

"I too trust in those points," Elder Eirian replied.

"Someone is targeting Becka, and I fear now that they've failed twice, they will only be emboldened to further attempts unless we stop them."

Becka slumped in her chair, regarding Calder as the council members talked amongst themselves. She'd believed he was the most likely suspect, but now that didn't feel right to her. Perhaps he had been arguing publicly in opposition to his closely held hatred of Becka to throw them all off the scent?

However, she didn't believe that someone who lost his temper at the drop of a hat could selectively mask his emotions. Did he even think before he blurted out his positions? Becka chuckled to herself.

But then, who did that leave as a suspect? They had crossed Astrid off the list because she didn't appear to fear Becka's powers at all. In fact, she saw Becka as a potentially huge moneymaker for the house. And they'd also eliminated Alain, but perhaps that was premature? Despite his interest in aligning with their house and bringing in a relationship coach, had the incident with Hanna changed his mind? Becka's death would free him from his obligations, as Calder was next in line.

Becka rubbed her forehead. Her mind was spinning with the possibilities, threatening an impending headache.

"Becka, do you need a break?" Maura asked.

The council had quieted around her; she assumed they'd talked the investigation to death without her. Oh wait, did that pregnant pause in the air mean she'd missed a question?

She shot Maura a forced smile. "I'm fine. Sorry, what did you ask?"

Concern lit Maura's eyes. "I asked for your thoughts. The

council could discuss this all day, but you're the one being targeted."

"I feel like I've already made that clear. I'm done getting poisoned." Becka looked each council member in the eye, one by one. "If we don't find the culprit, it's only a matter of time before they succeed. I support Quinn's proposal and having Brent's shifters working in tandem with the enforcers should wrap this up."

Lord Cedric's grudging nod was paired with frowns around the table.

"Let's put it to a vote," Maura said. "All for moving forward?"

Becka, Astrid, Calder, and Lord Cedric raised their hands. Maura, Lady Wynne, and Elder Eirian didn't.

Maura voting against furthering the investigation deflated Becka, the dire nature of the threat against her not enough to move her mother's hand. And what did Wynne and Eirian have against her?

"Against my better judgement, we carry the vote," Maura said. "We will consent to the indignity of this fishing expedition, because the alternative is unacceptable. We will have a council member present. If they cross the line, then we will find an alternative method of finding the poisoner."

Becka understood what Maura was demanding. Saving Becka's life was well and good, but not if it risked bringing an investigation down on House Rowan. It was a reasonable position for the head of the house to take, even though it stung a little to hear from her mother. The pressure on Maura had to be immense this past week, what with Vott comatose and the continued attacks against her heir. Becka knew Maura feared for her safety, evidenced by allowing the enforcers' investigation to continue despite the council's concerns.

One day that responsibility would fall on her. Becka hoped it would be a lifetime from now.

"I hear you loud and clear," Becka replied.

Maura's sad smile didn't reach her eyes, which were filled with cold calculation. "I'm glad we understand each other."

Becka rose to go. "I'll deliver the news."

She left the room, but as she closed the door Astrid caught it and slipped out with her. "Just a moment of your time?"

"Uh, sure," Becka replied.

Astrid's smile was refreshingly genuine. "I wanted you to know, we've confirmed Langdon's curses are gone while his powers remain intact. Your work is considered a resounding success by the healers and testers."

"That's fantastic," Becka replied. "I needed some good news."

"I am declaring you fully trained," Astrid said. "Guilded."

"Seriously?" Becka replied. "Doesn't training usually last much longer?"

"I filed the paperwork this morning. And although I encourage you to practice regularly to refine your skills, there's not much more I can do to help direct your learning." She smiled an encouraging smile. "It's not like I can show you the hidden secrets of a gift we've only just uncovered. It's on you to continue seeking and learning what you can along the way."

"What does it mean, that you filed paperwork?" Becka asked.

"It means you're ready to perform your civic service, as dictated by the Pax Hominid treaty. We're required to report on all gifteds' duty status as soon as we deem them trained. It's an unfortunate requirement, but even during that time of charitable work we can add in paying work, like you did for Langdon," Astrid replied.

It wasn't lost on Becka that Astrid had reported her ready for duty the morning after her second poisoning. The penalty for delaying must have been hefty for Astrid to be so punctual, considering Becka's condition.

"No doubt your civic service will help to spread the word about your abilities, which will increase the demand for your services," Astrid said.

"Fantastic," Becka replied. "But won't word of my hurting Hanna spread too?"

"Yes, but it might actually benefit you by adding to the reputed power of your gift," Astrid replied. "We offer your services for removing unwanted or outdated magic, like a magical house cleaner. We would never sanction requests for you to harm other fae as you did Hanna. We will not have you presented as a weapon. There will be outstanding questions as to the extent of your abilities to resolve, but that will sort itself out."

Again, Astrid's nonchalant waving away of the potential for others to see Becka as a threat concerned her. "I'm worried about my gift being seen as a weapon. How do we address that?"

"Well, we assure the other houses that some abilities are immune to your gift. Like the innate gifts of House Oak. It would behoove us to understand all of those exceptions, obviously. The artifact you broke was created with additive magic, and Elder Langdon's curse was formed with feminine moon magic. Therefore, not all powers are susceptible to your gift, although we don't yet understand why. No doubt we'll figure it out, given enough time."

"And enough injuries," Becka muttered. Learning what types of gifts were immune to her Nulling implied there would be more accidents like she'd had with Hanna.

Thinking of Hanna, Becka cringed inwardly. The brief meeting with the council hadn't afforded any opportunities to know what Maura's plans were with House Hawthorne. Surely, now that Becka was on her feet again, Maura would set up a meeting?

Astrid waved her off. "If an injury happens, we will forego the fee; that's standard practice amongst fae contracts. If it would make you feel more comfortable, we can initially seek clients whose need is extreme. They will be more open to the potential risks."

"I'd like that. Also, I don't know what else Maura has planned, but can we offer to pay a percentage of my fees to House Hawthorne as recompense for Hanna's injury? It seems only fair, considering Hanna's ability to work is hampered."

Astrid frowned. "I agree, perhaps the promise of ongoing monetary compensation will soften their ire."

"As you say," Becka replied.

Astrid turned and went back into the council room, while Becka headed down the hall. It wasn't long before she came face to face with an expectant Quinn and Brent. Luce and Saige had been waiting near the top of the main staircase for her return, and a pair of fae guards trailed behind her.

Thankfully, this part of the house was quiet now. Bright

sun filtered in through the windows, which ran the full height of the house across from the grand staircase. Perhaps everyone was off eating lunch or picnicking out in the gorgeous weather. She gestured to Quinn and Brent, and they moved closer.

Quinn's expression was once again stormy. "Did they shoot us down?" he asked in low tones, hands on his hips.

She shook her head. "You can move forward, but I recommend you do it quickly. In case they change their minds."

The men shared a palpable look of relief.

Quinn smiled at her, and it warmed her heart, despite her exhaustion.

"I didn't expect Maura to relent," Brent replied. "But I'm thankful. With Quinn's enforcers, we can make quick work of finding the poisoner."

"Agreed," Quinn replied, pulling out his phone. "I'll send for them immediately." He tapped a couple times and then slid it back into his jacket.

Did he have a message prepped to send, just in case the council relented?

"I am ready for that midday nap," Becka said, hearing the hoarse rasping of her voice.

Quinn offered his arm, and she grabbed it and leaned on him as they walked back towards her quarters.

They made it to her room almost without incident. When they turned the corner into the hall leading to her quarters, she knew a nap was not in her immediate future by the fiery look in Alain Hawthorne's eyes.

CHAPTER 22

A pair of House Hawthorne guards flanked Alain Hawthorne and his cousin Hanna, who she recognized at once by the crimson elemental flame insignia on their uniforms. All their postures were ramrod straight. Alain's chin practically sliced through the air as he turned to Hanna and shared a momentary glance.

Alain, as an honored guest in their home, was allowed two of his guards to accompany him as a nod to his status. This was the first time she'd seen the guards with him outside of his quarters on the far wing of the manor. Although they wore no weapons, she didn't doubt their ability to defend their lord without them. Becka had witnessed fire elementalists duel, and the results from even friendly altercations could lead to injuries with long healing times. Sometimes even scars. She didn't want to think about how bad the damage could be from a direct assault. Their powers were all the weapons they needed.

House Rowan guards stood between Becka and the Hawthornes. Becka came to a halt and released Quinn's arm, standing fully on her own two feet. Brent, Saige, and Luce stood behind them, their lithe forms tensed as if awaiting an imminent attack. Lorelai sported an expectant look of sheer pleasure.

To say the mood in the hall was tense would have been an understatement. This felt more like a parley with an enemy.

A fleeting thought crossed her mind: this confrontation style was not in alignment with her poisoner.

Also, Maura had directed her to wait before speaking with House Hawthorne, as her mother wanted to manage the talks. Becka swallowed hard, realizing Maura had missed her opportunity to control the narrative. What hope did she have to implore for peace against their steely gazes?

Alain stepped forward, meeting Becka midway between the two groups. They stood for a moment staring each other down. She didn't understand what he was doing, but the formality inherent in his actions gave her pause.

Becka spoke first, hoping to deescalate the situation. "Duchess Maura informed me we'd be meeting soon. Would you like to walk with me to the council chambers to discuss reparations?"

"The opportunity for civil discussion passed when you stripped my cousin of her powers." He reached down and pulled a scroll from his waistband, held it between his fingers for a deliberate moment, and then held it out to her. Not as an offering, but as almost as if he were striking a blow.

Becka had a moment of hesitation, looking from his eyes to the scroll, and then back to the cutting glare within his eyes. She held his gaze as she reached out and received the scroll into her gloved hands. She took it delicately, as if it might explode in her fingers if she mishandled it.

Alain grasped one hand in another, his chin cutting toward Hanna, who came to stand beside him.

"Becka of House Rowan, our engagement is broken. This document comes from Duke Eldinrod; I will deliver another one to Duchess Maura at the council chambers next, but I wanted to ensure you received the message first, and from me directly."

Becka's heart leapt! She'd hoped for an out to this arrangement, and the moment had finally come. But it was only due to the harm she'd dealt Hanna, who stood, arms crossed, glaring at Becka.

"I thought the engagement was a binding agreement and couldn't be broken?"

His voice was hard as honed steel. "There are provisions in most contracts that allow for one or both parties to cancel the agreement."

She shook her head. "I'm familiar with the agreement. Which section are you referring to?"

"House Hawthorne has issued a statement declaring you unfit and has advised other houses to follow our lead and not permit you within their territories."

Heat flushed Becka's face and Hanna smiled cruelly at her reaction. An aching sadness filled Becka, and although she didn't want to believe him, the accusation in his words hit her so hard in the solar plexus that Becka had to take a moment before she could breathe in again. She'd once considered *outcast* a horrible term to own. *Unfit* felt even worse.

Astrid had been wrong. Hawthorne's declaration named Becka's power a weapon and asked the other houses to take a stand. What fae would risk contact with her? Perhaps, as Astrid had said earlier, only the desperate.

"Unfit? How..."

He cut her off. "You're a danger to your own kind. Your house appears too blinded by the potential of the unique nature and raw power of your gift to realize you're an uncultured loose cannon who will destroy everything she touches."

Is he right? Was House Rowan so blinded by the monetary nature of her gift to see her potentially destructive power honestly? She did her best to keep her expression neutral despite the anger, frustration, and pain bubbling beneath the surface. All eyes watched her, waiting for her reaction.

"All right," she replied, endeavoring to keep her voice steady. "But how does this unfit claim break our engagement contract?"

"House Hawthorne contends that since you are unfit, you therefore cannot be the heir to House Rowan."

Becka pursed her lips. *What impact will Hawthorne's declaration have with Maura? The council? Other houses? How many houses could House Hawthorne turn against Becka, and by extension, House Rowan?*

Becka thought she could see the specter of reconciliation give her the finger, turn, and then saunter off. Calder had been right, waiting for Maura's oversight had been a mistake. Although even if she had acted promptly, Becka doubted the outcome would have been much different.

Perhaps I can still reason with him? I have to try.

"Alain, please. Let's not act rashly."

He smirked. "On the contrary, our action is well-reasoned and grounded in evidence."

Becka tamped down a flare of anxiety. She was determined to try harder. "It was an accident, an awful one, and I harmed your cousin. I am sorry for the damage I have caused. Please, let's find a way to move past this, for both our houses' sakes."

He rolled his eyes at her. Actually rolled them! "This is standard diplomacy, Becka. Not that I expect you to be familiar with standard fae culture."

Becka's composure shattered, she raised her arm and took a step towards Alain, pointing. "I am not..." she started, but a moment later Quinn and Brent grabbed her and pulled her back. Becka shook them off, confused, forgetting what she'd been about to say.

Alain assessed Quinn and Brent, surprise clear upon his face. "I'd heard you both were fearless, which you must be to touch this volatile creature without hesitation."

"I can control my gift!" Becka's raised voice carried the length and breadth of the long hallway. "I couldn't have known I would be tossed onto Hanna while my gift was peaked."

"No. You can't control it," Hanna replied. "Or have you forgotten the irreparable damage you've done to me and my house by your lack of control?"

"I haven't," she replied. "And I will never let myself forget the harm I have done to you. But throughout fae history there have been magical accidents, especially with potent gifts."

"After my injury, I convinced Alain that the dangers to his gift and his life were too great," Hanna said. She leaned in, fearless as only those who'd already lost it all could be, and whispered to Becka, "What do you imagine will happen to your lovers when you lose control in the throes of passion? Have you no conscience?"

Becka took a step back, Hanna's words a frightening image she had yet to consider. "I have hurt no one! I mean besides you."

Hanna turned to Becka. "Who would mate or marry you, knowing the price might be the loss of their powers? Our gifts are the very heart of what elevates us above the other races. No wise fae would risk it."

"I swear, there have been no other accidents. I haven't damaged anyone else," Becka repeated, not at all liking the direction this conversation had taken. Yet the truth of Hanna's words lingered. Who would want a partner who might maim them in a careless moment? "Haven't any fae within Hawthorne had magical accidents?"

Alain's countenance softened. "But we're here to discuss you right now, not them. It's not your fault, Becka. None of us chose the gifts our bloodlines bestowed on us, and for a select few, it's overwhelming. But others are due warning, and since your own house won't do the right thing, it forces House Hawthorne to step up for the greater good."

Becka remembered stories she'd read from her childhood of gifts so powerful they drove their vessels mad. Not everyone learned to control or manage their gifts, no matter how much training they had. Some got drunk on their power, it was so potent. Some lamented away their days, unable to use gifts without fear of harming those around them. In those tales, some were locked away. They sent others to live in hermitages far away from those they might harm. And still others took their lives to protect those around them.

She shivered at the thought. Astrid believed Becka had

adequate control, but did Alain have a pcint? Were Astrid and Maura blinded, uncaring about what might befall those unaware within Becka's immediate vicinity? But surely no! They'd sounded rational and reasoned over how to approach hiring her out and being cautious with the jobs she'd take.

Or did I just hear what I wanted to hear?

Seeing her lost in thought, Alain continued. "Calder warned me before we met that you were barely fit to visit this manor, much less live here. If I had taken his warning more seriously, perhaps my cousin wouldn't have suffered her injury. The least I can do is warn others, so they won't face the same fate."

She wanted to grab Alain by the throat and shake him. Make him listen to reason. But it was no use. He believed he was doing the right thing, not just for his house, but also for all the fae-touched. She'd been mistaken to think there had ever been hope for reconciliation between them after Hanna's accident.

At least she didn't have to marry this ass.

Alain turned and left, the rest of the Hawthornes following close on his heels. Their next stop would be a ceremonial visit to Duchess Maura.

Quinn stepped close to her, offering his arm once again. "For a moment there, I thought you were going to punch him."

Emotionally exhausted from the day, Becka barked out a humorless laugh. "I almost did! But now I'm going to nap. Hopefully, I can sleep straight through the bomb that'll go off in this house when Alain talks to Maura."

"Would you care for some earplugs?" Quinn offered.

CHAPTER 23

Soft, fluffy clouds ensconced Becka in a warm, safe haven. Her toes flexed, silken threads sliding against her skin. Lassitude weighed her limbs. Her body. The most comforting scent of musk and vanilla filled her senses. She curled against the warmth, feeling reciprocal movements pulling her closer.

Becka's mind sharpened. A weight sat, settled over her calves. She opened one eye, peeking around. Quinn's familiar form lay next to her, over the covers, propped up on a mass of pillows, his gaze focused on a tablet he held in his hands.

She didn't even know he had a tablet; most fae preferred not to depend on human technology and it was custom to not display such devices in public. He had kept the human-sourced tech hidden while within fae territory.

Becka closed her eyes and breathed deeply, luxuriating in the feel of silken sheets against her skin with Quinn's scent filling her lungs.

"How long are you gonna laze around, pretending to be

asleep?" his voice rumbled at her, intruding into her peaceful bubble.

She opened her right eye, peeking again at his reclining form. He glanced at her and then looked back at his tablet.

"Is it safe out there yet?" she asked.

"Not even remotely."

She closed her right eye and curled against him more tightly, pulling the sheets up over her nose. The weight on her legs hampered her motion. She wiggled her legs and was chastised with a sharp squawk.

Becka peeked down the bed to find Oriani glaring in her general direction.

"Does your cat know he doesn't sound like a cat? It's more like an owl. Or dog. Dog-owl?"

Becka chuckled, and then continued hiding under the covers, slowly undulating her legs in hopes Oriani would move off her.

Oriani, tired of her movements, stood and stretched as he yowled plaintively. After a lengthy lecture explaining his displeasure, he wandered off the bed, likely in search of treats.

Who'd been feeding him these past few days? Becka hadn't been. One benefit of being a fae of standing, the day-to-day maintenance of things got almost magically handled.

"He rules his empire fairly, but mercilessly."

"I'm impressed how you effortlessly overthrew his territorial claim."

"It's one of the few areas where I excel at finesse."

Quinn chuckled. "That's refreshing honesty."

Becka pushed back the covers, scooted up the hill of pillows, and then leaned her head near to Quinn's.

He set his tablet aside. "How are you feeling?"

"Oddly, fairly refreshed." She stretched again, relieved the soreness from yesterday had faded.

"You slept long enough. Do you even remember Healer Illan coming by yesterday afternoon?"

"I remember him giving me something foul to drink."

"Uh huh. He said it was for your own good."

"I'm sure, but couldn't he make it taste better?"

"The ways of healers are a mystery of foul potions. You'll be happy to hear he's coming back by this morning with another dose."

A shiver wracked her body, twitching to her fingers and toes.

He chuckled, the rumbling coming from deep within his chest. "I see you do remember."

Memories from yesterday came flooding back to her. The cruel expression on Hanna's face might haunt her dreams for some time, which she'd fully earned. "Ugh," she groaned. "The Alain situation went off the rails."

"That's putting it mildly."

A wave of anxiety washed over her. She didn't look forward to her next discussion with her mother after the falling out with Hawthorne. "Maura hasn't been by?"

"She stopped by last night. Said something like 'It can wait, there's no rush now. Let her sleep.' And then left."

"Thank goodness for small mercies. I needed the rest."

"On the upside, you're no longer engaged to marry that prick."

Becka smiled, reveling in the win for a moment. She rolled over towards him, crawling on her hands and knees until her face hovered over his. "That's the best news. Wait, why are we alone? Where are the shifter guards?"

"Right outside the door, I'd expect. I convinced them to back off a smidge."

"How did you manage that?" Becka asked.

"It might have involved a bribe to Brent. But I doubt it would have worked if they didn't already trust me." He shot her one of his winning smiles, and her heart melted a little. At least she told herself it was her heart.

An electric tension hung in the space between them. His heated gaze lingered over her, sending a thrill down her spine to her toes. He ran a hand from her shoulder down her arm. "I have even better news for you."

"Yeah?" She dipped her head down, brushing her cheek across his, the fine stubble on his chin tickling her skin.

"I have two enforcers arriving shortly. With them here, we can crank through the interviews and find the poisoner within a couple of days."

"That *is* fantastic news." She pulled back and shook her head. "Wait, how long was I asleep?"

"Not counting the few minutes where Illan poured gunk down your throat? We got back here early yesterday afternoon. You slept through the evening and night. You didn't even wake up to eat."

Becka's gaze drifted between his eyes and his lips. "Can I kiss you?"

His lips hitched with a smile, answering with a low, subvocalized "uh huh." And then he leaned forward into her and captured her lips with his own.

Becka pressed herself against him, reveling in the touch. The heat of his skin. The insistent hunger as his mouth danced against her own. The coarse feel of his shaved hair at the nape of his neck. The glide of his palms along the curve of her torso. The grip of his fingers on her hips.

Her world might be on the edge of chaos, but this moment was pure bliss.

A knock at the door brought them back down to earth with a hard stop.

They both sat bolt upright, Quinn lingering a moment to run his fingertips along the line of her chin. Then he jumped up to get the door.

Becka stood up, checking to make sure her pj's were still on right. They were.

He paused with his hand on the door handle. "Ready?"

"As I'll ever be."

Quinn opened the door. Illan stood there, bag in hand. "I figured I'd drop by again to see my favorite absent patient. How are you feeling this morning?"

"Like I finally caught up on sleep. And I'm not feeling sore and fatigued anymore, so that's a big plus."

Lorelai and Shamus followed the doctor into the room, walking around, checking to see if anything was out of place. Becka told herself she appreciated their efforts, even knowing their arrival meant there wouldn't be an opportunity to pick back up with Quinn after the healer left.

She needed a cool shower, and not just because she'd slept forever.

"I'm glad to hear it." Illan set down his bag on the sofa table, opened it, and pulled out a thermos. "The last dose I gave you had a sedative, so that should have helped you sleep. This is full of detoxifiers to help your body continue to flush the rest of the poisons out."

"Does it taste better than the last one?" She shuddered.

"I'm no chef, but it's not as bad."

Becka steeled her nerves and then walked over, picked up the canister, and opened it. She plugged her nose and downed the whole thing in a series of forced swallows.

Lorelai handed her a glass of water, and she downed that next.

"Thanks."

"May I check your pulse?" Illan asked, and Becka handed over her wrist. He did his usual routine, checking multiple pulse points, acupressure points, and the clarity of her eyes and tongue. "You're doing well, all things considered. Although your temperature is a little elevated."

Becka glanced at Quinn and then back. "I just got out of bed."

"It's likely nothing more than that."

"Do we know what the poison was this round? It didn't seem to be the same as the first," Becka asked.

"You're right, it wasn't. I know because you responded immediately to the tonic we use for accidental poisons."

"I thought Quinn had a special poison cure he brought in?" Becka asked.

"Oh, I gave you that one too. One after the other." He winked.

Quinn brought his tablet over and handed it to the healer. Illan hesitated and then took it.

"I know you did your own tests of the mints, but here are the results I got back from my labs," Quinn said.

Illan studied the screen for a moment, and then recognition dawned across his features. "Larkspur? Huh, I suppose it makes sense, but the concentration wasn't potent enough to kill."

"Larkspur?" Becka repeated. "You mean the flowers that grow down by the river?"

"Yes," Quinn replied. "They're common enough that House Rowan sends regular duty shifts to clear the area, as it's a place the horses and goats commonly use for grazing."

"There are several native plants poisonous to livestock and people alike," Illan replied. "But this is not the same as the first poison. I wonder why they used a different poison this time?"

Quinn rubbed a hand along the nape of his neck. "Perhaps they didn't have more of the first and improvised with the second dose? Larkspur is easy to find, and anyone who has worked in the fields here would know the consequences of consuming it."

"Which could also explain why it wasn't in the correct concentration," Illan replied. "Their skill was lacking. It's one thing knowing something is poisonous, quite another to manufacture a concoction or tincture. But it would also explain the timing delay between the two attempts."

Quinn nodded. "The initial poison was an amalgam of three different formulas, including the Treatment. That one wasn't made here."

"But the first poisoning didn't kill me, so they used what they could find on hand for a second go?" Becka asked.

"It points to the poisoner being within the household, with their knowledge of local lands," Shamus said.

"This confirms what you told the council yesterday," Becka said to Quinn.

"Thanks for sharing your report with me." Illan handed

Quinn back the tablet. "I need to get going." He packed the thermos back into his bag.

"How is Vott doing?" Becka asked. "I'm sorry I haven't been by to check on him more."

"He has regular visitors," Illan replied. "And he appears fully healed, but he's still in a coma-like state."

"That's encouraging," Becka replied. "Will you still let us know if he wakes up?"

"You'll be the second to know, right after the duchess."

"Of course."

Quinn's phone buzzed. He checked it, and then a mixture of tension and relief played over his features.

"Get dressed, Becka. The other enforcers have arrived."

"Can I catch up?" she said. "I still need a shower."

"No." The intensity of his gaze electrified her. "I'm not letting you out of my sight. Brent's getting them situated, and we already have a series of interviews scheduled for today."

She gave a quick nod and headed to her expansive closets. "Then I guess it's messy bun day for me."

"Do you ever do your hair fancy, like the other Rowan?" Lorelai asked, following her to the changing area but discreetly standing outside. "I bet with the pink it would look amazing, all shiny locks braided up."

"On my gosh, do I ever have better things to do with my time!" Becka laughed, tossing her pj's onto the floor and throwing on a brown peasant shirt over a pair of batik orange-and-yellow wide-legged pants. "Like anything else." Sandals, teeth brushed, face washed, and messy bun later, she was ready to go.

She would have preferred a shower but didn't want to hold up Quinn.

Becka returned to the bedroom, stuffing the Shadow-Dweller book into her bag and then hooking the strap over her shoulder. She donned her signature silk gloves, and then memories of yesterday flooded back to her. A heavy weight settled into her stomach. "Wait, are the Hawthornes still around?"

"No," Quinn replied. "The entire retinue left shortly after delivering their warning to Duchess Maura."

Becka glanced over to her bedside table, where Alain's unopened scroll sat, taunting her. "That's something, at least."

"The entire house is all a-murmur over it," Shamus said. "You'd think they didn't have murders and poisonings and better things to worry about."

"Oh, there's never too much drama for House Rowan," Becka replied. "And you're wrong, this news is worse than murder or poisonings. A break with House Hawthorne is tantamount to war."

CHAPTER 24

By the time Becka arrived at the library, the Enforcers had already transformed the space into a comfortable but serviceable interrogation room. A small, round table with a machine Becka didn't recognize sat next to a plush chair in the center. There were a pair of couches across from it, but someone had pushed most of the seating and extra tables to the outer walls, allowing for clear views to the center of the room. They had placed additional gear on tables along the outer wall.

Two of Brent's shifter guards stood outside the door, teamed up with a pair of fae household guards. Two more shifters, Luce and Saige, stood against a far wall, chatting quietly.

Entering the room, Quinn headed straight for the newly arrived enforcers who were fussing over the machine on the table. When they saw Quinn, both snapped to attention.

Just how does Quinn rank within the enforcers? She'd never wondered before now, other than knowing he reported directly to Chief Elowen.

Becka realized she'd met the female enforcer in the city after an altercation two years ago. She remembered Enforcer Caeda as both fair and fierce.

"Thank you both for coming," Quinn said to them, shaking their hands.

"How could we say no?" the large male replied. The fae enforcer laughed, a light, airy sound.

"Lady Becka, this is Enforcer Hamish," Quinn said, motioning to a tall shifter man whose pronounced jawline overwhelmed the other features on his face.

"Pleased to meet you, Hamish. Are you a member of Brent's pack, the Sawatch Enclave?"

"Nope," he replied, shaking his head. "I'm from the Bitterroot Enclave."

"You're a long way from home, then."

He squinted his eyes at her and then shrugged. "That's the truth."

"And this is Enforcer Caeda of House Poplar." The pixie-like fae was unusually petite, but the steely edge to her amber gaze belied any impression of her being a delicate flower.

Becka arched a brow at Caeda, who arched a brow right back at her.

"Enforcer Caeda and I met briefly in the city a while back," Becka replied.

"Nice to see you again," quipped Caeda.

"I suppose it is," she replied.

"Don't you worry. We'll get your poisoner," Caeda said in her birdlike voice. "And anyone else who might have helped them better be ready for the hammer."

"You can count on us," Hamish threw in. "Have you noticed this place is wound up tight as a virgin's knickers?"

Becka raised a brow, but no one else reacted to his colorful commentary.

Brent walked into the room, carrying a list on parchment. "Becka, glad to see you're looking better today."

"Thank you, Brent."

Brent handed over the list to Caeda. "Here's a register of everyone at the manor. No exception. There's been no one in or out, so we know the culprit, or culprits, will be on this list."

"We'll start at the top and work our way down," Hamish replied. "I bet we'll have it sorted in two, three days, tops."

"We should do the guards first," Caeda replied. "Then the higher-ranking family and staff."

"Agreed," Brent replied.

"What does that machine do?" Becka asked.

"It's an interrogator. Mostly, it puts the fear of transparency into the suspect," Caeda replied.

"It's a combination of human tech enhanced by fae magic," Quinn explained.

"What flavor of magic?" Becka asked.

"House Yew infuses them with clarity of the seen and unseen," Caeda replied. "And then House Elder does a little something which reveals shadowy aspects of character. It watches brain waves, pulse, temperature, respiration... things like that."

No wonder Maura didn't want the enforcers questioning everyone. Becka didn't want to sit in that chair either. Not that the magic would affect her, instead she might break their machine.

"I'll remind you both," Quinn looked to Caeda and Hamish, "there's to be no deviation from the focus of the investigation or the duchess will shut us down and throw the lot of us out."

"We both read the report you sent over," Hamish replied. "We'll keep it on track."

"They can't kick us out," Caeda replied, sporting a defiant smile. "We're too clever and cute."

"Caeda," Quinn said, drawing out her name into one long question.

She held up her hands. "You're so easy to rile up, Quinn. I'll stay on target. I'm your wee dragonfly with razor-sharp claws. I never miss my kill."

Quinn shook his head. "I have no interest in anyone here dying."

Hamish laughed out loud, looked around and seemed to realize Quinn hadn't told a joke, and then sobered up. "No! No, of course not. Let's get to it."

Becka headed to one couch and curled up, retrieving the book from her bag. No sooner had she settled before Astrid sat next to her on the couch.

"Good morning, Becka. We missed you at breakfast." Astrid's hair flowed around her, a mixture of perfect braids and glossy sheen.

"I had a special morning tonic from Illan. I'll eat once my stomach settles."

Astrid's face scrunched up in distaste. "I've drunk those too and I do not envy you. I swear that man keeps the medicine vile to scare us into staying healthy. Not that we get sick often, but you know what I mean."

Becka smiled and nodded. The fact that she and her Aunt Astrid could sit together on this couch exchanging pleasantries continued to surprise her. Over four months, she'd gone from outcast to heir. Ungifted to uniquely gifted.

What might the next four months bring?

"What's that book?" Astrid asked.

Becka looked at Astrid, trying to get a feel for whether she wanted a detailed answer or if she was just making small talk. By the rapt interest in her expression, Becka decided it was the former. "It's a Shadow-Dweller artifact. With my gift, I'm able to see messages. I've been trying to figure out its purpose."

Astrid's expression turned grave. "Surely any gains are not worth the risk to study such a dark tome?"

Becka shrugged. Compared to the prospect of being poisoned again, she preferred the book. Perhaps it reminded her of studying for classes, but it felt good to have a book in her hands again.

"For good or bad, I'm becoming accustomed to risk."

Astrid's brow furrowed. "A product of the unfortunate twists and turns in the path your life has taken. I don't envy you."

Quinn came over and leaned against the wall near the end of Becka's couch.

"Brent, can your guards keep a steady stream of people queued up?" Hamish asked.

"We're on it. Start when you're ready." Brent left the room, closing the door behind him.

Astrid stood up and walked over to Caeda, who stood next to the chair.

"Are you ready to start?" Astrid asked.

"We are, Lady Astrid. Would you like to be the first to give it a whirl?"

"I'll even insist upon it." Astrid sat in the chair, her movements graceful and elegant. "So, you know, I plan to remain for some time to ensure your questions do not cross the line of good taste."

Caeda picked up a loose cap attached to a tether and walked behind Astrid. "We welcome your oversight. You won't feel anything from this neural cap," she added, gently arranging the cap over Astrid's head. The display on the front of the machine lit up with waves of pulsing colors.

"How do you interpret the patterns?" Becka asked them.

"We take months of classes," Hamish answered. "But it boils down to catching blips in the flow, or abrupt or incongruous color shifts. It sounds easy, but there's a lot of finesse."

"People have a strong sense of self," Quinn said. "Lies run counter to our internal narrative. We invent explanations and narratives to cover them up, but the patterns are still there, if you're trained to see them."

"Unless they're a psychopath. Then the lies wouldn't bother them," Becka said.

"We have other ways of identifying those traits," Quinn replied.

"Besides," Astrid said. "Fae don't have the mental weaknesses humans do."

"I wouldn't be so sure about that," Becka replied. "Our genetics are part fae and part human. There's no proof that our magical gifts have fundamentally changed how our minds work. I took a comparative anatomy class my sophomore year, and although functional MRIs are different between the species, there's no significant difference between hominid brain structures."

Astrid frowned. "I do not understand some of the terminology you are using, but I think I have the spirit of it. You learned some odd things at that city school."

"Right." Caeda smiled. "May we begin, Lady?"

"You may proceed." Waves of tranquil blues and greens circulated on the display, creating a meditative and relaxing pattern.

Becka opened the book to a random page, resting it across her lap. Quinn glanced at her, but his attention was on the enforcers and their work. Between the two of them, she knew Quinn would listen for whether Astrid's words were true, and Becka would watch the book. Not that she doubted Astrid, but it was an interesting exercise.

Caeda and Hamish focused on the interrogator, and no doubt all three enforcers had also been trained on reading suspect behavior. Glancing around the room, she again noticed a pair of shifter guards, no doubt there for their ability to read emotion off others' scents.

She'd furthermore refer to this process as the gauntlet of truth, Becka decided, chuckling to herself.

This brought the three enforcers' attention to her, but she waved them off.

Hamish cleared his throat. "Please answer the questions directly and to the best of your ability. It's fine to answer with yes, no, or unsure. You're also welcome to elaborate if you want to, but it's not required. And ask us to repeat questions if you're unclear."

"I understand." A deep blue washed across the monitor before the colors flowed back to the light greens and blues.

"Do you dislike Lady Becka?" Hamish asked.

"No." A pink thread flowed across the monitor and then disappeared.

"Do you have larkspur, in any form, within your possession?"

She frowned, but the colors didn't change. "No, not to my knowledge."

"Did you poison Lady Becka?"

Red threads invaded the pulses of color. "Of course not!"

Becka watched the pages of the book, which felt heavier than usual against her lap. The squiggles moved with intensity.

"Have you assisted anyone who you think might harbor ill will against Lady Becka?"

"I would never do such a thing." Redder, and more pink this time, but the transitions were fluid.

"Do you suspect anyone of poisoning Lady Becka?"

Astrid frowned. "Well, yes. I suspect most everyone."

Becka looked to the tome under her fingers. The squiggles weren't just a word repeated, but a series of definite words. They read: Astrid's loyalty is absolute; protects you; protects family.

That seemed crystal clear.

Hamish shook his head. "Is there anyone you feel we should focus on?"

"I trust you will root them out on your own. No doubt my personal grudges wouldn't aid your process."

The screen was smooth as silk in bright greens and blues.

"She's good," Quinn declared. "And the device appears to be calibrated correctly. Let's get her out and move on to the next one."

Caeda removed the neural cap, taking care not to disturb Astrid's hair, while Hamish called in the next subject.

Astrid came to sit beside Becka again, tucking a loose braid back into place as she got comfortable.

Brent brought in one of the fae household guards and Caeda repeated the setup process as everyone watched.

"How are you doing today?" Astrid asked Becka in low tones to not disturb the enforcers. "I'm sure Alain's announcement last night must have upset you."

Becka sighed. Sure, she was upset, but did Astrid really think she'd wanted to marry that dolt?

"I hate what happened to Hanna. If I could take it back, I would in a heartbeat."

"Of course you would, dear. You're not a monster."

"How did Maura take the news?" Becka asked.

Astrid blew out a long breath. "How do you think she took it? I haven't seen her that angry in years."

"Glad I wasn't there."

"It's for the best. Alain wanted to grandstand, so he delivered the news to Maura as she came down the great staircase. He's got an impressive set of lungs. I'm guessing even Vott heard him."

"Vott's still in a coma."

"Exactly," Astrid replied. "Anyway, we received a letter from the House of Time—House Ash—informing us they stand with House Hawthorne. They refuse to do business with House Rowan while you're here, for the safety of their people, so they say."

Becka rubbed her temples. "Are there any Ash in residence here?"

"No, none by marriage, nor any here as tradesmen, so the immediate impact of their decision is minimal. But we can predict others will take up Hawthorne's banner on this issue.

Yew and Blackthorne are likely to follow, as they share the same territory and have long aligned."

"What's the plan for damage control?" Becka asked. She might not be able to heal the rift with Hawthorne, but Becka hoped she could help mend fences with houses swayed by Alain's charges.

"You think just like her." Astrid gave a halfhearted smile. "She's mulling it over, being deliberate and not reactive. We must wait to see where the other houses fall, but Maura will entreaty all to reason. Her plan to offer compensation for Hanna's injury is on the table, but it's not likely enough to mollify Hawthorne. I hear Alain gets his temper from his father, Duke Eldinrod."

"I'm not surprised. I mean, they are fire elementalists."

Astrid laughed, and then so did Becka. Caeda shot them a warning look, reminding Becka of her self-proclaimed status as the killer dragonfly. They quieted down, and Becka mouthed a sorry to Caeda, who shook her head in disappointment at them.

"We'll figure something out. Arguments break out between houses all the time."

Becka suspected it wouldn't be that easy and that Astrid was minimizing the situation. "If Hawthorne gathers enough support, won't that be dangerous?"

Astrid frowned. "They won't take it too far. The houses no longer war, not since losing the Great War with the humans. It taught us that other fae are not our enemies, and yet we appear versed in bickering endlessly."

Becka nodded in agreement, hoping Astrid was right.

The questioning carried on for a few hours, during which time they got through the entirety of the household guards, the shifter guards, and several council members. Even Maura had popped through, intent on showing cooperation, despite her distrust of the enforcers.

"Let's break for lunch," Quinn announced.

Becka stretched her arms and legs and then reached down to close the book. Three words stood out to her.

Home. Not. Safe.

She slammed the book shut. As if she hadn't already figured that one out.

CHAPTER 25

*L*unch comprised a platter of cut fruit, nuts, warm bread, and artisan cheeses. Everything Becka ate was checked twice. The shifters were taking zero chances.

She climbed the stairs to the rooftop garden to avoid the pointed looks and whispers from the fae she passed in the halls. Everyone had heard by now of the fallout with House Hawthorne and they'd all heard about the interrogations taking place.

Becka didn't have the impression she was anyone's favorite Rowan at the moment, unique and powerful gift or no.

Becka sipped iced tea and contemplated the Shadow-Dweller book's last message. Why would it bother to tell Becka her home wasn't safe, when such truth was obvious? Historically, it had shown her things she didn't know or suspected. Was it pointing out a new threat or was it emphasizing that the current threat hadn't yet passed?

She had no way of knowing.

Quinn, who had followed her to the roof and given her some space to eat alone, finished his conversation with Hamish and Caeda and then walked over and sat down beside her, resting his elbows on his knees. The three had eaten sandwiches while they walked and talked, which she assumed was a habit of working long hours as investigators and grabbing meals on the go.

"You're lost in thought," he said. "Anything you want to talk about?"

"Yes, can we walk?"

He stood and offered her his hand, helping her up. Becka threw her bag over her shoulder and led him down the stairwell at the side of the house and down to the meditation garden. Row upon row of short hedges formed a large labyrinth which was deserted.

"Tell me what's on your mind," he prompted.

Wasn't her anxiety patently obvious? "I'm afraid this drama with Hawthorne will blow up."

"Not to sound hyperbolic, but I'm sure it's just beginning to blow up."

"You don't think I'm overestimating the issue?" she asked.

"Not at all," he said. "Your gift, once known, always had the potential of being feared. That's just the nature of some powers. Ironically, Hawthorne's called the House of Thorns not just because it's a play on the name, but also because of the thorny and prickly nature of fire-based gifts."

"That's true. I suppose I'd come to think of Alain as prickly and dour, not prickly and a fireball," Becka replied.

"Why do you think their homes are all built of stone? Because you've got to work pretty darn hard to burn down masonry! Gods knows they've made a decent effort on multiple occasions."

Becka laughed at his joke. "Burning down your own home is definitely a vocational risk of fire elementals. Do you think their posturing is more about fae politics and that they're just using my gift as an excuse?"

"That's a question for your council, not me. But my gut says it's always politics first with the fae." He paused, appearing to gather his thoughts. "I'd be remiss if I didn't point out that your gift has the potential to disrupt the power balance between the houses. More so than anything else I've seen in our generation."

Becka stopped short at his words, her mind trying to wrap around the concept of that level of power. *What, you mean me?* He'd delivered his insight with unusual gravitas and she knew if he said it, Quinn believed it to be the truth. Becka would be unwise not to heed his warning.

"You think I'm that powerful?"

"You don't?" he asked.

She shook her head. "Not exactly. Nulling is a unique and new power, and I get why others are threatened by it. No one wants their magic taken away or destroyed. However, I've been completely focused on learning how to control my gift and trying to come to terms with being back here. When I think of my gift, I can't imagine being deliberately destructive with it. It's not who I am."

"I get it, but take a few moments to think about this from their perspective. What the other houses are thinking, knowing Nulling is in the world and they don't have control over it. If House Rowan wanted to, they could send you out to strip its enemies' powers at will," he said.

Becka groaned. "That's ridiculous. If I did that, someone would kill me outright for being a wild fae. Or dose me with the Treatment."

"Are you listening to yourself?" He reached out and touched her shoulder. "Someone dosed you with the Treatment! It's possible that motivation is behind your poisoning."

"But you said the poisoner is someone in this house," she replied, arguing because he *had* to be off base. Didn't he? "You and Brent both agreed on that when you presented your findings to the council."

"That's true, but that person settled for the larkspur on their second round of poisoning because they didn't have more ready access to the first poison they used. Therefore, they got the first substance from an outside source."

"Then we have to catch them to find out who provided them the first poison," Becka said.

"That's our plan. But that source could well be another fae house. Or humans. Even shifters. Even when we find the person who dosed you, we may not fully address the current threat. Anyone could act to prevent the emergence of your considerable power. Becka, consider that it's a bit terrifying to think of how you could abuse it, if you so choose."

"I would never willingly harm another! I feel ill when I think of what happened to Hanna."

He held up his hands. "I know you, and I know you wouldn't willfully cause others harm. But you're not well-known within fae society. You've spent half your life cozying up to college professors and living as a wild fae child in the city."

"I had no choice. I was an outcast." Becka couldn't

believe she was hearing this from Quinn. Calder and the others, sure, but not him. "Is that how you think of me?"

"Not at all. But most fae don't know you. They will hear a version of a story, likely from a long-time, trusted source, about how you maimed Hanna, permanently obliterating her powers. Do you think they'll even hesitate to ask for your version of events before acting reasonably to defend themselves?"

"So, then what do you propose I do?" She threw up her hands, hearing the shrill tone to her voice, but unable to rein it in. "How do I convince the world that I'm not just this destructive monster lying in wait for them?"

"I have a plan to protect you. I ran it by Chief Elowen yesterday while you were sleeping, and she gave it the go-ahead and set things into motion. It involves your civic service."

Fingers of ice gripped at her heart. It fluttered, skipping a beat, as the chilly sensation shot through her chest. "Did it occur to you to discuss this plan with me first before putting it into action?"

"I would have, but you were knocked out with the healer's concoction and I felt that time was of the essence."

She understood Quinn had done what he felt like he had to do, but Becka couldn't pretend she was okay with her life, yet again, being determined for her. Even by Quinn.

"Whatever you did, I'm sure it came from a sincere place, but I don't know that I want it."

Quinn's pupils flared, his shock at her reaction clear. He opened his mouth to speak and then seemed to think better of it. They stood there, facing off, for a few quiet moments,

Quinn's clenched jaw and determined gaze against Becka's raging independence.

"Do you want to hear my plan?" he said, his voice unusually flat.

She took another few, slow breaths. Quinn watched her, his expression tense and back ramrod straight, as if bracing for a fight. Which Becka supposed was what this almost was.

Becka looked into his eyes. This was Quinn. *Her* Quinn. He'd proven himself trustworthy time and again, and she knew he had her best interests in mind. He may have acted without her consent, but he'd done it to protect her.

When she'd calmed herself, Becka replied, "Yeah. Go ahead."

"You're right," Quinn replied. "I'm sorry, I should have talked about it with you before I spoke to the chief."

Her heart was heavy with sorrow. "I get your heart's in the right place, but you crossed a line, Quinn."

His expression softened. "I did. I know how being forced to be back here at the manor has been hard on you. I know you rankle at every order from Maura and Astrid. And you're practically allergic to the title of heir. I know you, and I knew better than to act on your behalf without speaking to you first."

"Why didn't you just wake me up?"

"Because things here are escalating quickly. Very quickly. The situation with Hawthorne is more volatile than Rowan might realize. I fear you won't be safe here once word spreads."

Quinn's warning echoed the last message Becka had received from the book, and that gave her pause. "Tell me about your plan."

He gave a quick nod. "Astrid filed the paperwork declaring you fully trained, so now the human government gets to decide where best to place you for civic service."

"Sure, I'm familiar with the procedure. I know Astrid and Maura are offering my Nulling services to other houses, possibly before I get called off to do civic duties or between assignments."

He shook his head. "That's a dangerous plan. The last thing you need is to be sent into a house that's sympathetic to Hawthorne and willing to arrange an accident."

Chills ran down her spine. "And I suppose being sent on any random civic duty assignment carries the same risks?"

"Unfortunately, yes. The fae fear your gift. Humans may fear you, but they are also apt to see you as a tool to use against your own."

"I hate the idea that other fae see me as something to fear. I'm just me!"

"But you have to think about how everyone else sees you. You must understand their perspective in order to outthink them and protect yourself."

"I suppose you're right, but I don't have to like it. So, what's the plan, Quinn?"

"My plan was to preempt the normal civic duty system by placing a request before the government even realized you were available."

"So you knew Astrid filed paperwork yesterday morning, and then what? You magically had a request in for me the same day?" Becka asked.

"It wasn't magic; it was Chief Elowen. And yes, I had her file the request yesterday afternoon. Hopefully, before anyone else even knew you'd become available."

Now the timing made sense. "Right after I fell asleep."

He shrugged. "Yeah."

Becka rubbed her temples. "Wait, what form of civic service?"

"Serving with the enforcers, specifically as a civilian consultant on certain cold cases the chief thinks your abilities might shed some light on."

Her heart skipped a beat. "You mean *Shadow-Dweller* cold cases?"

He nodded. "Do you still hate me? I thought you'd be interested in the opportunity."

"I'm still upset and emotional," Becka replied, hands on her hips. "I get to be upset. But I admit the job sounds interesting. Great, actually."

A weak smile tugged at the corners of his lips. "Do you want another apology?"

Becka pouted. "No, no. I understand your intent and I appreciate your swift action. I get it. But how does moving to the city and working with enforcers make me any safer? Won't my enemies have better access to me there?"

"Possibly, but it gets you out of fae territory, and when you visit fae, you will always have an escort."

She pursed her lips. "You mean... you?"

"The enforcers won't keep you busy all the time. And I won't necessarily be teamed up with you each case, but mostly. I know you've had self-defense training so you'll be able to take it up a notch with enforcer training, which will also keep you safer."

Becka groaned and began pacing back and forth. Luce and Lorelai became interested and Becka had to wave them off. It must make all the guards crazy, to see Becka so upset and just stand around, watching and twiddling their thumbs. It was weirder for Becka to know they were all watching, even from a distance.

"Let me get this straight. The fae will have less opportunity to harm me, but what about the Shadow-Dwellers? How would I be safer in human cities from them? There are plenty of fae in the city. I might avoid the political fallout of harming Hanna back in the territories, but there's nowhere in the world that I'll be protected from Shadow-Dwellers."

He flexed his shoulders. "You'd be with me."

He didn't even have the decency to blush.

She shook her head and sighed, barking out a single laugh. She loved his humor. "Your opinion of yourself might be just a wee bit overblown."

He laughed, but quickly sobered. "Look, I'm sorry. And be upset all you want, but think about it. Wouldn't you rather be out hunting down Shadow-Dwellers instead of sitting through council meetings and fancy dinners day in, day out, waiting for the next assassin to find you?"

She rolled her eyes. "You have a way of making all my options sound so appealing."

"Look, the letter will arrive shortly. You can talk to Maura and either encourage her to accept the option or protest it with the civic service. I'm guessing she, or the council, will follow your lead."

"Let me think about it."

"Thank you," he replied.

"One more thing," Becka said, hesitating to ask what had nudged at her thoughts since the beginning of this conversation. But she had to know. "Are *you* scared of me?" she blurted out. "Of my gift?"

He smiled a sad smile and took a step closer to her. "No, not at all. Why would you think that?"

"You said some fae will be terrified of me and what I might do. What I can do. Aren't you afraid I'll destroy your gift?"

"I'm not. If my gift was susceptible to your Nulling, it would have happened the first time I touched you, when we first met, and you ran into me."

Becka considered for a moment. "But, are you concerned that our more... extended touching... might not damage your gift?"

Humor twinkled in his eyes and he took another step closer to her. "That depends. What depth of contact are you considering?" he asked, a deep rumble in his voice.

Heat flushed her cheeks for the second time that day. She tried to come up with an answer, but her mind had blanked out.

Just then, Quinn's attention was drawn up and behind Becka. She spun around and saw a lone fae guard running towards them.

"What is it now?" she said.

They walked toward the guard. The rest of the shifters, including Luce and Lorelai, rounded the edge of the labyrinth to meet them.

Becka didn't get an opportunity to even ask why the guard was running.

"Hurry, Lady Becka! Duke Vott's awake!"

They jogged across the estate until Becka ran out of steam and had to slow to what felt like a crawl.

"You want me to carry you?" Quinn asked.

She was tempted, but then immediately thought about the face Maura would have if she saw Becka in Quinn's arms. "Heck, no."

"It wouldn't be any trouble."

Becka panted, sucking down breath. "I'm not about to let you carry me anywhere. I'm gonna walk myself all the way there."

His rich baritone rumbled through the air. "Either Luce or Lorelai could..."

"Nope. I've got this."

"You might be the most independent, stubborn fae I've ever met."

"I'll take it." Becka smiled, liking the compliment despite her ire.

"In this moment, that wasn't a compliment," Quinn said.

They arrived a few minutes later and Illan met them in

the main infirmary. The shifters and other guards waited out in the hall; only Quinn followed her inside.

"How's he doing?" Becka asked, breathless.

Frowning, Illan pulled on latex gloves and checked Becka's pulse. "Vott is weak but has his wits about him. Duchess Maura and Elder Alaetha are in with him now, but he said to send you right in as soon as you arrived."

She knew that was only half of the story. "What about his gift?"

"He reports that his gift has gone silent. It was the first thing he said upon waking."

Pain gripped Becka's chest and the corners of her eyes watered. "I knew it was likely, considering they dosed him with the Treatment, but I'd hoped."

Illan patted her shoulder. "We all did, Lady Becka."

She drew in a deep breath, held it a second, and then blew out slowly. The heat in her cheeks didn't fade. Vott and Hanna both had lost their gifts because of Becka's actions, accidental as they were. Was this how her life would be, a string of people injured because of her?

Becka couldn't let that happen. She needed to find a way for others to be safe around her. *Is perfect control too much to ask for?*

Perhaps Quinn was right, and others would rightly fear her. If she'd intended to harm others, Becka could have left a trail of carnage in her wake. She'd have to demonstrate to the masses that she was nothing like they feared, but how?

More importantly in this moment, did Vott blame her for his loss, as Hanna had? The possibility sat heavy on her heart.

Becka tried to plaster a smile on her face, but she just

couldn't, so she walked forward, teary-eyed. Quinn hung back in the doorway, out of sight but no doubt not out of earshot.

Vott lay on the bed in the corner, propped to nearly sitting on a stack of pillows. White linens surrounded him, and his long white hair stood at all angles despite obvious attempts to groom him while he'd been unconscious. Elder Alaetha sat on a couch which might have been brought into the room just for her, as Becka didn't recall it being there before. Maura sat on a chair pulled up close to the bed, his hands in her own, her expression full of rare tenderness. His pallor was almost ghost-white, and the sheen in his eyes had paled from his usual sunny gold to an unhealthy dull yellow.

To Becka's surprise, she wasn't the only one shedding a tear. Vott and Maura were sharing a rare, vulnerable moment together, their love laid bare to any who might see despite the others present in the room. How was it that people, in times of deep emotion, could appear so relatable? So real?

Becka paused. "Vott? May I come in?"

When he saw her his eyes lit with recognition, his light-hearted expression sobering into a frown. Anxiety gripped her solar plexus, making breathing difficult. Was that concern, or anger?

"Becka! Come in. Come closer."

Becka walked over, glad the windows in the stuffy, convalescent room had been opened. Vott held out his hand, and Becka hesitated, despite wearing the gloves. Despite knowing he'd already lost his gift.

Her gut burned with the sinking weight of guilt, yet she took his hand. Out of the corner of her eye, Alaetha frowned.

"I am glad to see you well," Vott said

A tear ran down her cheek, a combination of guilt over her role in his inadvertent poisoning and relief beyond measure that he didn't appear to hate her as Hanna did. "I'm so sorry, Vott."

"No, no. You have nothing to be sorry for. You didn't take the song of the wind from me."

"If I hadn't poured my tea into your mug..."

"Don't be ridiculous, Becka," he said, the sharp edge of his words cutting through the room. "Now, Maura just told me someone poisoned you a second time?" he asked.

"Yes, but I've recovered." When he frowned at her, she continued. "Mostly. I'm still fatigued."

"Becka has risen to the occasion," Maura said. "She's even started attending council meetings and assumed oversight of the shifter guards while you were catatonic."

"Have you?" he asked, a doubtful frown painting his brow, and Becka shrugged. No doubt he knew Brent managed the shifters himself, but she wouldn't explain that to Maura now. "I'm glad to hear it, but that's not why I called for you."

"What did you need?" she asked, surprised he didn't appear interested in her activities, as it had been the focus of so many of their discussions.

"Maura has been explaining the investigation's findings. I understand you haven't found the poisoner yet?"

Fatigue kicking in after her sprint-walk here, Becka pulled up a chair and sat down. "No, they continue to elude us. What do you remember about the poisoning?"

"I remember seeing that ancient tea set out and ready for use. I remember feeling overjoyed to get to use it. And I was so pleased to have the lapsang souchong to share with you."

Driving the questioning was a reversal of roles for them, but Becka couldn't help her curiosity, and Vott seemed eager to help. "Did you see who put the tea set out? Or anyone in the rooftop garden before I arrived?"

He shook his head. "Only fae and shifter guards were there. But I remember which ones."

Quinn stepped into the room. "Can you list them off for me?"

"The enforcers are doing interrogations now," Maura explained.

Vott's eyes widened. "Interrogations at House Rowan?"

Elder Alaetha whipped open a hand fan, closing her eyes against her self-generated wind. No doubt the vitriolic elder was appalled, but Becka was grateful she hadn't jumped into the conversation.

"It's no worse than a poisoner." Maura replied, and then sighed dramatically. "Besides, the council outvoted me."

"Ahh," he said. Vott turned to Quinn. "Shamus and Luce were with me, but they arrived when I did. There were a pair of house guards, Beore and Oba, who appeared to be walking perimeter and watching the distance for... whatever it is guards watch for?"

"Thank you, Duke Vott," Quinn replied. He pulled out his phone and stepped out of the room. Becka heard the rumble of his voice speaking in short, clipped tones.

No doubt those four would be next for the hot seat, assuming they hadn't been there already.

"It's unfortunate you didn't see anyone else," Becka said.

Vott started to say something, and then coughed, a deep, rattling sound. Maura held out a cup for him to take a sip, which seemed to help.

"I am in agreement," Vott whispered, his voice hoarse from lack of use. "But there is one conversation I remember which stands out in my mind."

Becka leaned forward on her elbows. "What conversation?"

"When dear Hanna Hawthorne delivered the tea, such a touching gift, really, knowing my proclivities for fine teas, I wasn't alone. Your brother, Calder, and his paramour, Alvilda, were in my study visiting. I'd mentioned to Calder that I planned to share the tea with you, and then I had talked about how well you have been progressing in your training."

"Astrid declared Becka guilded just yesterday," Maura replied.

"I'm so impressed with you. You've been doing so well." He smiled up at Becka, looking every part the proud father.

Becka nodded, basking in her father's long-sought praise. The moment of joy was tainted by the knowledge that he'd hear about the accident with Hanna and the subsequent impending political war with House Hawthorne.

"Anyway, after Hanna left, Calder spoke to me at length, questioning your position as heir and returning to the manor. His words were heated, and his demeanor unseemly."

Vott's admission hit her with the cadence of truth. "Calder and I have spoken a couple of times recently. Although I know from our early exchanges when I'd returned to House Rowan that he didn't want me back, it seems he's come to a level of acceptance. Just this morning he behaved in a borderline gracious manner towards me. I can't imagine he would have poisoned me the night before and then been so kind today."

Unless he was playing me.

Vott shook his head and threw up his hands. "I could have read it wrong, Becka. But when Maura told me you'd been poisoned yet again, he was honestly the first person to come to mind."

"I can't believe you'd point an accusatory finger at our son," Maura replied, scowling. "He's a passionate lad, and given to delusions of his own importance, but no poisoner."

Vott smiled at Maura, and they grasped hands more tightly. "I'm sure you're right, my dear. Goodness, his paramour, Alvilda, is well-matched for him in that department. She had nothing kind to say of Becka either."

A chill ran down Becka's spine. "Whatever do you mean?"

"Oh, every time Calder would lament something, Alvilda would chime in with gusto, parroting his fervor. She sounded like she disliked you more than Calder did, which is ridiculous, as you barely know each other."

Becka looked up, seeking Quinn, who stood just inside the doorway listening to every word. Becka gave him a "no, it couldn't be" shrug. He arched a brow and pursed his lips with a "maybe" reply shrug.

Maura shook her head. "Then she's exactly the wrong partner for our son. He needs someone who's grounded and level-headed to counter his emotional outbursts."

Vott's perspective of Alvilda didn't fit with Becka's. Alvilda had always been standoffish or polite to Becka, but instead her father painted her as hateful.

"I've seen her hanging on Calder's arm, and I was at a picnic with her a day or two ago, well before the second poisoning. She wasn't overly warm, but not quarrelsome either," Becka replied. "We should speak with her," she said to Quinn.

"You should let Vott get some rest," said Illan, strolling into the room with a large glass of something likely vile for Vott to down.

Becka released Vott's hand and rose to leave before the healer might get any ideas on another similar dose of tonic for herself.

"It's good to see you well again," Becka said. "I'll be by again tomorrow."

Vott eyed the healer's concoction with due concern. "Yes, dear. Maybe bring some tea?"

She gasped. "After what it's done to you, you'd drink tea again?"

He smiled a weak, sad smile. "One cannot blame the tea for the poisoner's actions, and I love it too much to give it up."

Becka nodded. "I can do that."

Becka and Quinn walked out of the infirmary and headed back towards the library where the interrogations were happening.

"Do you think Calder is involved in the poisoning?" Becka asked.

"No, but he's up to be tested soon," Quinn replied. "We'll want to be there for that."

"Definitely," Becka replied. "You heard Vott speaking of Alvilda and how much she dislikes me? Could she be a suspect?"

"Yes. Your arrival back into the house prevented her lover from becoming heir. She might have thought, with you out of the way, that Calder would be back in his rightful place."

"If Calder was heir, she might end up as duchess one day.

Who knows, perhaps his anger even spurred her into action? But how would a fae who lives in the territories get access to the Treatment?"

"That's the key question. There's no way Alvilda would have been able to access it here, so she must have acquired it on a trip into the city for work. Even then, the Treatment is kept locked up under strict protocols, only distributed and used with authority of the judicial system. She'd have to have very interesting friends."

"What's next? Do you think we should schedule her for after Calder and the guards?"

Quinn gave her the side-eye. "We've started with guards and immediate family first. We could send for her after we're done with them."

"Why not check her next?"

"If she senses we're on to her, she might run or destroy evidence. I will have Brent put a watch on her, and when she's away from her room we will see what evidence we can find."

"Also check Calder's room," Becka said. "As his lover, she might have left evidence there as well. We also need to find out what Calder knows. Either he's working with her or he's blind to her motivations. I'm not sure which would be worse."

"Fair point. Plan to keep that book handy for Calder's questioning, assuming you still think it's safe to use."

"I'll bring it," she replied. "We'll see if it helps, but I still don't trust it."

As they neared the library, a woman approached them. She was a cousin of Becka's, but Becka couldn't remember her name.

"Fair day," the lady said, holding out a letter. "This came for you in the post."

Becka held out her hand and took it. "Thank you."

The lady walked away, errand done. Becka turned over the letter in her hands. The front read "Civil Service — Official Mail."

"Fairy balls!" she shouted, her curse echoing down the crowded corridor.

$\mathcal{B}$ecka sat curled up on a couch in the library, now an impromptu interrogation room, with the Shadow-Dweller book open upon her lap. Astrid was next to her, continuing her oversight of the process to ensure the enforcers didn't cross any lines.

Becka surveyed the room. Fae, enforcer, and shifter alike milled about. Many were still coming back from lunch, but no doubt they were awaiting Calder's arrival before jumping back into the interrogations.

Becka flipped a few pages, continuing to watch for anything unusual, but the pages were quiet for now.

Astrid frowned at the book. "Is that a letter you're using as a bookmark?"

Becka looked at the edge of the envelope stuffed between the pages of the book. "Yes."

"You get little mail. Is that your Civil Service notice?"

"I suppose it is," Becka replied, continuing to page through the book.

Astrid's eyes widened. "That was unusually quick. Have you read it?"

"I'll get to it," Becka replied. "Life is a little busy at the moment for me to worry about it."

"I look forward to hearing about the notice when you do," Astrid replied. She leaned over and opened the bag that sat at her feet, pulling out a skein of delicate gray fingering-weight yarn.

Becka looked askance at Astrid, never having imagined her patient enough for a slow craft like knitting. It was something she associated with elders, not ladies in their prime.

Astrid caught her look and let out a heavy sigh. "What? Can't a master illusionist have pedestrian hobbies?"

"When I think of you, it's your position as head of the Illusionists Guild or your position on the council. I guess I figured if you wanted something knit, you'd use your gift or buy one."

"Illusion won't make this shawl warm nor soft against my skin. Sure, I'll construct designs upon it for my amusement, or to go with an outfit, but I've got to have something of quality to start with."

"You're a practical lady in everything you do," Becka replied, surprising herself with the compliment.

"It's kind of you to notice," Astrid replied, a smile gracing her lips as her fingers fell into a steady rhythm with the needles and yarn. "Knitting also keeps my hands busy and lets my mind focus on the task at hand. You should try it sometime."

Becka stifled a laugh. "Maybe I will. But it seems a slow and laborious craft."

"As you say," Astrid replied.

Calder arrived, escorted in by an eager-eyed Caeda. "If you'll just take a seat here," she gestured, "I'll get you hooked up."

"How long is this indignity going to last?" he asked, his feathers ruffled like a strutting rooster.

"It takes as long as it takes," Hamish replied. "But it'll take longer if you stand around whining about it."

Calder sat, his cheeks flushed. He noticed Astrid and Becka, eyes widening. "What are you two doing here?"

"I am here," intoned Astrid, "to oversee the proceedings."

"You're here to protect me?" Calder asked Astrid.

She shrugged. "Maybe. I mean, I'm here to protect the interests of House Rowan and ensure the enforcers don't overreach." Hamish put a hand over his heart, mocking offense, to which Astrid rolled her eyes. "They've behaved themselves so far, so you have nothing to worry about."

"That's gracious of you to say, Lady Astrid," Hamish replied. "All right, Caeda. Are we ready to put the screws to him?"

She finished settling the cap on his head, fiddled with the device for a moment, and then nodded to Hamish. "We're ready."

"Wait," Calder said. "Why is Becka here?"

Quinn, who'd been leaning against the wall by the door, spoke up. "She goes where I go. And I'm here."

Becka blinked at Quinn's borderline-possessive statement. She should dislike the tone, or the sentiment, but a fluttering sensation hovered in her belly, disproving her desire to dislike his insistence. *I'm still mad at him*, she reminded herself.

"Fine, whatever," Calder replied, his tone snappish. The

interrogator filled with swirls of yellow and orange. "Let's get this over with."

"Happy to," Hamish replied. "Do you dislike Lady Becka?"

"Yes," Calder replied without hesitation. The colors swirled in yellows and whites.

Caeda stood to the side, her grin bordering on predatory. Becka wasn't sure what it was about the spritely fae that worried her, but she was glad Caeda was on Quinn's side.

"Do you hate her?" Hamish pressed.

Calder's gaze met Becka's, emotions shifting across his face. "When she first returned, I hated her. I missed Tesse dearly. You know everyone loved her."

"As did I," Becka replied, feeling connected with him through their shared loss of Tesse, despite their differences in style and temperament.

"And you were just, everything Tesse wasn't." Calder looked up at Hamish. "Becka didn't fit in here. She's crass and uncultured. Dressed like city trash. Still does."

It surprised Becka the enforcers were allowing her to hijack the investigation, but perhaps Quinn had directed them to go with the flow. She glanced at the book in her lap, but for once, nothing was happening.

Becka rolled her eyes at him, amazed she could go from commiserating with Calder to irritation in a heartbeat. "Tell me what you really think, why don't you?"

"Attached to this thing," he gestured to the interrogator, which continued to swirl steadily in yellow and orange despite his vitriol, "I have no alternative but to be honest with the enforcers, and by extension, you. I didn't feel you'd earned the honor of being the heir. Having opinions isn't a crime."

His smug expression grated on her, but she didn't rise to the bait. "I didn't just return. I also displaced you as potential heir after Tesse's death," Becka said.

"I've admitted I hated you, Becka. But I can see that you're trying. You've adapted a bit, and you've accepted your responsibilities. I don't hate you anymore. You've faded to a mere frustration."

Becka sighed. At least the sentiment was mutual. "Do you have larkspur, in any form, within your possession?" She looked at the book, which again wasn't reacting.

Calder looked to Hamish. "Is she in charge now?"

Hamish shrugged. "Regardless of who asks it, it's the script. Answer the question."

Calder shook his head. "No, I don't have any larkspur."

The colors swirled smooth as silk.

"Did you poison Lady Becka?" Hamish asked.

"No, I did not."

Calder's colors were level as a reflecting pool.

"Have you assisted anyone who you think might harbor ill will against Lady Becka?" Hamish asked.

"Never," Calder replied.

"Do you suspect anyone of poisoning Lady Becka?"

"No."

Hamish looked at the interrogator, then at Quinn, and shrugged. It was clear he didn't think Calder knew anything, but he kept going. "Is there anyone you feel we should focus on?"

"No one. Are we done yet?"

Before anyone else could answer, Becka had to ask one last question. "Wait. Do you know of anyone else who is upset I'm back?"

Finally, she had movement on the pages of the book. Familiar squiggles moved to and fro, but didn't yet coalesce into a message.

His brow furrowed. "Everyone knows I am emotional at times, sharing my feelings on the situation. Several people have supported me, but I don't know if that means they're also upset. Do you know what I mean?"

"You rant about me to get it off your chest?" she said, feeling aggravated that this was his default, normal behavior. But was she upset because he openly vented his emotions, or because he didn't like her? After all, she wasn't fond of him either.

"Sure, to willing listeners. Perhaps I've gone a bit far. I know Alvilda has encouraged me to calm myself a number of times when I became overly upset, but that's what good friends—lovers—do."

Words formed in the squiggles. *Anger is an infection.*

Becka shivered. "You might be an asshole, but you're not guilty of poisoning?"

"I'm being honest, and you are still crass."

Astrid nodded at him in apparent agreement, which didn't help Becka's mood one bit. Her gaze flicked to the interrogator, whose screen continued to exhibit smooth ribbons of color. "That's something we can agree on."

The words had disappeared from the book.

"We're done with him," Quinn announced. "Luce, can you bring in Alvilda?"

Luce disappeared out of the room and returned a

moment later, ushering Alvilda in. The lady stepped cautiously into the room, hands wringing, but her expression appeared carefree and relaxed.

Caeda removed the neural cap from Calder and he jumped up, a wide smile across his face at Alvilda's arrival. He walked over and stepped in close to her, uncaring of others watching their movements. He ran the outside of his hand down her jawline.

"I'll wait for you outside. Perhaps after you're done, we can go for a walk to clear our heads?"

Becka wondered if a walk was indeed what he intended. She suspected it was couple-speak for a rendezvous.

Alvilda nodded, her smile not reaching her eyes. Her movements were jerky, and she appeared relieved when Caeda motioned for her to move to the hot seat.

For all that Becka wanted to believe Alvilda was the poisoner, she'd yet to even notice Becka. Instead, her focus was on the enforcers and shifters. And Calder. Becka looked at the book and wasn't disappointed.

Mask.

Alvilda moved toward the chair, but Calder caught her by the arm. "Wait," he said. "What's going on?"

Becka closed the book and jumped to her feet. Astrid, who'd stopped knitting to follow the interaction, set her partial shawl aside and stood up, crossing the room to where Calder and Alvilda stood. Even the enforcers stepped back to give her space, but Becka followed her forward.

"Calder! Let go of me!"

Calder continued to hold Alvilda's arm. "Your birthmark is missing! Who are you?"

Astrid took a moment, looking to Calder and then to

Alvilda. She then stepped in close to the girl, raised her hands in the air before her, and, through a series of hand gestures, dismantled the illusion surrounding the girl.

"Yaeli?" Calder said, confused, releasing her arm. "Where is Alvilda?"

Without the illusion you could see the fear on Yaeli's face. Now the stiffness in her movements made more sense.

"I didn't mean to do anything improper, Lady Astrid. Alvilda asked me to cover a duty shift for her while she ran an errand away from the manor. She left just this morning. I didn't think there would be any trouble."

"Do you know where Alvilda went?" Astrid asked.

"I'm not sure. She'd said she needed to pick up a delivery from Nadal's dairy farm at the far meadow. Said she'd forgotten about it and would get in trouble if anyone knew she was gone."

Immediately Becka thought of the grazing land near Nadal's farm and the larkspur that grew near the river. Her bile rose, the sour juices burning her throat. Was Alvilda getting more larkspur to poison her with right now?

"Brent," Quinn called out, and the shifter opened the door and stepped into the room. "I need your help hunting a stray."

Brent smiled, his wolfish grin reminding Becka of Caeda's predatory look earlier. "I thought you'd never ask. Where do we pick up the scent?"

"Calder," Quinn said, "take us to Alvilda's room."

He gaped. "Wait, you can't hunt her down like a dog! This is just a misunderstanding. She'd never have harmed Becka!"

"We can, and will, hunt her down," Quinn spat out. "But I promise we won't harm her, unlike what she might be planning right now in some twisted attempt to further your standing. Now, take us to her room."

CHAPTER 28

Becka watched as the enforcers searched Alvilda's room. Located on the first floor of the manor, her room was oddly smaller than Becka had expected. She'd always lived in and visited the quarters reserved for the immediate family of the duchess. While Alvilda's room was well-appointed, it lacked the luxury of rooms just one floor up. On the upside, as the room was about the size of Becka's en suite bathroom, there was much less space to search.

The small, modest room implied that Alvilda wasn't a high-ranking fae and also that her gift wasn't powerful enough to command substantial income for the house. No wonder she'd been so aggressively courting Calder; the alternative was remaining in her meager station.

Calder stood just outside the doorway, fuming as he watched the enforcers rip apart the room and Brent pick out clothing from her laundry to be used in tracking. Becka left the room and stood next to him, trying to imagine what he was thinking. Somehow his blatant honesty during the interrogation had dissipated her remaining frustration with him.

Becka didn't care if he liked her; she'd long ago gotten used to being the odd one out in the group. Now that he'd been honest, there was no longer any pretense hanging between them.

Becka liked to know where she stood with someone, even if it was alone in the desert.

"How did Alvilda come to live at the manor?" Becka asked.

Calder's expression was grim. "She's the daughter of Padrig, cousin to the duchess. She grew up on his estate, just down the road."

"I remember him. He's renowned for his dressmaking."

He nodded. "When Alvilda came into her powers, they brought her to the manor so she could study with Astrid. She's good, but not an adept."

Becka could have mentioned how Alvilda's illusion at the tea party was well done, yet the first to be called out. But she thought better of it.

"Few are," she replied.

"Anyway, that's how I met her. When she finished training, she stayed on at the manor to continue our affair. She took on duty assignments as a lady's maid for Sigfrid and Ingrid, doing dress alterations, even working in the kitchen. It's how we first met."

"She sounds devoted to you." Which was syrupy sweet, if possibly also a smidge mercenary. Had it ever occurred to Calder to wonder at his lover's motivations?

Calder wobbled his head from side to side. "Mother wouldn't approve the engagement; said she's aiming higher for my prospects than a village girl. We'd hoped if Alvilda conceived then Mother might change her mind."

"If Alvilda was pregnant, Mother would allow her to stay here, near you," Becka replied.

Quinn emerged from the room followed by Hamish, who carried a box filled with jars, containers, dried herbs, notebooks, and whatnot. Brent was close behind him, carrying a handful of socks.

"Get those items inventoried and set off to testing," Quinn said to Hamish, who gave a sharp nod and then headed off in the library's direction.

Quinn turned to Calder and Becka. "Things were already in disarray when we started. It looks like she left in a hurry. I found dried herbs that I think are larkspur, but our lab will confirm. There were several tinctures and unguents which we will also test."

Calder ran a hand through his hair. "I still can't believe she'd hurt Becka. Alvilda knows how important family is to me."

Becka didn't point out that Calder himself hadn't considered her one of the family for some time, only grudgingly tolerating her presence for weeks. No wonder Alvilda had disliked her; he'd emotionally poisoned her against Becka, day in and day out for months.

Quinn extended a piece of folded parchment out to Calder. "She left you this letter."

Calder snatched it from Quinn's hand, turning it over and revealing a broken seal. "You dare read our private correspondence?" he replied, his cheeks instantly ruddy.

Quinn put his hands on his hips. "I do. Read it."

Calder fumed, but opened the letter and scanned it, paling as he did so.

"I meant," Quinn continued, "read it out loud."

Calder's lips formed a hard line and Becka wondered if he'd yield. "As you say."

He took a deep breath, and then read.

My darling Calder,

I regret leaving you under these, or any, circumstances, but I fear fate has caught up with me.

The arrival of the new enforcers can mean only one thing. Therefore, I must flee before they find me.

Never doubt in my unending and enduring love for you, my light. I would have done anything for you. Even in leaving, I do so confident you will be held blameless.

I freely admit I poisoned Becka. I grieve Duke Vott's poisoning, but that was at Becka's hand.

Never fear, my love. One day soon I am confident you will take your rightful place as heir. It's only a matter of time before Becka brings destruction upon herself and threatens House Rowan, and then your opportunity to shine will present.

I only wish I could have remained by your side. Although you may miss me, please do not try to find me. I understood the risks and now I travel the Helvegr for my redemption. Perhaps one day we will meet again, free of our present constraints.

Ever yours,
Alvilda

Calder's tears fell freely. "I swear to you, Becka. I knew nothing of her plans. I would never have asked this of her."

"You didn't have to," Becka replied, her voice quiet. He might not have poisoned Vott and herself, but by his relentless ranting he'd persuaded his lover to do it on his behalf. Becka wanted to hate him for it, but he'd have to live knowing his lover had poisoned his beloved father and scorned sister. Calder was too pathetic to hate. "Your hate did it for you."

Calder was stricken into silence by her words.

"Are you up to riding with us?" Quinn asked Becka. "We must make every effort to find her before she passes beyond our reach."

"Ride?" She bit her lip. "I haven't ridden since I returned to the estate, but sure, I want to come. Wait, do you know where she went?"

Quinn gestured for her to lead the way. Caeda followed them out. She guessed Hamish would be busy with inventorying evidence. Brent, Luce, Shamus, Saige, and Lorelai ran ahead, already committed to the search.

The stables were out back next to the garage, not that Becka had been there in some time. As they walked down the hall, the fae gave them a wide berth. Calder tagged along, much to her confusion.

"May I accompany you?" Calder asked.

"No," Quinn replied.

"But she knows me," Calder replied. "I can make sure everything goes smoothly."

Quinn stopped short, stepping up close to Calder. "It's non-negotiable. We have a small window of time where we might be able to save her if we can find her before they do."

Calder's earnest expression filled with fear. "Whatever do you mean?"

"The phrase she used, 'travel the Helvegr,' is one we've seen associated with the Shadow-Dwellers and those who cross the road into the underworld to join them," Quinn replied.

At the mention of Shadow-Dwellers, Becka felt a shiver of fear trickle down her back. *That... can't be good.*

"So she's off to meet some mythic boogeymen? Then there's time!" Calder replied.

Becka rubbed her temples, so very, very tired of hearing the threat of very real Shadow-Dwellers minimized into mere boogeymen.

"I can assure you, if she does meet these very real persons, that she will not be fine. She will most likely be dead."

All color drained from Calder's face.

CHAPTER 29

FAE TERRITORIES - HOUSE APPLE

Quinn placed a hand on Calder's shoulder. "Leave this to the professionals. We'll do our best to bring Alvilda back alive."

Calder's jaw clenched and he shrugged off Quinn's effort to comfort him. "Becka's not an enforcer nor a guard, yet you are taking her."

Quinn smiled, but it lacked all warmth. "Becka's with us because I say she is."

"Fine." Calder took a few steps back, and they continued on their way. "I want to talk with Alvilda when you find her," he called after them.

"Of course you do," Quinn said under his breath.

Becka walked beside him, relieved Quinn had insisted on her presence. She felt safest by his side. "Do you think she's gotten far?"

He shook his head. "By all accounts she left on foot this morning."

Becka quieted as they walked down the great staircase. The house had been disrupted by the investigation, and

287

while fae had perfected the art of watching while looking otherwise preoccupied, none of those lingering in the common areas appeared to bother hiding their interest. Crowds had gathered, voices fell silent as they passed on the stairs and in the foyer. Becka saw fear in their eyes, hate directed at the enforcers, and a bit of distrust when they looked at her.

Nothing about this aided Becka's ongoing image problem. Perhaps Quinn was right. Perhaps some time away from the house would help? It would give her a chance to earn money for Rowan and prove she had control over her power at the same time. Then she could return as a proven asset.

Assuming I don't have any more accidents.

The walk to the stables felt like a bizarre fashion show with all eyes on them. The shifters were nowhere in sight, but they or someone must have alerted the stable hands to their arrival, because three horses were prepped and ready to go.

Caeda walked right up to the tallest horse, a dapple-gray stallion, and stepped up into the saddle with ease. Quinn walked up to a black mare and held out his hand to help Becka up.

"Is now the time for me to mention my general dislike of, or at least lack of familiarity with, horses?" Becka asked. What she wouldn't give for a bike or pair of good running shoes right about now. Too bad she'd thrown on sandals this morning; they wouldn't do her any favors now.

The stable hand who held the reins frowned.

"Would you prefer to stay here?" Quinn asked.

"No. I'd feel safer with you until all of this is over."

Becka poked her sandaled foot into the stirrup, grabbed the pommel, and dragged herself up into the saddle the hard way. She flung a leg around the horse's rump and would have went over if not for Quinn catching her.

"I didn't realize you had so little experience with horses," Quinn said.

Becka straightened herself in the saddle. "I haven't ridden since I've been back at House Rowan, and there aren't exactly horses in the city. Don't worry, I'll be fine now that I'm up." The stable hand handed her the reins, his expression pensive.

Quinn's look was equally dubious, but he mounted the chestnut horse next to her, and then led them down the road, away from the manor and stable.

"How far could she have gotten on foot?" Becka asked.

"Up to a dozen miles," Caeda answered. "Assuming she stayed on foot and went in a straight line."

"That's still well within House Rowan's lands," Becka replied. "Unless she went to the river and crossed over into House Birch's territory?"

"We'll know soon enough," Quinn replied.

A soft bark caught her attention. Becka looked to the right, where a pack of five very large gray wolves had emerged from the trees. They ran alongside for a few moments, before pulling ahead and loping down the winding road ahead of them.

"Looks like they found the scent," Caeda called out.

Becka hadn't seen a shifter in animal form since her fight with Woden after Tesse's funeral. As always, the sight did not disappoint. Their burly forms moved with grace and flow she associated with the predatory hunters. Were regular wolves this large? She guessed not, but wasn't about to ask now. She wasn't sure which one was which, but assumed the largest, with the brilliant white coat, was either Brent or Shamus.

Every so often a wolf would fall back and run next to them for a short while, only to yip and then run forward again at full tilt, rejoining their packmates. Becka had the impression the wolves were going slower than they'd like so the horses could keep up, and that these brief interactions were their way of saying, hurry!

Becka wasn't surprised when they passed Padrig's estate. Becka had expected the excuse Alvilda gave Yaeli, that she had something to pick up from his house, was a cover story.

They rode a few miles down the road at this pace with an occasional warble or yip from the wolves. Becka's lower back and thighs ached lightly from being unaccustomed to the movement of the horse under her, but she appreciated the feeling of the wind against her skin. They passed a pair of fae with a horse-drawn cart headed towards the manor with a load of fall squash in the back, their eyes large as they took in the wolves and enforcers. Becka waved but wasn't surprised when they didn't wave back.

Another mile down the winding road and the wolves split left, heading into the forest. They followed, the land sparsely treed so they were able to maintain a trot and keep up with the now loping wolves.

Becka's hips groaned at the added unevenness to the bounce in her mare's gait. The wind whipped her face, her hair getting into her eyes and mouth. How did anyone enjoy riding?

They passed rocky outcroppings and copses of aspen surrounding boulders. This land lay at the border between

Birch and Rowan, separated by a shallow river. What would have brought Alvilda all the way out here?

Rounding a boulder-filled outcropping, Becka spied the river, and beyond it, a small rustic cabin with a dirt road next to it. In minutes they reached the water's edge and stopped. The wolves yipped and howled at the river's edge, waiting for the enforcers to catch up. The largest instead growled deep in his throat. She was fairly sure that one was Brent.

Quinn stared at the wolves, who looked back and forth between the enforcers and the cabin. "They smell something. We need to cross and check it out."

"We don't know how deep the river is," Becka replied. "And that's House Birch territory. Crossing without sanction could cause problems."

Quinn did a double-take. "Look at you, caring about customs."

Caeda let out a short, harsh laugh. "We're enforcers first, Lady Becka. The shifters' concern is all I need to follow the investigation across this river. Besides, the water is slow and I'm a good swimmer." Caeda urged her mount into the water. His whinny conveyed doubt, and his eyes went wild when the wolves followed him into the water.

When Caeda had reached halfway without getting in past the stallion's flanks, Quinn turned to her.

"You can stay here if you want. I can get a wolf to stay with you."

"I don't want to be separated by the river," Becka replied, and urged her horse into the water. The mare was careful the first few steps, but then moved with the confidence of experience. Quinn followed and soon they were neck-and-neck in the clear water.

The large white wolf howled, urging them to move faster.

When they exited the river, Becka realized she'd lost a sandal in the crossing. If she spent more time around enforcers, she'd have to wear more practical footwear. At least the standard enforcer attire was sleek and practical, unlike the floofy House Rowan standard.

The conclusion hit her out of nowhere, but she thought about it as her horse followed Quinn's closer to the cabin. Working with the enforcers would also mean more research, more hunting down clues, more figuring out puzzles like the book now in her bag.

Plus, if her work was based out of the city, then she'd have an opportunity to circle back with Professor Traut regarding her internship. Surely, she could juggle the internship, part-time enforcer duties, and periodic jobs from the council?

Surprising herself, Becka realized she liked the idea. But how would she convince Maura not to fight it, especially the enforcer element?

"Do you see it?" Caeda said, pointing to the cabin. She dismounted a moment later and Quinn followed suit.

Becka pulled hard on the reins, stopping her mare. She studied the cabin. Nothing stood out as odd at first, but then she saw it too. She spied a pair of feet and legs, prone on the ground, the rest of the body hidden by the outline of the cabin. She dismounted, the ground cool under her one bare foot.

The wolves growled and paced, eager to investigate. Quinn and Caeda both pulled out stun guns, which Becka knew were standard issue, but had never seen them carry.

"Saige, will you stay here with Becka?" Quinn asked.

One of the smaller, black-furred wolves whined and shook its head, but then padded over to Becka and sat down.

"I want to come with you," Becka said, anxious at being left alone. Not that she didn't trust Saige, but Becka felt safer by his side.

"No," Quinn replied, his clipped tone brooking no argument. "You'll be safe here with Saige while we investigate."

Becka's hands balled into fists. Why had he brought her along just to make her watch from the sidelines?

Caeda nodded to Quinn, and then they headed off towards the cabin, the four wolves flanking their progress. Becka and Saige stood there with the horses, watching them go.

"This blows," Becka whispered.

Saige yawned in response, again shaking her head.

She watched them split into even teams, and one moved around the front of the cabin.

For a moment there was quiet, and then she heard a scuffle. Becka saw flashes of movement through the windows and around the corners of the cabin but couldn't make out any detail.

"How do you think it's going?" Becka asked the shifter.

Saige cocked her head and let out a high-pitched whine in return.

"Well, isn't this a lovely surprise?" came a low, rich feminine voice from behind her.

Becka's heart rate spiked as she whipped around to face a curvaceous fae-touched woman standing maybe twenty feet away from her. She wore fitted slacks and a bright, color-blocked blouse like a city dweller. Her hair was short and layered in a carefree manner. Her smoky-eye makeup and shock-red lips matched her self-assured stance. The flash in her amber-toned eyes held no warmth.

Saige stood at her side, hackles raised, teeth bared, and snout wrinkled. The woman didn't appear at all frightened of the shifter, as her eyes didn't leave Becka despite the wolf's warning.

How did the fae sneak up on us? Especially Saige?

She knew she should be afraid, but curiosity got the best of her. "You didn't expect us to come after Alvilda?"

The sounds of fighting continued behind her. How many were there in total? Becka didn't dare take her eyes off of the woman in front of her to check how things looked at the cabin.

The fae took a step closer, and Saige growled and snapped, moving between the two of them. Becka took off her gloves, shoving them into her pocket.

"Oh, I did. It's why I waited for the enforcers to arrive. But I never expected them to bring *you* along, but I'm pleased we have this opportunity to meet, face to face, as they say."

She'd hoped I would be here?

Terror gripped her stomach at the woman's blatant confidence despite the shifters and enforcers closing in. How had she appeared out of thin air, casting no shadow despite the sunny day? Although this fae looked nothing like Woden, Becka was sure of one thing.

She stumbled a step backwards. "You're a Shadow-Dweller!" And by the ongoing sounds of the fighting nearby, she hadn't come alone.

The fae raised her hands with flourish and gave a half bow. "I'd heard you were clever... although I suppose not quite clever enough, because here you are."

The woman took a step towards her, and Saige snapped again, yet the fae continued to inch closer. Becka's head ached, her telltale that fae magic was nearby. What did this fae have up her sleeve?

Waiting for an opportunity to strike, Becka brought her focus to her hands, extending the reach of her Null gift as far as she could.

"The others will be back soon, and I'm not about to go down without a fight," Becka replied, hands up defensively in front of her. If the Shadow-Dweller attacked, she'd be ready. "Who are you, and why are you meeting Alvilda?"

"I'm not here to fight you, Becka." She inched forward. "You can call me Mimir, and I'm here to exact payment due from Alvilda."

Becka recognized the name from fae myth. "You're named after the ancient Keeper of Knowledge?"

Mimir smiled, her blood-red lip curling up in a macabre mask of joy. "Something like that."

Becka noticed the woods behind her were silent. "The fight's over. They'll be coming back here to check on me."

No doubt Saige had noticed too, as she let out a low, keening sound, but remained in front of Becka, blocking Mimir.

Mimir laughed in a carefree manner, taking another step forward. "I doubt that."

Why are they silent?

Panic flooded her veins.

This isn't how things were supposed to go.

"Are there more Shadow-Dwellers back there?" Becka asked. She kept trying to move around Saige, but the wolf continued to block her path to Mimir. "Dammit, Saige!" she whispered.

At this point, Mimir stood a mere six to seven feet away. Could Becka reach Mimir and Null her powers before the Shadow-Dweller had a chance to react?

"No. It's just me here today," Mimir replied, her smile widening.

Becka breathed a sigh of relief, but then her heart skipped a beat. "Wait, what? Then who are they fighting?"

Mimir scrunched her nose and winked, holding her hand over her chest in a faux-demure manner. "Me!"

Try as she might, Becka's mind couldn't wrap around Mimir's puzzle. Frustrated and fueled by fear, Becka launched at Mimir, hands going for her throat. Saige was right beside her, jaws snapping.

Instead of making contact, Becka and Saige fell forward and through Mimir's apparition which dissipated on contact. Both remained on their feet, but it took Becka a few steps to catch herself.

What had just happened? Becka scanned the forest around them. Mimir was gone! She'd been speaking to an illusion! That's why Mimir had no shadow!

Fear, which had fueled her attack on Mimir's apparition, now urged her towards the cabin. Becka took off at a run, despite the pain in her one bare foot. Saige ran alongside, quickly outpacing her.

Becka was utterly unprepared for the sight which greeted her when she reached the back of the cabin.

CHAPTER 30

Blood was everywhere.

The bodies of shifters and enforcers sprawled out on the scene before her. In front of the cabin was a lovely set of lounge chairs next to an overturned bistro table. Underneath the table Becka spied Caeda's body, facedown and unmoving on the ground. Brent's large white wolf form slumped across the stairs leading up into the cabin, bright red stains spattering across his fur.

Quinn! He lay lifeless, predictably in the middle of the fray, with two of the wolves laid out next to him. Was the blood from the wolves? From Alvilda? Becka couldn't tell if those on the ground were dead or unconscious. Her heart ached to see them all helpless, faces pale as death.

I can't tell the other wolves apart. And where is the fifth wolf?

The only one moving was Mimir, who dragged Alvilda's lax, bloody body towards the open door of a black car. Mimir's clothes had a little dirt on them and her hair was disheveled, but she didn't appear to have gone through the same battle everyone else here had.

The hair on the back of Becka's neck raised. This Shadow-Dweller had incapacitated all of them while barely breaking a sweat.

Saige, who had stopped short alongside Becka as she mentally digested the scene, surged forward with a growl, teeth bared for Mimir's throat. Mid-leap, Saige's body froze and then crumpled to the ground.

"No!" screamed Becka. She rushed towards Mimir, hands up and ready to attack. A headache slammed into her as she crossed some sort of boundary. Unlike Saige, she wasn't knocked out, but the pain in her head was near crippling.

Mimir laughed a mirthless laugh, raked a hand through her hair and then tucked it behind her pointy ear. "At least my magic slowed you down." She paused to pull Alvilda another few feet, a wide trail of blood left in her wake. "I knew better than to think you'd be vulnerable. But Becka, I'd advise you to stop right where you are and let me go in peace."

Becka staggered forward. "No!" she screamed again. "You will drop Alvilda and break this spell that does... whatever it is you're doing to everyone, right now!"

"I have no intention of stopping."

"Why are you taking Alvilda?" Fear gripped Becka, and she glanced to Quinn hoping to see motion, but there was none. Had Mimir already killed them all? But if so, why was she taking Alvilda with her? "What's she to you?"

"Oh, you know. She took a vow. She failed me. I'm calling in her debt. Same old, same old." Her heel caught on a rock and, unbalanced, she momentarily lost her grip on Alvilda's legs. Sighing, Mimir righted herself and resumed her gruesome task.

"*You* wanted her to poison me?"

"Oh, definitely!" Mimir replied with a quick nod and broad smile.

Becka couldn't understand Mimir's cheery response, and it filled her with deepening dread. "But... that doesn't make any sense. Don't the Shadow-Dwellers want to consume my power? How is that supposed to work if I'm dead?"

"According to our prophecies, if you are who we think you are, then there's only one way to kill you. And it's not by poison."

She's insane...

Becka rubbed her aching temples. "I didn't drink enough poison to kill me, *that's* why I'm not dead! Your prophecies are a bag of bunk!"

Mimir stopped dragging Alvilda and met her gaze. "No, Becka. My attempt failed, just as I thought it would. The prophecy has spoken."

"Argh!"

Mimir resumed dragging Alvilda's body to the car.

Becka followed her, edging closer and watching for an opening to step in and use her powers on Mimir while she was distracted, but the woman kept an eye on her.

"Stop! You can't take her. Break the spell on my friends, now, or I will hurt you!"

Mimir reached the vehicle and dropped Alvilda's legs, her focus singular. "As I see it, you have two options." Mimir moved to Alvilda's head and scooped her up under the shoulders, dragging her partway into the back seat. Having walked through the blood trail, Mimir's heels tracked obscene smears with every step. "And you're going to pick option number two."

Becka continued to fight through the pain in her head and walk towards Mimir, barely able to think straight.

How is Mimir so physically strong? Is it more magic? Some acquired powers from feeding on her victims?

"One," Mimir continued. "You come at me now, knowing I have resources at my disposal you probably cannot comprehend. You might take me down, but chances are I'm leaving with Alvilda regardless."

"Your magic has no power over me," Becka replied, confident her Null gift would shield her. *Unless the Shadow-Dweller knows something I don't?* "I won't let you take her."

Mimir, having loaded Alvilda's head, shoulders, and part of her torso into the car, moved around, picked up her knees, and shoved her body in further. "I appreciate your dedication, but the strain in your voice says otherwise. If you come after me now, you'll never be able to save all of them." Mimir gestured to those on the ground. "Option two, which I suggest you take, is allowing me to leave and then attempting to save your friends."

Her heart leapt in her chest. "They're still alive?"

"For now..." With one last heave, Mimir pushed Alvilda into the car. She stood up and stretched her back, which let out an audible pop followed by her satisfied sigh. She slammed the car door shut and squared her shoulders towards Becka. "But they won't be for long."

She could try and save Alvilda or save the others. Stomach churning with guilt, Becka realized part of her longed for the first option because she wanted to fight Mimir now and not let her get away, not because she cared about saving Alvilda.

But Quinn... Saige... Brent... Shamus... Lorelai... Luce!

"How do I save them?" Becka asked, reining in her anger.

Mimir smiled, opened the front door of the car, and then slid into her seat, closing the door and leaning out the window. "Break the spell. Something which should be a cinch for your unique gift. Just don't dawdle!"

Becka nodded and walked to Quinn, dropping down to sit next to him. She felt around him, searching for the layers of magic Mimir claimed to have encircled him with.

"Oh, and Becka?" Mimir called, her voice a playful singsong tone, like a child's. Becka paused and looked up at Mimir. "Find me."

With those final words and a smirk, Mimir's car rushed off down the road towards House Birch territory. Immediately the throbbing between her temples lessened, like a weight had been lifted from her shoulders.

Once again, Becka focused on Quinn, his body slack and lifeless. She focused her thoughts, feeling the space around him for the telltale threads of magic. There! Around his chest there was this tangle of energy she knew was new and malignant. A single thought and swipe of her fingers disintegrated the magic, and Quinn sucked in a deep, needed breath of fresh air.

Wiping tears from her cheeks, Becka crawled to the pair of wolves lying next to Quinn. She trusted Shamus's claim that her Null magic couldn't harm a shifter's innate power, but this incident with Mimir and the jasmine flowers Ingrid had blossomed in his hair proved shifters weren't immune to fae magic. Moments later, she'd broken through the magic encircling the shifter pair and they too were once again breathing normally, although their breath sounds were haggard.

Quinn coughed and groaned. Becka wanted to go to his side, but instead she rushed over to Caeda, pulling the bistro table off of her supine form. Bruises covered her exposed skin, and her right leg was bent at an unnatural angle. Remembering her mishap with Hanna, Becka faltered. What if she misjudged her magic and broke Caeda's gift?

Caeda needed healers, pronto!

"Quinn! Wake up and call for backup. We need healers. And Hamish. And whoever else you can get!" she yelled in his direction.

Ever so gingerly, Becka leaned over Caeda, seeking out the same tangled net of magic around her chest. She Nulled the magic, thread by thread, until Caeda gasped in a breath. With her inhalation, pain distorted Caeda's face and a high-pitched keening sound issued from her throat.

"Hang in there," Becka whispered. She wanted to touch Caeda with reassurance, but was afraid to do so with her bare hands.

Had Quinn called for backup yet? Was he able to, was a better question. "Quinn!" she yelled again, panic fraying the edge of her focus, "I need you to rally and make that call. If I stop, they could die!"

"I'm calling," he mumbled back at her.

Relief surged through her. She could do this!

Next, she ran to Brent on the stairs nearby. She slipped on the blood painting the steps and landed hard on him.

"Shit," she ground out through her clenched jaw.

He'd have to forgive her for his future bruises. Trying to

shrug off her anxiety, Becka deftly raked her hands through the web of magic encasing Brent's chest. It was thicker, deeper than the others, and for some reason she knew he'd attacked first or otherwise borne the brunt of the attack. Moments later he sucked in air, followed by a halfhearted yip on the exhale.

She patted his fur. "Work it out, buddy."

"But they won't be for long..."

Mimir's words echoed in her mind. She had to hurry. Who else was left?

Saige!

Becka stumbled to her feet and ran over to Saige, who had fallen near Mimir's vehicle. She slid to the ground, feeling the gravel cutting into the sole of her bare foot. She worked her Nulling magic, and in seconds Saige heaved in a deep breath, shook her head and sat up, and then worked herself up onto her paws.

Saige nuzzled her face, and Becka threw her arms around her friend for a short, rough hug. Saige didn't appear as heavily affected as the rest, but then she hadn't been under the influence of the magic as long, either.

When Becka pulled away, Quinn was sitting upright, his pallor gray. He looked around, disoriented, as if he wasn't quite sure what had happened.

"Did I get everyone?" Becka asked. Quinn and Saige looked around. Caeda lay flat on her back, while Brent and the other wolves were up and in sitting positions.

"Luce?" Quinn asked. "She got thrown into the trees at the start of the fight." He pointed to the area beyond Caeda and Brent, where Becka knew she hadn't yet checked.

Becka's heart sank into her stomach. She leapt to her feet, Saige at her side, and sprinted towards the trees.

Please let me not be too late.

Saige found Luce first, her nose guiding them to a nearby copse of trees surrounded by juniper. Pushing back the sticky, prickly branches, Becka went right to work, ripping her way through the bundle of magical threads wrapped around Luce's chest. In seconds, they were gone.

But Luce didn't inhale.

"Luce!" Becka screamed at her, compressing the wolf's chest in an attempt to make her breathe.

Saige whined and nosed at Luce's fur. Quinn and the other wolves had risen and came to watch, all waiting for Luce to come to.

Seconds passed. Then minutes. Becka couldn't see through her tears. Saige lay down, nestling herself against Luce's body, and let out a high-pitched, keening howl.

Becka sat back on her heels and then stood. She'd saved most of them from Mimir's magic, yet today felt like a loss. They hadn't been able to bring Alvilda home, and now Luce would never go home again either. She backed off, giving the wolves space to grieve their packmate.

Quinn had done the same and was squatting next to Caeda. Becka moved to join him. Caeda's pallor had returned. He fished a packet out of his jacket and withdrew a prefilled syringe, which he injected into her broken leg. After a few seconds, her eyelids grew heavy.

Quinn stood and moved close to Becka. "At least she's resting comfortably now. Help should be here shortly. Enforcers are sending in an airlift."

"Do you think they can trace the car?" Becka asked.

"I gave them details and they're making an effort, but I'm not holding out hope. That road leads through heavy forest and the day's waning on us. She could hide and wait us out, switch transport, or just outrun us. The Shadow-Dwellers have remained hidden this long for a reason. I bet she's got any number of tricks up her sleeve."

"I can't believe how powerful she was," Becka replied, a heavy sigh escaping her lips. "What magic was that, anyway?"

"I think it was the binding magic of House Ivy. I didn't feel like I could breathe, move, and it even seemed my heart was moving slower." Quinn grabbed her by the shoulders and looked her in the eye. "You did well against a more skilled opponent."

She cast her gaze over to where the shifters still surrounded Luce. "Not well enough."

"That's on me. I should have anticipated that Alvilda could have been going to meet someone."

Becka shook her head. "We discounted Shadow-Dwellers from this a while ago. You couldn't have foreseen it."

He dropped his arms. "You're right, but we'll figure out what happened here."

Quinn walked straight to the cabin and through the open door with Becka close on his heels. It was a small, one-room affair with a wood stove, sink, bed, and kitchen table.

"Oh my gods," Becka whispered.

Blood covered the wooden table, oozing in rivers onto the floor below. It was still fresh enough to be dripping.

Brent's white form hovered in the doorway behind them.

"Do we know the blood is Alvilda's?" Becka asked.

The white wolf yipped. Quinn nodded, so Becka assumed that was a yes.

"Why would Alvilda have come here?" Quinn asked.

"Mimir said Alvilda had broken her oath," Becka replied.

"Mimir?" Quinn replied, digesting her words. "You spoke with her?"

Becka nodded. "Alvilda was supposed to poison me and failed. Although according to Mimir, Alvilda failed due to some sham prophecy and she chose to punish her for it anyway."

"Prophecy?" he asked. "You'll have to fill me in after we get Caeda patched up. No doubt they'd met here before."

Becka looked around the small space, noticing a shelf behind the bench on the far wall holding a few well-worn books. She walked over to it, taking care to avoid stepping her bare foot into the blood on the floor. Reaching out to the books, Becka felt the pressure of a headache threatening at the base of her skull.

"This is something," Becka said, picking up one book, her gloves and her mental control shielding her and the book from each other. Flipping through the pages, she realized they were journals written in a foreign language she didn't recognize. Becka held the book out to Quinn. "Look, it's the same script as the Shadow-Dweller book you gave me."

Quinn's expression turned grim. "Which we still can't decipher."

"Why would Mimir have left this here?" Becka wondered aloud. Was this like the book Quinn had given her? Did it also have the ability to communicate underneath these odd glyphs?

"Who knows?" Quinn replied. "This place is far enough

away from House Birch's main holdings to be of little consequence, and likely let them work without interruption. I
wonder how Alvilda met Mimir, how they decided to meet at
this place."

"She must have known of this cabin, as she grew up
around Padrig's farm. As she got older, she started attending
parties and events, and then she's been hanging off Calder's
arm for the past year or so."

"If you wanted to get close to those running House
Rowan, Alvilda was the perfect target," Quinn said, running
a hand through his hair. "I bet she was being manipulated by
Mimir even before Tesse's death. It couldn't have just been
Lagan, Woden, as he's dead. Now Alvilda's dead too."

Becka looked around the room. "We don't know she's
dead." Quinn stared at her like she'd lost her wits, and Brent's
furry head was cocked to the side. "Okay, this *is* a lot of blood.
So mostly dead? But why take her body? Who needs a dead
fae?"

"Killers only hide bodies to hide clues."

A revelation hit Becka hard. "Perhaps her body was
covered in glyphs, like Tesse's was?"

Quinn shrugged. "We can't know now."

Stymied, she needed to act. She had to, or the horror of
this day would drive her to darkness. "What do we do?"
Becka asked.

Quinn blinked, a ghost of a smile crossing his face, which
was otherwise painted with frustration and grief. "We?"

"Yes, what do we do with this investigation?" she asked,
clarifying.

"We..." Quinn whipped out his tablet and began taking
pictures. "Catalog the evidence."

Becka picked up the rest of the books. "Can I keep these?"

Quinn's brow furrowed. "Sure, but let me take some pictures of them first." His phone rang. "I need to grab this." He stepped outside.

Becka stowed the new books in her bag and took one last look around the cabin, only to note what looked like blood smeared across the kitchen table. She drew closer and the words came into sharp focus.

FIND ME

A shiver ran down her spine. Mimir had left her those words, perhaps as a taunt? Perhaps as a threat? On a whim, she pulled the three new books and the original one out of her backpack. She opened them, one at a time, and flipped through the pages.

A vice-like pain gripped her heart. The words FIND ME were repeated, page after page, in all four of the books. Tears streamed down her cheeks yet again, but this time she didn't wipe them away.

Becka returned the books to her bag. She shook her head, mopped the tears away on her sleeve, and then walked over to the table. She wiped the bloody words away into one giant smear. Becka used a drapery in the kitchen that was mostly clean to wipe her hand off.

What was she hoping to accomplish by destroying evidence? Guilt washed over her, followed by a wave of confusion. Becka didn't fully understand why she'd done it, just that it had needed doing. Becka suspected the message, which Mimir had also spoken to her directly, was for her and her alone. She didn't want anyone else getting caught up in the Shadow-Dwellers' obsessive interest in her. Becka didn't want there to be more Votts or Luces hurt in the crossfire.

She suspected the new book of glyphs was a clue to finding Mimir. She was familiar enough with how the one Quinn had given her worked and was already starting to develop a plan to study them further.

She turned and headed outside, again taking care not to step in the blood. She walked up to Quinn as he finished up his call.

The wolves remained circled around Luce's quiet form, but their ears and eyes made it clear they were on high alert.

"What do we do now?" Becka asked.

"The chief is sending out a team to process the site and a crew to transport Caeda and Luce. After they get here, we should head back to the manor." His expression was dark and stormy.

"What are you worried about?" she asked.

He looked at her, and Becka had the impression he was choosing his words carefully. "I'm surprised we have another Shadow-Dweller after you just months after Woden's death."

"Woden said they had a network."

"Yes, but I now suspect there are more of them than we'd estimated."

Becka let that sink into her consciousness, the added weight of the books in her backpack especially heavy at this moment.

"Mimir took Alvilda, presumably so we wouldn't see her body, but then why leave the books?" she asked.

He nodded. "Exactly. They would know we'd identify that script as used by Shadow-Dwellers."

Tightness gripped her chest. "They want me to know they're right next door. Waiting for me."

He shook his head. "I don't know. But what do I know? You're definitely not safe at House Rowan. And maybe not anywhere."

FAE TERRITORIES - HOUSE ROWAN

Becka paced the length of the council chambers, for once alone in the opulent room. She crossed to the windows and opened a pane, breathing deep the fresh air drawn on the crisp fall evening breeze.

The door opened behind her, and Becka glanced back to see Maura close the door behind herself. As glad as she was for this private audience, her stomach was doing flip-flops. The fist clenched around her chest hadn't abated since earlier in the day when she'd realized the poisoning had been directed by a Shadow-Dweller.

"How are you holding up?" Maura asked, coming to stand near Becka.

She took a moment to consider how to put her thoughts into words, but she appreciated Maura starting the conversation by showing concern. "It's been a rough day at the end of a series of rough days," Becka replied.

Maura appeared to take her measure. "Would you like to have a seat?"

"I'm too on edge."

Maura took her gloved hand in her own and walked her over to the table. "All the more reason to sit. No one will interrupt us, I made sure of it."

Becka relented, sitting in her chair, but then turning it to face Maura's.

"Not even Calder?"

Maura rolled her eyes. "He wouldn't let off his ranting and wild accusations towards the enforcers and shifters over losing Alvilda. I sent him on a walk to work out his anger."

Becka wrung her hands. "It would have been nice if he'd been reasonable, but I can't say I'm surprised."

Maura shrugged. "No worries. I have thick skin, and he couldn't say no, so off he went."

"Have you heard from House Birch yet? I'm worried we may have upset them."

Maura nodded. "We've had runners going back and forth all afternoon. They aren't upset at Rowan because enforcers crossed into their territory without warning, but they aren't too happy to hear that someone killed a shifter on their lands, home to the House of Healing."

"The irony..."

"I don't think it's lost on them. They claim the Shadow-Dweller can't be hiding within their territory, that all fae are accounted for."

"The enforcers' investigation will confirm or deny that fact." Becka supposed she should be grateful they weren't accusing them of making up boogeymen, but was exhausted by the immediate denial, nonetheless.

"As you say," Maura replied. "But I had the impression you have other things to speak of?"

"I do," Becka replied, steeling herself. "My civic duty letter arrived."

Maura's brows raised. "That was fast, but certainly a good next step. It'll give you the opportunity for a change of pace to distract you from all of this mess. Who've you been placed with?"

A breath hung in the air between them.

"As a consultant to the enforcers," Becka replied, hearing the trepidation in her tone.

Maura blinked. "We can protest. The last thing you need is to be exposed to more traumatizing events like you saw today!"

Becka held up a hand, and Maura frowned. "I don't think Rowan should protest."

A silence settled between them as Maura digested her statement. "Why would you want to work with them?"

Becka didn't want to offend her mother, but now, of all times, she needed to stay strong and be direct. "You must realize I'm not safe here. Alvilda might have delivered the poison, but the Shadow-Dwellers were behind the attacks."

"But if you work with them in the city, it can't be any safer. Here we have guards. Magical defenses. Measures we can take," Maura replied, her expression concerned but her tone terse.

"Sure, but more requests will come in for my civic service and I could get pulled around fae and human locations alike. A longer-term assignment will surround me with enforcers. I can't take fae guards with me everywhere, but I can be side-by-side with enforcers for the foreseeable future. It's a much safer option until the Shadow-Dweller threat is managed."

Maura sat back in her chair. "What if your next

requested assignment sends you right into the lion's den?" She pursed her lips. "But I understand you want to take on the Shadow-Dwellers head-on, and there will be risk no matter the assignment. At least we assume the Enforcers would be able to protect you."

Becka let out a nervous laugh. "I never thought I'd hear you say something nice about them."

Maura sighed. "That may be the first and last time. But they do have their uses and they didn't try and overstep during the interrogations, which was a pleasant surprise."

Encouraged by her mother's positive shift towards the enforcers, Becka pressed forward. "I'll also have access to portable scanners for checking my food, and self-defense training."

Maura tapped her fingers on the table. "It sounds like you've had time to think this through."

Becka shook her head. "I just got the letter at lunch today."

"I'm surprised Quinn didn't give you any warning," Maura said, eyes narrowed.

"Oh, he did. First thing this morning. If you heard me yelling earlier, that would have been why."

Maura laughed. "Busy day."

It felt good not only to laugh with her mother, but also that they were seeing eye-to-eye. "Yeah, busy day."

"Look," Maura said, leaning forward, an elbow on the table. "You're bound by law to do civil service; we don't have a way around it. I can't complain if you're surrounded by armed enforcers, especially if the alternative of spending time at other houses is too dangerous right now. If this is where you want to be, then I won't fight it."

"Thank you, Maura," Becka replied, relieved beyond words to have her consent. The last thing she'd wanted was to have a new argument between them.

Maura raised a finger in warning, as if Becka needed a lecture. "You need to be aware this assignment won't solve your image management problem."

"Wait, what?" Becka said, feeling like she'd taken a blow to the gut.

"The incident with Hanna goes well beyond House Hawthorne." Maura stood, pacing the length of the table. "Hawthorne is claiming you're unfit and a danger to others, and other houses are moving to support them."

Her anxiety wouldn't allow her to sit still, so Becka stood and walked back to the open window. She couldn't blame Hawthorne for being upset over Hanna's accident, but what would Becka do if they wouldn't relent on their mission against her?

"Then perhaps after I've worked with the enforcers for a while, and they can state I've been in control of my gift, that would counter Hawthorne's claim."

"Assuming all goes well," Maura replied. "Yes, that would certainly help."

"Yeah, assuming." The tightness in her chest warred with the sinking sensation in her gut. *No pressure, Becka, just don't screw up.*

"Additionally," Maura continued coming to stand next to her, "you need to use this opportunity to better understand fae society and your place in the world, which being in the high-profile position of consulting to the enforcers should more than adequately provide you. In fact, I would bet you're in for a rude but necessary awakening."

"Society?" Becka stammered.

"I don't blame you at all, but we're in a delicate position. Outcasts are never brought back into the fold, Becka. You're the first, and not surprisingly, due to your ordeal you lack a degree of empathy for your own kind. So why would you care about fae culture or society? Why would you care to dress and present yourself according to your station? None of this mattered to you for eight years. But you took on other challenges and, by all accounts, performed admirably before the carpet was pulled out from under your feet."

"I never knew you were paying attention during my time away," Becka replied, touched and surprised at Maura's words. "Thank you for understanding my perspective."

Maura shook her head. "It doesn't matter that *I* understand. *You* need to understand. For other fae to accept you and take you seriously, you must treat them as peers worthy of respect. Right now, you're a wild card who may well be a danger to them."

Becka rubbed her temples. "I'm aware things are in a precarious position, especially with House Hawthorne."

"I have the feeling serving with the enforcers is just the challenge you need right now."

"As long as I don't have another incident with my gift." Saying the words aloud sent a shiver down Becka's spine. *Just don't screw up again or it'll be bad for the entire house!*

"I knew you'd understand if I was blunt about your situation." Maura put out a hand and squeezed her arm gently through her sleeve. "You have my blessing to work with the enforcers."

Becka stood, gaping, trying to process what was happening at this moment.

Maura turned and walked toward the door, talking as she went. "Oh, I'll send up the porters to help you pack and I'll send word to your Aunt Lydia. Of course you'll return home for holidays and events, but you might as well get started ticking down the years towards your civil service quota." Maura opened the door and paused. "Safe travels, dear."

Becka blew out a long breath. "I got what I hoped for," Becka said to the now-empty room. "And I don't even know how to feel about it."

DENVER - MIDWEST REGION

Becka collapsed against her bed, surrounded by suitcases and boxes of things she couldn't begin to dig her way out of. She closed her eyes and breathed deep, recognizing the smells, the sounds, the feel of home.

Oriani jumped up onto the bed next to her and mewed a plaintive cry. She rolled over and scratched him behind the ears.

"Sorry, little fella. This might be home to me, but it's got to feel pretty crazy to you."

But whoa, does it feel good to be back at the townhome! She didn't have other fae underfoot constantly or listening to everything that came out of her mouth. She'd get some alone time again, too!

There was a soft knock on her bedroom door.

"Come in!" Becka called.

The door swung open, her Aunt Lydia leaning on the door frame.

"How are you doing?"

"I don't even know how I feel. Did I really just arrive

here under the cover of darkness this morning?" Becka glanced out the window. It was already dusk out and she'd been resting in her room all day, luxuriating in the solitude.

"It was more like under the semi-cover of dawn, but yeah. Be glad I didn't rent out your room while you've been gone."

"Doesn't this townhome belong to House Alder?"

"Yeah, yeah, it's a figure of speech. How's the cat managing?" Oriani pranced to the end of the bed and mewled in Lydia's general direction. She held out her hand and he headbutted it, displaying no shame in his hunt for attention. "He seems okay."

"Yeah, he's just gonna whine for a while, but I didn't want to leave him at House Rowan. Every time I scratch his little chin, I think of Tesse."

"Aw, that's sweet. I can't blame you for keeping him with you." Lydia looked her over and cocked her head to the side. "How's the unpacking going?"

"I pulled out my pj's for tonight, but I haven't gotten any further yet." She could have explained about the hours she'd spent pouring over the Shadow-Dweller books but decided against it. Becka didn't want to pull Lydia into that world.

"I wouldn't worry about it. Hey, you busy?"

"Only sort of," Becka replied. Those books weren't going anywhere, and besides, she'd missed hanging out with Lydia.

"Then let me tempt you with bingeing episodes of the latest season of *Baking Wars*. I hear the hosts actually swear once this season and the bakers all walked out in protest over the incivility."

"No!" Becka shouted. What could have happened to drive the hosts to swearing? "Oh my gods I've missed that show! It's the best!"

"Yes! Or, there's also new episodes of that old-timey human show where they reenact how royalty used to live in an old manor house?"

"Hmm, no. As in, never again am I watching that tripe." If Becka wanted to see an old manor house, she'd go back to House Rowan to visit.

"But you used to love it."

"You know, that was before I had to live day in and day out in proper, cultured fae fashion. It's only entertaining when it's on television."

Lydia wobbled her head back and forth. "So, it's the baking show, then?"

Becka nodded. "But only if you have Oreos."

"What do you think I emergency shopped for at two a.m. this morning after Queen Maura's phone call?"

Becka laughed. "Be careful, she might just show up here someday."

"Let's hope not." Lydia held out her hand, and after a pause, Becka took it, and Lydia hauled her up off of the bed.

"I forget, are we allowed to binge-watch before dark?"

"Girl, you have been gone far too long if you can't remember the house rules."

Becka laughed along with Lydia, who seemed to know just how to break her out of her funk. She curled up under her favorite fuzzy pink blanket, ate Oreos, and laughed at episode after episode of great bakes that invariably went horribly, awfully wrong.

At eight o'clock, there was a knock at the door.

Lydia set aside her tin of chocolate sandwich cookies and paused the show.

"Are you expecting someone?" Becka asked.

"No, but you are," Lydia replied, sashaying her way to the front door.

"My lady, I'm afraid you must be mistaken." Becka stuffed another Oreo into her mouth. "Gods, how I missed this creamy, crunchy, chocolatey goodness!" Becka mumbled around the cookie.

There was a second knock just as Lydia got to the door. "Hold up, I'm here."

She opened the door while Becka watched from the couch. Somehow she managed to stuff a fresh Oreo into her mouth at the moment Quinn walked through the front door.

"Hey," she said around a mouthful of cookie, smiling reflexively at his arrival. She'd expected him to check in on her, but she hadn't even had a full day back to herself to enjoy. Nonetheless, it was good to see him.

"Good evening," he said, dropping a large duffel bag to the floor.

"Good evening," Lydia replied, and then closed the door and returned to her perch on the couch.

Quinn walked up behind the couch, taking in the empty Oreo tins and fluffy bunny slippers. "Are you busy?"

"Yeah, sorry, I'm catching up with this season's *Baking Wars*. It's macaron week."

"Macaroon?"

"No, macaron. Super important. Perhaps let's catch up on the case some other time?" Becka raised another cookie to her lips. Quinn raised an eyebrow at her, so she bit into the cookie extra slow.

He shook his head. "Where's the room?" he asked Lydia.

"First floor, down the hall and all the way to the back." Lydia pointed, helpful as always.

Becka ate another cookie, watching him closely.

"Cool, thanks." He grabbed his bag and walked down the hall out of sight.

Becka turned to Lydia. "What's going on?" she asked, muffled by the cookie in her mouth.

"He's renting one of the guest bedrooms," Lydia replied. "And he's not the only one."

"What?" Becka shot to her feet. "Since when do you actually rent out rooms?"

"Since Duke Vott ordered it. Or it might have been Chief Elowen. Maybe both." Lydia shrugged.

Becka sucked in a breath around another cookie, feeling her heart rate spiking. *Oh my... he's going to be living here?*

"He gonna be a problem?" Lydia asked, brow arched.

"Yeah, he's trouble." The temptation of not just working with Quinn, but also living with him day in, day out?

Lydia pinned her with her glare-stare. "You need me to handle it?"

Who is this woman, and what is she planning?

"No, no." Becka waved her off. "He's my trouble."

Lydia's tense stare softened, and she raised a curious brow as a smile tugged at her lips. "*Your* trouble?"

"I mean, I've got it."

The doorbell rang again.

"Oh, for Pete's sake!" Becka exclaimed, then moved to open the door.

Saige, suitcase in hand, stood on her stoop. "Fair evening, Becka." She walked in, glancing around the space. "Room's at the end of the hall?" she asked Lydia.

"On the right," Lydia called back.

Saige turned to Becka and placed a hand on her shoulder.

"I'm here to help you hunt down Luce's killer. My cub-mate died being true to her own skin, and I'm here to be true to mine."

Becka's eyes teared up. "I never said..."

"You didn't have to," Saige interrupted her. "I'm going to unpack." She gave Becka a quick squeeze and then headed off down the hall.

Becka wiped her hands free of crumbs, took a deep breath to dispel the sudden heaviness in her heart, and stomped down the hall. When she reached the first guest room, she stepped in.

Quinn stood unloading clothes into the dresser. "How's the reentry been so far?"

"It's been a quiet day, until now. I was liking the quiet."

He let that pass without comment. "I see Saige has arrived."

"Did you two coordinate this invasion?"

He shrugged and then looked at her side-eyed. "You're upset I'm here?"

She shrugged back. "I guess I thought when they sent me back to Lydia's I'd have a few days of normalcy before jumping into working for the enforcers."

Quinn stopped what he was doing, turned, and crossed the room to her. Becka backed up, running into the wall. Quinn stopped just as their bodies touched.

"Even if Saige and I weren't here, do you think that would be possible?" he asked.

Between the sugar on her lips and the smell of his skin, she couldn't remember what she thought. "That what was possible?"

His lips hitched a grin. "Normalcy." When she didn't

answer, he continued. "Do you think after you've become who you are now that things could ever go back to how they were?"

Becka sighed. "No. I'll always have the Null gift and I'm heir to House Rowan unless they kick me out again. But I can want what I want."

He leaned in and took a deep breath. "There's what we want, and then what life throws at us."

"Uh huh," she answered.

"So, I'll ask again. Is me being here a problem? Because if it is, I can get another room somewhere nearby."

"You can stay," Becka replied. "I know it's safer and smarter all around. But you have to get your own Oreos."

He laughed. "Noted. Have you looked at those journals yet?"

Becka nodded, but then pressed a finger across his lips. "I know there's a mountain out there waiting for me, but can you just give me tonight to do something mindless so I can stop worrying about who will try to kill me next?"

Sadness flitted across his expression, but was soon replaced by a heat burning deep in his amber eyes. "I can think of a few mindless activities to pass the time."

Her lips grazed against his cheek, the heat between them electric. "I'm confident you can," she whispered. Becka slipped sideways out from underneath him and backed out of the doorway into the hall. "But for tonight, it's all about *Baking Wars*."

THE END

Thank you so much for reading Poisoned Shadow! It would mean a lot to me if you could leave a review. A single line or two makes a big difference for other people when deciding if a book is a good fit for them.

The next book in the series, Shadow Underground, is available for preorder now.

Unwilling to wait until the Shadow-Dwellers attack next, Becka and Quinn take the fight to them. But can Becka save her friends, Quinn, and herself from Mimir's hunger for power? Turn the page to learn what fate has in store for Becka and Quinn.

Read on for an exclusive excerpt from the next book in the series:

Shadow Underground

They say you can never go home again, especially when an all-powerful psycho is lying in wait to steal your magic.

I'm not the same Becka Rowan who left the city. I'm back with new powers, a new job, new roommates, and a list of dead fae that's getting longer by the hour

That last part sucks.

Still, I'm excited about my future, especially now that I have Quinn by my side as my live-in bodyguard? Boyfriend? Partner in solving crimes? All the above? My will power is damn near ready to crack with Quinn. By the way he looks at me when he thinks I'm not paying attention, he knows it.

When my missing cousin turns up dead, the mystery isn't who killed her, it's who the Shadow-Dwellers will target next.

Spoiler alert? It's me.

They've proven they'll do whatever it takes to reach their goals, including attack those closest to me. I don't know what's worse: knowing all of my loved ones are in danger, or the guilt that I could protect them if I just give in to a psycho's demands for my blood.

Which I shouldn't do, right?

Turn the page to preview the first two chapters or
click here to pick up your copy today!

SHADOW UNDERGROUND PREVIEW - CHAPTER 1

DENVER - MIDWEST REGION

Becca stared into her closet, hoping for inspiration. She glanced toward the outfit hanging on the back of her bedroom door which had been there for the last week, still sheathed in plastic. A black blouse, black pants, and black jacket uniform were hers for the low, low price of a consulting interim placement with the Enforcers Guild. It wasn't like she could turn down the gig which fulfilled the conditions of her civic service. Chief Elowen had said she could take a few days and start once she was ready.

But was she? Becka hadn't even left the townhome in the week since she'd been back.

Oriani mewled plaintively for his breakfast, seeming to understand the exact level of ear-piercing noise required to spurn her fae-touched hypersensitive ears into action. The plump gold-and-brown tabby didn't care one iota whether she wanted to get dressed, what she wore, or when she started her new job. All he cared about was his stomach.

"Okay, okay, fine," she replied. She pulled out a spring-time green blouse and brown pair of slacks, wanting to look her best for her meeting with Dr. Traut today. As she dressed, Becka told herself everything would be alright. It wasn't like there were Shadow-Dwellers lying in wait around every corner.

Were there?

"Mraw," Oriani repeated, his plaintive tone escalating in pitch. Becka slid on a pair of sandals and tucked her sea silk gloves into her backpack, checking to make sure she had a full bottle of hot sauce in the side pocket.

She glanced at her bedside table, where the Shadow-Dweller glyph book sat next to the two journals she'd picked up at the Shadow-Dweller Mimir's cabin hideout a few weeks ago. Becka had continued to try and decipher them, but every time she'd picked up one of them or the glyph book they had the same message on every page. Even without asking any questions. Even after asking unrelated questions. Even after she'd cursed and sworn at them.

But Becka couldn't help herself. She reached out and picked up one of the journals, flipping it open to a random page.

FIND ME

The same message Mimir had left for Becka at the cabin where she'd killed the wolf-shifter Luce, Saige's packmate.

But there was a second message in the journal. One Mimir hadn't left for her at the cabin.

TELL ANYONE AND THEY DIE

An ever-present anxiety lived in her stomach, coiled up

like a serpent poised to strike. She hadn't yet figured out what to do about the Shadow-Dweller books or this message, which had to be from Mimir. Becka didn't want anyone to get hurt, so she'd kept her mouth shut about the message. She didn't have a death wish, so Becka hadn't gone to find Mimir by herself either.

Becka threw the journal against the wall and it thudded to the floor. She picked up the next journal. Wash. Rinse. Thud. Repeat. Becka picked up the glyph book and slid it into her backpack, not bothering to check the pages. She knew what she'd see.

When she opened the door to her bedroom, Becka came face-to-face with Enforcer Quinn.

Oriani whooshed out her door and down the stairs, not waiting for her to follow.

Becka's heart skipped a beat, longing for the comfort of his touch. She'd have thought after a week her heart would have gotten used to having Quinn in the room next door, but no such luck. Having him so close without acting on their mutual attraction or divulging the journal's messages was wearing down her defenses.

"I heard a series of thumps. Journals disappointing you again today?"

"Just like every other day."

His amber gaze flicked to her outfit and then back to her eyes, and the intensity of his focus on her had her feeling like they were the only two people in existence, living within their own private universe. "I thought you might want a ride?" This had become Quinn's gentle way of asking if she was ready to start working at the guild with him. "I know Elowen is looking forward to getting you on board."

Becka bit her lip. She'd been keeping her distance from Quinn, but that hadn't stopped her from remembering their kisses or dwelling on the moments she'd slept peacefully curled up next to him.

"I don't think I'm quite ready yet," Becka replied, tucking a stray lock of hair behind her ear.

He nodded, as if he'd expected her continuing avoidance. "Are you going out?"

"Yes, I have a meeting scheduled with Dr. Traut about my old internship with the Interspecies Department. It sounds like there's been some progress, so I'm going to see what's up."

"By yourself?" Quinn asked, a frown furrowing his brows.

"Yeah. I mean, it's the middle of the day and the institute is a place I know well." She'd been avoiding leaving the town-home, but hated to live in fear. She had a target on her back and who knew how many Shadow-Dwellers Mimir had out there watching her?

His frown turned stormy. "I could give you a ride. Wait for you until you're done?"

"No, that's not necessary," Becka replied, forcing a smile. "I know you've been busy. Besides, I need to get out on my own sooner or later."

His eyes widened. "You don't, actually. The guild has the resources to have you always accompanied."

Which she knew to be true. After all, they'd had Quinn move in with her and posted guards out front and back twenty-four seven. How that made financial sense when she was just a consultant for the guild, Becka didn't know. Although she always felt safer when Quinn was around,

Becka couldn't say the same for the guards, who she barely knew.

"Whatever you think is wise." Becka crossed her arms. "But I'm going. That's not negotiable."

A smile passed over his face, but then he masked it with his "I'm taking you seriously" expression. "I can see it isn't. But an enforcer will go with you, nonetheless. Andre is on shift today, and a solid enforcer."

She'd put her foot down and she wasn't at all surprised Quinn had done the same. If she was the epitome of stubborn, he was the pillar of determination.

"Hey up there," Aunt Lydia called up the stairs. "Breakfast is ready!"

"Coming!" Becka called back.

Becka sidestepped past Quinn, knocking shoulders with him. He put a hand out, touching her arm lightly, an electric thrill running along her skin at the contact. She paused, wanting nothing more than to curl up into his arms, breathe in his scent, and let her anxieties fade away.

After his first night there, Quinn had moved into the room at the top of the stairs, next to Becka's room and across from Lydia's. Becka hadn't complained, preferring the security of his presence close by. The sweet temptation of having him just next door could have pushed her back into his arms, but the warnings from the glyph journal never left her mind.

"I look forward to hearing about how your meeting with Dr. Traut goes," Quinn said. "I have some leads I'd like to run past you."

"Yeah, of course," she replied, thinking the last thing she wanted to do with Quinn was talk about a job interview or Shadow-Dweller cases. Despite sleeping next door to each other, they'd both been cautious, keeping their dynamic light and flirtatious. Then there was the matter of his gift, his ability to know if others spoke the truth, which made keeping the secret of the depth of her Mimir concerns from him tricky at best.

Quinn was so easy to talk to, Becka feared she'd tell him about the messages in the journal, placing this life at risk. So she'd kept her distance, much to both their frustration.

When they arrived downstairs, her Aunt Lydia was setting out a stack of plates and silverware. She wore a flowy deep-blue blouse and a sea-green skirt over her lush figure, her long, golden hair cascading down her back. On the table, a mound of doughnuts filled a large serving bowl and a smaller bowl was filled with a colorful fruit salad. Two large French presses were on the counter, mainly because Lydia had a fear of running out now that both Quinn and Saige had moved in.

"Doughnuts!" Becka said.

"No, they're beignets!" Lydia replied, holding a hand to her chest in mock horror. "Look at all of that powdered sugar! It's like a signpost pointing to decadence!"

Becka shook her head and laughed. "I'm looking, and I'm liking," she replied, pouring herself a cup of coffee.

"Sit, you two!" Lydia hummed along, her cheerful demeanor always a breath of fresh air to Becka. "Hmm, is Saige up?" Lydia said to herself, and then wandered down the hall and knocked on the door to Saige's room. Then knocked again.

When Lydia returned, Becka and Quinn were both sitting at the table. "Where has that wolf gotten herself off to?" She sat down with a flourish, leaning forward over her coffee cup and diving into the beignets.

Becka shrugged. They'd barely seen Saige since she'd moved in, so it was anyone's guess. After Luce's death, Saige had taken a leave of absence, citing a need to grieve her pack-mate's death. Lydia had happily offered her a room at the townhome. From what Becka could see, grieving looked a lot like trying to hunt down the Shadow-Dwellers responsible for Luce's death.

Not that she blamed Saige. Becka's mission was the same: find and stop Mimir and the others.

"She doesn't report to me right now. Brent gave her some time off to mourn Luce, so her time is her own."

"I should be relieved she's not moping around, but I suspect we both know she's out hunting down leads on her own," Lydia replied.

"Likely, but good luck getting her to admit to it," Becka said. "You're all fancy. Where are you off to?"

Lydia positively beamed. "I have a wine tasting downtown."

"Isn't it a little early in the day for a wine tasting?" Quinn asked.

Becka barked out a laugh. Quinn had a lot to learn about Aunt Lydia.

"I'm a cosmopolitan woman, enforcer. Besides, it's a charity event, it's not like I picked the time. And none of your judgment about it lasting all day, either! I mean, there's cheese too. Cheese fixes everything." Lydia took a sip of her coffee. "What about you two? Any mysteries to solve? Together? In—"

"I'm headed to see Dr. Traut," Becka replied, interrupting her. "He phoned yesterday and said he has something lined up for me."

Lydia's heels bounced a staccato beat on the floor. "Oh, I'm so happy for you! You must tell me all about it tonight!"

When Becka had been tossed out of House Rowan as a teen for being ungifted, Lydia had been there for her. For each hardship Becka had endured growing up in the city, Lydia was there for each one, from Band-Aids to broken hearts.

"You know I will."

"And you, Quinn?" Lydia asked, looking back and forth between them. "Big plans?"

"Just continuing to chase down leads on possible locations Mimir might have taken Alvilda Rowan."

Becka didn't miss the sag in Quinn's shoulders or frustrated tone in his voice. It had been just a week since they'd returned to the city and they hadn't pinned down any solid leads on Alvilda's location so far. Becka assumed the chances of finding her kidnapped cousin alive were slim to none.

"Any luck?" Lydia asked.

"Not much on her, so I've been mostly reviewing old case files."

"Riveting, no doubt." Lydia's phone beeped, and she swept her dishes to the sink in a rush. "That's my ride. I've got to run. Please make sure Saige eats when you see her!"

"Have fun," Becka called out as the front door slammed shut.

"Did Lydia always cook for you before?" Quinn asked, beginning to clear the table.

Becka got up, filled a mug to take some coffee with her, and then helped with the dishes. "She loves to cook, but no, it was sporadic. I think she's trying to make you and Saige feel welcome."

"Has she always been so eccentric?"

Becka put together a plate for Saige, hoping she'd eat it later. "She's quirky but I love her. Actually, she's been more predictable since I returned. Less busy. Around more too."

"Perhaps out of an abundance of caution for you?" Quinn asked.

If that was true, and she had to think it could be, Becka didn't know how to feel about it. She didn't want Lydia changing her ways, but no doubt her aunt would welcome a return to normalcy after all this was over.

The front door opened and Becka assumed Lydia must have forgotten something. When she looked up, it was Saige walking through the door.

"Hey Saige, were you out all night?" Becka asked.

Her appearance answered for her. Saige had dark circles under her eyes and looked like she'd been traveling rough, with dirt on her clothes and unkempt hair. Saige's need to avenge her packmate and dear friend had driven her to exhaustion hunting for leads on the Shadow-Dwellers.

"I had a lead to chase down," Saige replied, her voice rough.

"You find another shifter to question?" Becka asked.

"I did, a jaguar shifter on the north end of town," Saige replied. "They didn't have any leads, but did give me a number for a pair of bear brothers across town."

"If you need help, my resources are at your disposal," Quinn said.

"Thanks, Quinn," Saige replied, turning down the hall. "I'm going to get some rest."

"Lydia made doughnuts and fruit for breakfast. I made you a plate," Becka said, holding it up for Saige to see.

"I'm going to get cleaned up and rest," Saige replied. "Can you put it in the fridge for me?" She didn't wait for a response and continued down the hall.

"Yeah, of course," Becka called after her, and then put Saige's plate away.

Quinn moved close to Becka. "I'm worried about her. She hasn't taken Luce's death well at all."

"You think?" Becka replied, her tone sharper than she'd intended.

Quinn raised a brow and stepped closer to her. "I'm not sure I deserved that."

"You didn't. Sorry. I'm just frustrated." *In more ways than one.* "What can we do for her?"

"I'm not sure," Quinn replied. "We need to get Saige to come out of her den and talk to us."

Becka sighed. As much as she loved being back home, Becka had brought her problems back with her from House Rowan.

He leaned in even closer, lowering his voice. "I'd love to find out what you've been able to learn from the Shadow-Dweller glyph book and journals too. If you have ideas on how I can get you to talk to me about that, let me know."

Becka glanced up at him, pursing her lips as she gauged his mood. "The sarcasm is new for you."

"Did it work?" He smiled down at her, so she knew he wasn't really pushing her hard.

Quinn's ability to read truth and falsehoods in others' speech was again at the forefront of her thoughts. Becka didn't want to lie to him, but especially didn't want to get caught lying.

Had she been reading the journals? Well, yes, she had. Had she tried to find out information on Mimir or Alvilda? Well, yes, she had. But Becka was also keenly aware Mimir was out to kill her. And maybe her friends. Maybe Quinn.

Becka especially couldn't bear to think of losing Quinn.

She'd lost so much. Her sister. Her friend Luce. She'd almost lost her father, Vott. Even Alvilda, whose betrayal had caused such conflict between Becka and her brother, Calder.

Sure, she was concerned for Alvilda, at least as concerned as she could be over someone who had tried to kill her and her father. But Becka knew Mimir had taken advantage of Alvilda, no doubt leading her down the dark path she'd traveled. She didn't wish Mimir's attention on anyone.

Becka took a deep breath, trying to shake off the mental images of Luce's blood flowing and the threatening messages from the books. "I haven't wanted to think too much about Mimir and Alvilda and the Shadow-Dwellers," she replied, which was totally a true statement. "The entire incident with Luce still weighs on me."

Quinn placed his hands on her shoulders, squeezing her gently, and she found herself leaning into his touch. "I don't blame you, but we don't have any other leads and if Alvilda wasn't dead when Mimir took her, she's likely running out of time. We have to assume there's a possibility of saving her until we know otherwise."

"I've been asking the books questions, and they haven't given me anything useful about Alvilda." Which was mostly true.

His eyes narrowed. Did he intuit she was withholding information?

"Perhaps you're not asking the right questions? I bet we could get something useful out of the books with the team helping to guide your questions."

Guilt over not helping Alvilda and withholding information from Quinn flooded over her, souring her stomach. "Yeah, maybe." Becka checked the clock, knowing Quinn was not going to let this one go. He was too tenacious to let any clue go. "I've got to get going for my appointment."

He nodded, but his eyes were back to stormy. Quinn wrapped his arms around her and she melted into him, wishing the moment could last forever. "Be careful. Andre will be with you. Call me if you need anything."

Despite Becka's overwhelmingly positive interactions with enforcers, she'd grown up within fae territories where distrust of them ran rampant. She'd learned to trust not just Quinn but a few of the others, although the human Andre was still new to her. But if Quinn trusted Andre, so would she, despite her misgivings.

Unfortunately, the Shadow-Dwellers weren't going away anytime soon, so she'd need to move past her discomfort and embrace her new reality of twenty-four-seven guards.

*B*ecka lifted her hand to knock on the door and was struck by a moment of deja vu. How long had it been since she'd last visited Dr. Traut? Had it really only been less than six months?

Her life had changed so much since then that it felt like years had passed.

"Is everything alright?" Enforcer Andre asked, standing just a few feet behind her.

Clad in trademark enforcer black and looking like he'd spent all of his off time at a competitive boxing gym, Andre was just as intense as the other enforcers she'd met. Except Andre was human. Becka had witnessed human enforcers with fae over her time in the city, and they never seemed to lean towards giving fae the benefit of the doubt they gave to humans or shifters.

Curiously, Andre didn't seem to mind being assigned to bodyguard duty for a fae-touched. Then again, Lydia had been taking the guards coffee, lemonade, and fresh-baked cookies multiple times a day, so she might have softened them up for Becka.

In fact, Lydia's overall generosity was one of the things Becka loved most about her. Regardless of living as an unguilded fae in the city, Lydia embraced life with unrepentant joy.

Becka exhaled and then knocked on the door. "Yes, I was just gathering my thoughts."

Andre nodded, all business.

When the door swung open, Becka felt a smile flash across her face.

"Lady Becka of House Rowan, I'm so glad you could make it today!" Dr. Traut exclaimed, his beaming smile framing his face in well-worn creases. He had the same poofy, wiry hair, the same off-kilter horn-rimmed glasses, and the same brown-toned outfits that might have been older than he was. But from the time of her twin Tesse's death and Becka's subsequent time back at House Rowan, it had only been a few months. Maybe four months in total? What had she expected to change?

Becka stepped into his office, butterflies of excitement fluttering in her stomach. "Dr. Traut, it's so good to see you again."

"Look at your gloves," Traut said. She'd put them on in the car, as it was her practice to always wear them when away from home to help protect others from her Null gift.

"Why, thank you. They're a gift from my father, Elder Vott of House Alder."

"Just exquisite," Traut replied, his attention wholly focused on them.

Enforcer Andre followed, sweeping around her and into

the office, no doubt checking for access points and other people inside. Traut frowned, but didn't interfere, his attention focused on Becka's gloves.

"I suppose you always have someone with you now?" Traut said.

"For the time being, yes," Becka replied. She hoped the guards would be temporary, but given the continuing interest in her by the Shadow-Dwellers, most likely she'd have to accept a permanent enforcer guard long-term.

Andre reappeared from Traut's storage room in the back. "It's clear."

Becka gave a stiff nod. "Could you wait outside?"

Andre's response was unequivocal. "No."

"Please, won't you come sit?" Traut continued, as if having an enforcer check out his office and stand guard was an everyday occurrence.

Traut grabbed a manila file folder off his desk, and then motioned for Becka to join him at a pair of faded yellow upholstered chairs in a little guest area he had at the other end of the room, complete with a bookshelf, side table, and teapot on a lace doily.

For his part, Andre closed the door and stood guard. The chairs were a bit lumpy and threadbare but Becka didn't care. The Institute of World Politics and, in particular, the Interspecies Department headed by Dr. Traut, was an area of her prior life she intended to reclaim.

"Could I get you some tea?" Traut offered, setting his folder on the side table.

"Nope, I'll pass," Becka replied, hearing the firm edge in her tone.

Traut didn't appear to notice. "Oh, okay. Let's get down

to it, then, shall we? I must say, Lady Becka, it's an honor to have your continued interest in the institute. We're excited to have you on board again with our efforts."

Why is he calling me Lady? Well duh, I am one now. Traut had always been deliberately formal to the fae, and now Becka was a fae of merit and position. Still, she didn't quite know how to feel about it. When last she'd spoken to Traut, it was as an unguilded, ungifted fae student in his program. Now she'd been declared gifted, accepted as a guilded member of House Rowan, and even further, named heir.

But inside, Becka didn't feel like a different person.

"The work you're doing here at the institute is fundamental to the journey to further relations between humans and the fae. I believe in your mission, and I want to help make sure it succeeds."

"It's so kind of you to say so," he replied a touch of pink coloring his cheeks. "I look forward to working together with you towards that goal." He picked up the folder, paging through it until he found what he was looking for. "Now, let's discuss what that could look like. Ah yes, the formal offer is right here."

The sinking sensation of disappointment hovered around her. Traut's stiff demeanor wasn't exactly broadcasting good news.

"First, did you get the letter from Chancellor Evans regarding your doctoral studies?" He looked up at her over the rim of his glasses. "It was sent to House Rowan a few weeks ago."

"Uh, no. No, I didn't." Becka suppressed a few choice

words. Had her mother, Duchess Maura, or Aunt Astrid kept it from her?

He frowned momentarily, but then forced a smile. "Well then, let me catch you up. The chancellor has placed a hold on your doctoral studies pending a review as to your change in status. As you know, fae-touched have historically not been allowed to study at the institute, although an exception was made in your case, as you were unguilded at the time."

The possibility should have occurred to Becka, but she'd gotten so used to thinking of herself as the exception to the rule. She knew humans didn't allow fae access to the human education system. This was ostensibly because fae had their own schools and gifted training within the territories, but Becka suspected it was to prevent fae from becoming too educated. Too prosperous. Too influential.

Too much of a potential threat.

What had she expected? Sure, she wanted back the life in the city that she'd left behind the day her twin Tesse died. But just because they'd bent the rules before for her, under different circumstances, didn't mean they'd do so again. Especially not just to humor her.

"And now I'm guilded," she said, mirroring her thoughts.

"Which is wonderful for you, I must say! It must be such a homecoming to be back at House Rowan and have a magical gift like others of your kind." He again beamed at her.

Wonderful was not the term Becka would have used, but it made sense he'd think so.

"But it does put our policy people in a pickle, if you know what I mean," he continued. "I've written a statement arguing for you to be allowed to complete your studies, and for the goodwill it would generate. I'm hopeful for a positive outcome."

Disappointment flooded Becka. So she was back to limbo land? "Where does that leave my internship?" she asked, guessing the answer.

Traut's expression turned contrite. "Well, as you can imagine, that was also put on hold, pending the outcome of the review. However, I simply could not fathom passing up on an opportunity to work with you, and by extension, House Rowan. So I came up with a proposal and the chancellor approved it straight off."

"That's surprising," Becka replied, wary of hearing the details. "What's the plan?"

Traut held up a paper for her, covered with signatures and stamps. "I've had you declared a fae liaison to the Inter-species Department!"

Becka laughed at his raw enthusiasm, his ebullient joy chasing away her anxiety. "That sounds promising, Dr. Traut, but what does that mean, exactly?"

He set aside the paper and folder on the table and leaned forward, practically bouncing with excitement. "It means, my dear, that you are being offered a formal position with the department as unpaid adjunct faculty. When there are opportunities to consult or teach on fae-specific matters, you will be the first one we call. And it means you can continue to access the institute's resources. I know you're a fan of the library." He winked at her. "So, will you accept the offer?"

"Thank you, Dr. Traut," Becka replied, her throat suddenly tight with emotion. It wasn't what she'd hoped for, but perhaps it could be almost as good? And was he seriously dangling library access as an incentive? "That's so considerate of you. I'd love to be your fae liaison." Saying the words, she had to blink back the tears of joy suddenly welling in her eyes.

"Fantastic!" Traut exclaimed, throwing his hands up in the air in exaltation, and Becka heard Andre shift behind her. She glanced back at him and shook her head, letting him know this was typical behavior for Traut.

"What will my duties be as liaison?" she asked.

He shrugged. "I haven't quite gotten too far down that road yet. When I heard from you of your return to the city and your continuing interest working with us, I rushed to get this approved."

"I appreciate you finding a way for me to continue my relationship with your department, but I'm sure my house, particularly the duchess, will want a written job description to review."

Traut nodded. "Certainly. I can have that to both of you later this week."

"Wonderful. I'm so happy for the opportunity."

"I am thrilled to have you! Oh! I have a Q&A panel next week that I'd love to have you attend. Assuming you're available?"

"I'll make time!" Becka replied, not at all caring what questions she'd have to answer. "Hopefully, over time, when the administration sees my willingness to help, do you think they might allow me to finish my doctorate?"

Traut leaned back in his chair, half-smiling and frowning at the same time. "I'm curious, Lady Becka. Now that you're guilded, why would you want to complete the program?"

Becka opened her mouth to answer, and then closed it again. She'd had many conversations with Traut over the years, so he knew how driven she was. How could he question her motivation?

She glanced at Andre, who shrugged with a "don't ask me" vibe. Traut was kind enough, or perhaps curious enough, to wait for her response, anticipation glittering in his eyes. Perhaps he just wanted to hear her say it again?

"I feel the initiatives the Interspecies Department is exploring will aid the future of human, fae, and shifter relations. I'm dedicated to seeing a future where the scars of hate no longer hold us back, and I hope for a future with greater cooperation and peace."

Traut nodded, his nimbus of wiry hair bouncing as he moved. "An esteemed goal, to be sure, and one which I applaud, especially coming from a fae. But, that doesn't answer my question. Why now, with your current standing, do you want to complete the doctorate?"

Hadn't she already answered? "So I'm better equipped to bring change?" Becka answered, hearing the question in her own voice as she searched for the truth.

"Right." He nodded again. "May I be direct, Lady Becka?"

The honorific hadn't bothered her at House Rowan, but here, in the world she'd grown up in, it grated. In the city she'd always been Becka. Never Lady Becka. She wanted to be Becka, just Becka, here again.

"Yes, Dr. Traut, but only if you call me Becka."

"I suppose I could, Becka, but only if you call me David."

She nodded. "Certainly, David." It sounded weird, but it was a smidgen of prior normalcy, and Becka would take all she could get.

"Your life has changed dramatically since you were last at the institute. You're now the guilded heir to House Rowan."

That was a smidge of an understatement, but she didn't want to delve into the various finer points with Traut. Er, David. No, she'd stick to Traut.

"It's true," she replied.

"Perhaps now, with your newfound status, you have different avenues to reach your goals? Avenues even more influential than a doctorate from this esteemed institute would provide?"

"To be honest, after so much time away from House Rowan and fae territories, I don't have the relationship clout and political connections others do to make change happen."

He shrugged. "You've only been back within the fold for a short time. Now, I don't want to dissuade you from working as my liaison. It's in my best interest, after all. But perhaps, in thinking of your path with the institute, you're aiming too small-fry?"

"Excuse me?"

Traut held up his hands. "I don't mean to overstep..."

"No, please. Go on. What did you mean by small-fry?"

His expression was cautious. "From your papers and our conversations, I know you want to use your voice and abilities to do good in the world. Working with the institute is certainly one path, but you have others available to you now as well. If you broaden your scope and consider all of the resources under your influence now, what's the most impact you can have to bring positive change?"

He has a point.

Perhaps she'd been thinking about her future and goals all wrong? She'd been playing defense, angling to get back home and reclaim her scholastic past, trying to defend herself against the hidden Shadow-Dwellers, and waiting to feel safe again. Traut was right, she needed to focus on positive impact again.

She needed to go on the offensive.

What was the biggest thing she could do to use her powers and influence for good and make the world better? She could bring down Mimir and the Shadow-Dwellers by working with the enforcers. Not just to stop them from coming after her, but to keep them from hurting anyone else, ever again.

After that, she could focus on reviving peace talks between fae and humans. The two races had never moved beyond the Pax Hominid Treaty, which Becka considered nothing more than a glorified ceasefire agreement. If fae and human could be convinced to develop cooperative partnerships, and work together, what might the world be like in another 150 years?

"Thank you, Dr.... David," she replied. "You've given me a lot to think about."

His smile was broad and heartfelt. "I'm just glad my position as your advising professor still comes in handy. Now, let's go make you official!"

An hour later they walked out of the admissions building, Becka holding a shiny new picture ID with the title "Fae Liaison" and "Adjunct Faculty" under her name. Andre had been with her every step of the way, and, perhaps because he was a human enforcer, no one seemed to pay him much mind.

"I think that gives you access to the faculty breakrooms, should you ever need it," Traut said. "There's always coffee available."

"Is it any good?"

"The coffee is... coffee?" He chuckled, and she laughed too.

The midday sun was bright, the skies were clear, and Becka had a part of her old life back. "Will you send me details about the Q&A session?"

"I'll get you the details once they are finalized."

"I want to stop by the library and check on the status of some requests I've made," she said.

"If you don't mind, I'll walk with you."

"That'd be nice."

They crossed the courtyard, Becka taking in the bird song, the chatter of groups of students passing by, and the familiar buildings and brick walkways she'd become so fond of over her years here.

A scream rang out, shattering her idyllic moment of reflection. Then another.

Andre grabbed Becka's arm, his intense gaze scanning the crowd. "For your safety, we should leave."

Becka knew he was right. Whatever this was, it had nothing to do with her beyond satisfying her curiosity. Or did it? She pulled her arm out of his grip. "This can't be mere coincidence. I need to get closer and see what's going on."

She took off in the direction of the crowd, both Traut and Andre close on her heels. When they rounded the corner of the building, the library and its courtyard came into view, along with a growing crowd of people standing around the large fountain that stood in the center of the courtyard.

But then the group in front of them parted, and Becka saw what had drawn them all to the fountain.

The water was the color of black... no, that wasn't quite it. It was the color of shadow absent light. The deeper or thicker the water, the darker the shade. Suddenly Becka's heart was pounding and her head ached like it only did when she neared magic. Then she saw the outline of a person propped up against the middle, under the sprays of dark liquid, unmoving. Becka froze where she stood, heart in her throat. Whoever it was didn't appear to be alive.

"Oh my goodness!" Traut exclaimed. "We need to get the students out of here." He pulled out a whistle and moved into the crowd, directing everyone to leave.

Andre swore as he pulled out his phone. "Dispatch? I need a cleanup team for a body at the Institute of World Politics in the library courtyard. Send a shield and investigation unit too, stat."

Becka had her phone out too. She called Quinn and he picked up in one ring. "I'm okay, but we've got a situation at the institute's library."

"I'll be there in ten," he replied, and then the line went dead.

Get the rest of Shadow Underground now!

AUTHOR'S NOTE

If you loved the book and have a minute to spare, I would really appreciate a short review on the page or site where you bought the book. Your help in spreading the word is greatly appreciated. Reviews from readers like you make a huge difference to helping new readers find similar stories.

Thank you so much for reading and supporting my work!

Candice

P.S. If you'd like to know when my next book comes out and want to receive occasional updates from me, then you can sign up for my newsletter at candicebundy.com. I promise I will never sell your email to the daemonic marketing hordes.

WRITING AS CR BUNDY

The Depths of Memory Series

The Dream Sifter

Dreams Manifest

For a list of my full catalog of available titles, visit my Amazon
Author Central page.

ACKNOWLEDGMENTS

Thanks to Zippy Wizard Redaction and 5280editing for their editing services.

Special thanks to Jen for her support, critiques, and insight.

And to my friends and family who've been a source of unending strength, laughter, and wine over the years: thank you for the inspiration.

And lastly, to my partner, Lee. Thank you for running alongside me in this journey. Your enduring support and candor mean the world to me.

ABOUT THE AUTHOR

Candice lives in Denver, Colorado with her son and their cat Newt. A professional hedonist, rabble-rouser, winemaker, and goat-herder, she adores archeology and mythology. Candice focuses on habit hacking to meet minimalist, health, productivity, and positive mojo goals, and sometimes even blogs about it. An unrepentant epicurean, she grows heirloom tomatoes and ferments a variety of sauerkraut, sourdough, kombucha, pickles, and water kefir.

If you would like to know when she has new books out, please sign up for her newsletter at candicebundy.com. Or, email her at candice@candicebundy.com if the mood strikes you.

* 9 7 8 0 9 8 5 4 1 8 5 6 4 *